THE LIES THAT SECRETS DESIRE

By Sara A Miller

I would like to take this opportunity to say a huge thank you to my wonderful girl Friday Val Hannah, without you I never would have done this so thanks for the constant support and encouragement.

I would also like to express my gratitude to Laura Hannah for the fantastic cover design, I don't know what I would have done without you.

I would like to dedicate this book to my wonderful husband Gary. You have the patience of a saint, you pick me up whenever I'm down and for always supporting my dreams and always having complete faith in me.

You are MY one true love

Sara x

CONTENTS

PROLOGUE

Savas Remizov was born in the old USSR, behind the iron curtain. He had been raised in the United States, Detroit, Michigan to be precise. Even with his American accent and all the perks that came with living in the western world, his heart still and always would belong to the Motherland.

Growing up in the tight knit and very strict Russian community where family was important, the Brotherhood or *Bratva* meant more. Savas' Papa was the head of the Michigan syndicate, *The Pakhan* and one day that mantle would be handed down to his eldest son, Savas. From the age of thirteen, Savas was groomed for the position, learning the mantra *The Brotherhood is more important than the blood of life.* He had witnessed his first kill at fifteen and by sixteen had made his first. On his seventeenth birthday he had been fully initiated and branded with the most coveted tattoo every Russian male longing to join the Bratva desired.

Savas' best friend and confident was Nikolai Bazin. Nikolai's father was Savas' Papa's 2nd, his under boss or *Sovietnik*. So like Savas, Nikolai had been groomed from a young age, destined to follow in his fathers footsteps and was initiated and branded on the same day. They were the next generation of the Brotherhood. Nikolai had a sibling, a sister called Natasha and between the Remizov and Bazin clans she had been the first female born in decades. The only girl amongst eight boys and so she was treated like the princess she was. Savas always knew she would one day be his; he'd fallen in love with her long before the decision had been made to unite the families and keep the bond between them strong.

Natasha was beautiful, literally perfect in every way, tall and slim with long, honey blond hair and the bluest of blue bewitching eyes, basically she was the fantasy of every straight teenage boy who set eyes on her. Still Savas knew she would be his and his alone, he couldn't even remember when his feelings changed from being a protective big brother, to seeing her as the seductive, mouthwatering goddess she had become and who he wanted so, so badly.

On a cold dark day in the heat and sunshine of mid July, Natasha had been gunned down and killed in a drive by shooting in broad daylight, apparently retribution for someone in the Albanian mob, an eye for an eye. She was only seventeen and it had been the first and thankfully last time a minor had been targeted. A summit had been immediately held with all the heads of the different organizations, meeting at a secret location. New laws had been put in place immediately and instantly enforced, and these are still in place today.

Getting over Natasha had been the single most painful thing Savas had ever had to deal with. It had changed him, not only had Natasha died but something inside him had died too and it made him cold, dark and very dangerous. By the age of twenty he was a force to be reckoned with and his status inside the Brotherhood had grown. People feared him and his reputation preceded him, there were no second chance with Savas Remizov.

At twenty five, Savas became the youngest *Pakhan* in the history of the Brotherhood. The sudden death of the patriarch, strangely enough of natural causes, had thrust him to power, he was the new *Pakhan*. He had gained the trust and respect of the elders a long time ago and they all had faith in him. Savas made changes, all for the greater good of the Brotherhood. His first priority was to get someone he trusted inside the Police department, an ally from within. The only person he trusted beyond a shadow of doubt was Nikolai. It had been easy to forge papers and documents to change his ID and family history that was before it all became computerized. Sergi was Savas' tech guy, come bookkeeper, the *Kassir;* he had falsified everything, including a full background check that was faultless.

Nikolai Bazin no longer existed; he was now Nicholas Bays, a twenty five year old from Redford, Detroit, whose parents had been killed in a car accident on vacation in the UK five years ago. He had no other living relatives and had been left financially secure. His application to the Police academy had been accepted and so Savas' plan had been set into motion. The only regret Savas had was losing his best friend and comrade in arms, there could be no connection between them for this to work, like a sleeper cell, which could take months or even years to yield the goods. Savas would have to rely on his trusted soldiers; his *Boevik* to relay Nik's Intel there was simply no other way.

At twenty seven Savas married Petra Orlev, the daughter of Borya Orlev, *Pakhan* of Illinois, based in Chicago, and once again all for the greater good of his Brotherhood. Love was not on the cards at first but eventually he buried the past, laying the ghost of Natasha to rest and his love for Petra grew, she blessed him with three wonderful sons and a precious daughter.

Nikolai or Nicholas had progressed well through the Detroit Police department and was now Detective Sergeant, all to the delight of Savas; Nik was his prize hidden possession. Savas had heard his friend had married to keep the ruse going, to an all American elementary school teacher named Jessica but he had broken the one golden rule, which was to never fall in love. He worshiped the ground she walked on and he absolutely hated the fact that his whole life was a lie. The day she told him he was going to be a father was the happiest day of his entire life.

An undercover operation had been in place for months, the surveillance on the Albanians had gathered tip offs about a huge drug shipment scheduled to arrive in just two days time. They had been encroaching on the *Bratva* territory and they would have to be put in their place. Savas was happy to give the scumbag Albanians their comeuppance. Nik had sent word through the channels that he needed to see Savas and left instructions in a code that only Savas could decipher on where to meet him.

At eleven a.m. at Patties diner on Miller Street in Dearborn, Savas sat in the back booth sipping a hot, strong black coffee when he saw his childhood friend walk in. It had been close to a decade since they had last seen one another but Nik had never changed. They embraced before sitting and chatting in Russian, just in case any eavesdroppers were listening. Nik told Savas about Jessica and his unborn child.

"Tomorrow will be a war zone and I have a really bad feeling. Savas promise me one thing, if anything happens to me look after and protect them. Jess knows nothing and I want it to stay that way, I don't want her to know the truth about me."

"Brother I swear on my life I will do my best for them, I will find a way into their lives. They are your family and so that makes them mine."

"Thank you Savas, I needed to hear that."

"So when is the baby Bazin or should I say Bays due?"

"August 16th," Nik smiled.

Savas chuckled, "Petra is due August 1st."

"Wow, so how many is that now?"

"Four and finally at last we have our Princess," Savas said so proudly.

"I don't even know what we're having; I want it to be a surprise."

Time was up far too soon and once again the two friends had to part, it was so hard watching Nikolai drive away in the opposite direction and he knew that it would never get any easier.

The Detroit Police department had done a fantastic job of eradicating the Albanians from first the City and then the entire State. Savas was over the moon as the information started to filter through the channels. Soon though, all his delight was demolished when he had heard the news of three officers' deaths, one of them being Nicholas Bays.

Savas was alone in his office and simply crumbled to his knees and wept uncontrollably for the first time since the death of his beloved Natasha.

CHAPTER ONE

I could not recall a single memory from my life that did not include Jasmine Remizov. She was more like a sister than my best friend and her large family was an extension of my own. Her Mom Petra and Dad Savas had first met my Mom, Jessica when they were both pregnant with us. I had listened to my Mom tell that story countless times; she'd say Petra was her guardian angel and Savas; well he was just a gift from God.

It had been a real dark and painful time for my Mom. My Dad had just been shot and killed in the line of duty; he'd been a detective in the Detroit police department. A week after his funeral she'd had a prenatal appointment, and as she was walking out, her emotions had gotten the better of her and she broke down sobbing. That was just as Petra and Savas had walked in for their own appointment. Petra had been so concerned that she helped her get herself cleaned up, then made her promise to wait for them while they went in to see the doctor.

By the time they returned, my Mom had composed herself a little and apologized for causing such a scene. Petra and Savas had driven my Mom home and over coffee she had explained the reason behind the break down, she had just found out I was a girl, the girl my Dad had wished for. That had literally broken Savas and Petra's hearts. From that day forward a bond had been forged and was never ever broken.

Petra and my Mom were six months pregnant; Mom had been so terrified about giving birth and raising a child alone. Petra had already given birth to three strapping boys, Mikhail who had been eight, Luca six and little Alexei just two, she assured my mom it was normal to be scared the first time, as well as putting an end to the fears of raising me alone. On August 4th, Jasmine Zoya had been born, she was the first female to be born into the Remizov family for decades, everyone had been ecstatic and Jazz had been dubbed Princess from her first day on earth. I followed ten days later on the 14th, weighing in at 8lb 2oz, 6oz smaller then Jazz and named Isabelle Natasha Bays. When Savas had held me on the day I was born, he'd said with my big blue eyes, fair skin and chubby cheeks, I looked like a little cherub, so like Jazz, I was always referred to from that day as Angel.

My childhood had been wonderful, full of love and laughter. That was until I was ten, when my beloved Mom had died from breast cancer. It had been the only time in my short life that I felt truly alone and lost, even though I had been surrounded by people who loved me. I was eight and a half when she had been diagnosed, she had sat me down and promised me she would fight her hardest to beat the deadly disease, she was the bravest person I had ever known, even when we found out it was terminal she still fought to the bitter end, not wanting to leave me. On the night she passed away, I had been by her bedside, sitting in uncle Savas' lap, when she took her last breath with aunty Petra holding her hand. Looking back on it now, I'm pleased she hadn't died alone. Savas picked me up into his arms and carried me to the window.

"Open it Angel and let her soul find your Papa." I had flipped the catch and felt the air rush out.

"Bye Momma, I love you."

Savas had taken me from the room and left my Grandmother and Petra with my Mom and that was when I finally cried myself to sleep in his protective arms.

Grandma had wanted me to move to Milwaukee and live with her. I had hated the idea from the moment she'd told me. Not only had I lost my Mom but I would be losing the only family I had ever known. Jazz and I had cried for hours and had even talked about running away. After the funeral service, everyone had returned to the Remizov's home. Mika, who was now eighteen, never left my side, with his huge arms wrapped around me pulling me close into him. He gently kissed the top of my head.

"Angel I'm so, so sorry."

I felt so safe and secure in his embrace and from that day I always knew I would love him forever. Luca and Alex had Jazz in a sibling sandwich, a protective shield. All three brothers hated seeing us so upset.

Savas had taken my Grandma into his office for a 'chat,' which meant do not disturb. When they had returned about an hour later she looked happier and a little relieved, I could tell she had been crying by her puffy eyes, she called me over.

"Izzy, I've talked to Savas and have decided it would be best if I moved here, would you like that better?"

The way that I threw my arms around her was clearly my answer. It was the first time in days that it felt a little less bleak. I never did find out what had been discussed behind the closed door of Savas' office, even years later she took that to the grave with her.

I didn't see much of Mika after that, he had left for college where he studied hard in preparation for taking over the family business one day, I always knew he'd make a brilliant CEO. Over the next few years we waved goodbye to all the boys as they left one by one for college. It was a relief when Alex finally left, it was hard trying to flirt and date boys when you had two overly protective big brothers in the shadows. The pair frightened off every potential hook up Jazz and I ever had.

In the holidays all the family would congregate together, the Remizov's always included Gran and I. Sometimes Mika would come home with a girlfriend in tow, which nearly killed me to have to put on a friendly face. There was one woman in particular I hated, I'd been practically green with envy, Yana Kozlov, and she was becoming a permanent fixture in his life and my arch enemy. Mika seemed quite smitten with her and that only splinted my heart even more. I was now counting down the days until Jazz and I left for college.

Just before we turned eighteen, Jazz and I received our acceptance letters from Berkeley in California. Her folks and my Gran hated that we had chosen somewhere so far away. I couldn't wait to stretch my wings and taste independence at last.

I had always been close to Savas and some days I'd catch him staring at me. He'd smile saying "you caught me." I asked him once why he would look at me like that, he told me a story that was still emotional for him to recall.

"I once had a very beautiful friend, she meant the world to me and you Angel look so very much like her that you could be twins. Sadly she was killed many years ago now," he had smiled as he remembered her.

"What was her name?"

Before thinking about it he answered, "Natasha," he looked like he could have kicked himself.

"That's my middle name, how spooky."

Savas' smile didn't reach his eyes.

"Yes," then he cursed in Russian, quickly changing the subject.

Something didn't sit right and it had niggled me for years, I'd seen a few people look at me then talk about a Natasha, whenever I would walk into a room and always in Russian, a language I wasn't supposed to know but from being little, Jazz had taught me and I was as fluent in it as if I was a native. That had been mine and Jazz's' secret. She as well as her brothers had been told to only ever speak to me in English, I never understood why? But I had pestered her until eventually I had worn her down, I'd been so sick and tired of Luca and Alex talking about me and not being able to understand what they were saying. I knew it was a big thing that Jazz had done by defying her Dad and I had promised her that I would never tell.

CHAPTER TWO

Savas and Petra had not wanted us to stay in the dorms so had bought a two bedroomed apartment, just a few minutes walk from the campus, it was wonderful and we had the time of our lives.

We had some of the same classes, Jazz wanted to go into hospitality and the entertainment side of their family business, eventually she wanted to run one of the families bars, while I had more of a head for math's and accounting, which thankfully I found easy. We both made up for lost time enjoying the attention of the opposite sex and going out on dates without the fear of bloodshed. Jazz was more out going than me, full of confidence and being absolutely stunning with her long, dark, glossy hair and caramel eyes with thick lashes, she was a total exotic beauty, features which she shared with her siblings. Watching guys falling all over themselves was entertaining. I on the other hand was still pretty shy and a little bit prudish.

We had started our sophomore year and had only been back a month when we spotted a black SUV with tinted windows parked outside our apartment. As we got closer, the doors opened and out stepped Mika, Luca and Alex, all looking very somber. Jazz froze and instantly the color drained from her cheeks.

"WHAT! What are you doing here?" she screamed, knowing something terrible was about to come crashing down around her.

Mika approached her.

"Princess," was all he managed to say.

"No! No! No!" She sobbed as all three brothers ran to her. I stood there, completely numb, watching this scene play out until tears cascaded down my cheeks. Luca pulled me into him, and all five of us stood in the street, clinging to one another.

Alex took my keys and opened the door; Luca helped me in while Mika carried in Jazz. She was a total wreck, and my heart ached for her, for all of them. Once we were seated, I asked what had happened. Mika held on to Jazz, cradling her, so it was Luca who spoke.

"Our parents were in a helicopter on route to a meeting in Chicago, when it was brought down in an electrical storm, there were no survivors." Gasping in horror I watched Jazz cling to Mika tighter.

"I'm so sorry," I choked out before the emotion over came me, Luca embraced me once more.

It had been the worst twenty-four hours, we'd all flown back home and hardly anyone spoke, still to raw and all in shock. I had held Jazz's' hand, not saying a word but she knew I was there for her. We all stayed together at the family home, I had slept in the same bed as Jazz and cuddled her till she had cried herself to sleep, it was the least I could do for her.

Eventually I left her sleeping and headed to the kitchen desperate for a drink of tea, maybe something stronger! I was surprised to find the lights on and Mika sat at the breakfast bar with his head in his hands and a glass of scotch to the side.

I coughed not wanting to startle him, he looked up and a single tear dropped on to the counter top.

"I'm sorry Mika; I didn't want to make you jump."

He wiped his face roughly with his hand, "No, no you didn't."

I walked towards him and opened my arms, wondering if he would accept my gesture? He did and this time it was me consoling him. He was seated so we were nearly eye level with each other, instead of him towering above me at 6'5 to my 5'3.

I held him close to my chest and could smell that citrus spiced cologne he wore. I kissed his cheek and heard him take a deep breath, not wanting to let him go.

"I'm here for you Mika, if you want to talk or just want a hug."

He sniffed softly, "Thanks Izzy, you are a real Angel, anyway what are you doing up, it's nearly three o'clock?"

"I needed a strong drink."

"You are a year to young for that, how about a sweet tea with honey, that will help you sleep?" he winked as he made it. We sat and chatted while I drank my tea; I reached out and squeezed his hand.

"We'll get through this."

He raised it and kissed my knuckles pulling me up out of the chair.

"We will, now sleep time Angel," he whispered as he kissed my cheek.

Over the next few weeks there was so much activity, official looking men in suits had been coming and going from the Remizov house and in and out of Savas' office where Mika had taken up residence.

After the funeral Mika changed, it sounds like a strange thing to say but he had. He became more of a man if that sounds at all possible.

I'd over heard one man greet him in Russian as the new Pakhan? That meant boss, well I suppose he was now. Again Natasha was mentioned with eyes looking at me and the men would nod and smile, I pretended not to understand and simply smiled back before leaving the room.

I was so pleased when Jazz said it was time to return to college. Luca drove us to the airport, it was going to be hard, especially for Jazz, but I would always be there for her. Getting back into the swing of things and establishing a routine helped to keep our minds occupied. Those first few weeks were the toughest for her, all our friends had rallied around us and it was real touching and so heart felt, I was truly grateful, we both were.

Mika called Jazz everyday to start with, he'd been so worried about her, and his roll in the family had changed to the father figure, even if he didn't want it. He adapted to it for the sake of his siblings. My respect and love for him only grew.

Over the months things changed, we matured became more independent and less reliant on one another, but we were still as close as ever. The build up to Christmas had been awful, Jazz wanted to cancel it; she didn't want to go home or do anything. She had already cancelled Thanksgiving this year, and I was determined not to let her do it to Christmas. So one night when she came home from class I had opened a bottle of Zinfandel and we talked. I did get her to agree to go spend the holidays with her brothers, but she argued with me until she was blue in the face when I had told her it should be just the four of them, they all needed to reconnect. It was killing me because I could see the cracks forming inside their family but she couldn't. She really didn't like the fact that I wasn't going with her to Detroit.

"So you are spending Christmas here with your Gran?"

"Yes, she's really looking forward to the warmer climate, it helps with her arthritis apparently," I smiled, "but I will miss you."

She pouted, "We'll Skype everyday."

I promised that we would and she hugged me before leaving the room to go run the bath. That had given me a chance to text Mika.

"Done, she's coming."

"Thx babe u r an Angel."

"U r welcome :)"

"Let me know what time u land so we can pick u up."

Oh shit!

"Only Jazz, Gran is coming out here to me but I'll get Jazz to give u a call xxx."

Two minutes later my cell rang – it was Mika.

"Isabelle, you and your Gran should be spending it here with us!"

Christ he was using my full name.

"No Mika, the four of you need this time together, you need family time!"

"You are part of this family."

That did make my heart grow.

"That's real sweet, but it's all arranged and Gran is looking forward to the warmth and sun shine."

"It's been a long time since you have been back home, I, I mean we miss you."

"Next vacation I promise."

That seemed to appease him a little.

"OK but you should know that you should never break a promise to a Russian! It could be dangerous," he chuckled.

"Merry Christmas Mika."

"You too Angel."

Gran had decided to move back to Milwaukee once I'd left for college. I seriously doubted she had ever really settled properly in Detroit, she'd only relocated for me. So I would usually go there and stay with her in the holidays. A few times Jazz came with me but other times Jazz and I had hit South Beach in Miami and once we did Mardi Gras in New Orleans and oh my God, what a week that had been in The Big Easy, we had collected so many beads her brothers would have had coronaries if they had seen us flashing our stuff.

Jazz had giggled, "We can cross that off our bucket lists!"

I'd been a little confused.

"What Mardi Gras?"

That only made her laugh harder.

"No public nudity dummy."

We had returned back to college with the same amount of spending money we had left with; news- flash, show naked flesh and men will buy you the world, who knew! Back in my bedroom I had a clear glass bust statue of a lady who now proudly displayed all those glittery beads I'd earned and which, by the way, I still have today and it still makes me smile every time I see it and remember that fabulous week.

Jazz started seeing a real cute guy called Rob Parker, he was so sweet and fell hard for her. I'd asked her once if she'd told her brothers about him. By the way her face contorted I guessed no.

"God no! You do remember what they are like? In their minds we are still pure, lily white with intact hymens, untouched by any male hand."

I chuckled and thought mine is, but not so much on the pure lily white, when it came to it I'd always chickened out, nobody so far had been worthy enough to claim it, but I had done other things and even if I do say so myself, I'm pretty good at the old blow job.

Jazz spoke again snapping me back to reality.

"Anyway, it's not serious with Rob, we're just having fun. Once we graduate he's going back to Houston to work for his Dad and we're going home, so why put him through the torture of those three goons?"

It made sense and the last part made me laugh because it was so true. Rob and his buddies made the last two years of college so much fun. We partied like the old song said 'like it was 1999.' Bradley Roth was Rob's best friend and who had tried his luck with me on numerous occasions and failed, we did have a few make out sessions but that had been it. Eventually he'd accepted the fact we'd only ever be friends.

We all hung out together at a bar called 'Chaplin's,' it was like Cheers and we thanked the Lord on many occasion for our fantastic fake ID's. I would sing karaoke all the time, singing was a true love of mine, I'd sung in the school choir and always got the solo lead, and I could sing anything with the exception of opera. Jazz had always been my number one fan.

"I'm so jealous of you! You can sing like your nickname," she'd say.

My favourite genre was classic rock, you cannot beat a little AC/DC and I would blast 'Back in black' and 'Highway to hell' out of my bedroom, much to Jazz's dismay.

CHAPTER THREE

The last Christmas before we finished college I spent with Gran in Milwaukee. Over the past few months she had worried me to death, something was definitely amiss. She'd told me I was being silly, but when I had talked to Jazz and she'd agreed with me I knew I needed to do something. So when Rita, Gran's friend called me out of the blue one day, my suspicions were confirmed.

Rita had told me she had been concerned about her behaviour and had taken her to the doctors, where they had run tests and she was diagnosed with the early onset of Alzheimer's. It had crushed me and I had sobbed when I told Jazz about it. She offered to come with me for the holidays but I had said no and I think she was a little relieved and I couldn't blame her. I would have been too if the boot was on the other foot.

This would probably be the last Christmas I had with her, who knows just how long she'd remember me for, that's what hurt the most. Arriving in Milwaukee I was dreading what I would be walking into. But as the cab pulled up to her driveway I saw the decorations and lights adorning the eaves of the house and I smiled.

Seeing her standing there in her apron, she'd been cooking while waiting for me. She waved all excited, I had to wipe away a sly tear before getting out, and at least I still had her for now.

To my surprise Jazz met me at the airport on my return.

"What are you doing here?" I hugged her tight.

"I missed you, how's Gran?"

I filled her in, I was still worried she'd had a few episodes of confusion while I'd been there, but Rita had promised to keep an eye on her, which reassured me. Before I left I was given power of attorney over her financial and legal things, I signed all the paperwork for her lawyer, and that alone was a daunting prospect. I was only twenty two and now was responsible for another person. It had been Gran's idea and while she was still of sound mind she'd had her lawyer sort it all out for her.

Jazz held me while I cried. "Listen, I talked to Mika and he said not to worry about anything and to call him, he will help you with everything." That had been such a burden lifted.

Back at our apartment Jazz told me all about her Christmas present; she had been given one of the family's bars, her own little business to run as she wanted to, with no interference from Mika, Luca or Alex. The only clause had been that she had to graduate with honours and to say she was happy was putting it mildly, she was fit to burst.

All she had talked about when we were younger was having her own bar, serving home cooked food during the day and being known for hosting live bands at night, I had lived her dream with her and was so happy it was finally coming true.

The bar was called *Red Square* and was in a real trendy part of town. Then she handed me an envelope.

"What's this?"

"It's your present from the guys."

I had to reread it twice before I really took in what was written.

"Oh my God!" I gasped.

"What, what does it say?"

"It's a job offer, at the head offices' administration department."

Jazz clapped her hands, "That's wonderful, but I had wanted

you to work with me looking after the books and legal stuff," she giggled.

I handed her the letter and watched her eyes bulge out.

"I couldn't offer you that salary!"

The pay was fantastic and all the perks that went with it, how could I refuse? It also had the same stipulation Jazz's had about graduating.

I had just placed my pen down when the Professor shouted "time." Talk about perfect timing. That had been my final exam and deep down I knew I had done really well. I floated out of the room on such a high. Jazz had been waiting for me in the quad, she'd sat her final the day before and as soon as she spotted me she ran over, yelling "freedom." I screamed and everyone cheered. We linked arms and skipped out of the campus leaving Berkeley for the last time as students. In five days time we would be on a plane Michigan bound.

Everything was nearly packed; I was sitting in my room bubble wrapping my glass bust, reminiscing about the last three and a half years. It was astonishing just how much had happened, good as well as bad. In our first year we had become good friends with a foreign exchange student called Anka Bjorkman, she was from Sweden and was the typical Nordic Goddess, tall blond and gorgeous, she lived in Malmo just outside of Stockholm.

She had already done one year of her two year placement. She had taught Jazz and I Swedish. The day Jazz asked her if she would and explained the reason why to her, I had nearly pee'd myself.

"Can you imagine the reaction we'd get back home, it will piss off my brothers' big time? Play them at their own game and beat the pants off them."

All three of them still didn't know I was fluent in Russian. Luca and Alex would talk in Russian to wind me up and I would play along pretending to get annoyed. I'd gotten so good at masking my reactions to what was being said, it did bite me in the ass a few times over the years, hearing things I shouldn't, that's what you get for eavesdropping, but I never did repeat what I heard.

"Izzy, seriously though just being able to talk to you about men and sex without being spied on," she sighed.

I knew full well what she meant, no matter how quiet we'd whisper, one of them would always hear.

"Are you sure there are only three of them?" I'd laughed. It took us just shy of a year to learn to speak Swedish, well to get by enough for Jazz and I to understand each other, reading it was a whole different matter. I couldn't wait to mess with Alex and Luca, that was going to be fun.

Mika had already sold the apartment. I had asked Jazz if we were shipping the big furniture out with the rest of our things and she'd said no.

When I asked why she said, "We don't need it."

"I do, for when I find a place back in Detroit."

Her face fell, "Izzy you are ruining my surprise," she sulked, before begrudgingly telling me about my homecoming gift from her.

Mika had moved into the other side of the house and Jazz had had his old room redecorated and furnished for me.

"It was your graduation gift, I knew I had to live at home and how could I survive that with out my BFF close at hand. The bonus being there is no rent to pay, so you can save all your money and eventually buy your own place out right."

I had nearly strangled her I squeezed her so tight.

"Aw, thank you."

"I love you girl."

Rob had already left California, he'd begged Jazz to go with him, he was devastated when she'd said no and explained why, saying this was a whole new chapter of their lives and new beginnings for them both so it would be best if they ended it now. She did not want the long distance relationship and I totally understood why, we were too young for that and life was far too short.

Waking up in a cold sweat with your heart racing and gasping for air is not a pleasant experience and it wasn't something I had done since I was a child. My dream or more like nightmare was, I had been working my hardest and failing miserably.

The boss was a horrid man who constantly shouted at me, 'If you can't do the fucking job you shouldn't be here.' When I'd begun to cry he just continued the abuse, 'that won't work on me little girl,' he'd spat. I had run out catching a glimpse of my reflection in the glass window, I was dressed like a child with pigtails. That was when I had woke up, wiping the sweat from my brow, "stupid dream."

I was trying to laugh it off when I suddenly had an epiphany. We had three days left in California and I needed a complete make over, new wardrobe, new hair, shit, new everything. For the past six or seven years all I had worn was jeans and T shirts, hoodies when it got cooler and my hair was permanently tied up in a pony tail. It was time to look like the career woman I was going to be.

Jazz came with me to the shopping mall, she didn't need asking twice and I needed the help. Finally I had bought seven work suits, three with pants and four with skirts, umpteen blouses in pastel colours, all cut and fitted beautifully making my boobs look lush and the finishing touch was the matching shoes that completed the new look.

I was booked into the salon at one o'clock; Jazz took my bags and left me saying, "I want a fashion show when you get back."

"Get the wine chilling and call me Tara Banks," I giggled,

shouting at her.

Four hours later I walked out with gorgeous ash blond high-lights and about five inches cut off the length, so it now sat on my shoulders and had been flat ironed straight. I loved it so much I even bought a pair of straightening irons. The beautician had waxed everything, may as well start out as you mean to go on. She had applied natural tones in the make-up and nail polish; I felt like a new woman and didn't recognise the person looking back at me in the mirror.

Walking into the apartment, Jazz was in the kitchen.

"Hi," I sang.

"Holy fucking Christ, Izzy you look amazing, WOW! Twirl, twirl," and I did.

"You are stunning, you look so grown up, fuck me!"

"Jasmine!" I chastised her, but I did look fucking fab, and it only cost me what $3000, now fuck me!

CHAPTER FOUR

The Present Day

The day had arrived, time to bid farewell to California and the place we had called home for the past three and a half years. It was pretty emotional and we were both quite weepy. By the time we were dropped off at the airport, our sadness had been replaced with excitement. Jazz was practically buzzing about all the plans she had for her bar.

"I want to give new bands a chance, be famous like the Cavern Club in Liverpool for discovering the next Beatles or even bigger, and during the day be a family friendly place that serves great food. My first task will be to hire a chef."

Her enthusiasm was contagious; I just sat back and listened to her, enjoying the company and the smooth flight.

Luca and Alex were waiting for us in arrivals. It had been over a year since I'd last seen them, it was nearly two since I had saw Mika last. The pair had not changed, still attracting the attention of females and loving it, I was so happy to see them again. I heard Alex speaking to Luca in Russian.

"Holy fuck bro, what's happened to little Izzy?"

"Wow, she's grown up and filled out real fine."

"Look at those sweet tits."

Jazz hit him round the head then turned to me and played our golden ticket.

"Jag tror att de godkanner den nya dig!" which translates to "I think they approve of the new you!"

"Jag kan inte skylla pa dem!" or "I can't blame," them I laughed.

The looks on Alex and Luca's faces were priceless.

"What the hell was that?" Luca asked.

Jazz replied smugly, "Oh just something we learnt. Now you know what Izzy feels like when you do it to her," she winked at me, I loved it.

Eventually after the hugs and nearly having my ribs broken by them, we were finally in the car on our way home. I was dying to see the room Jazz had prepared for me and wondered if it still had Mika's sexy scent in it.

"Is Mika home?" Jazz asked.

"No he's away on business but will be home on Friday."

I tried to hide my disappointment, but then what's another two days after two years.

"How is he? Is he still seeing that cow Yana?" Jazz scowled.

Luca chuckled while Alex shook his head.

"Only for the occasional hook up, she wants more but Mika doesn't. I think he's feeling the pressure from the Brotherhood to settle down though."

Luca swerved and nearly crashed the car; he glared at Alex and in Russian growled, "Shut it Alex for fucks' sake!"

I looked out of the window, trying to look carefree, what the hell was the brotherhood? That kind of killed the moment and the rest of the drive we were all quiet.

"Come Izzy, let me show you your room, the guys will bring our bags up," she said, blowing them kisses as she dragged me up the magnificent staircase.

Finally we stopped outside Mika's old room, which was literally opposite hers.

"Christ, I hope you like it!"

I couldn't believe she sounded nervous, and that she was worried about me! She smiled and opened the door and I was blown away, it was absolutely perfect, all my favourite colours, pale aquamarine, creams and gold. A huge king-size bed, matching walnut furniture, the dressing table and mirror was simply to die for. I couldn't wait to put all my trinkets and things on it.

"Jazz, I, I," was all that came out before the tears started to roll down my cheeks.

"Oh Izzy, I'm guessing you like it then," she hugged me.

"No, I love it, it's more than I ever imagined, so much more. God thank you."

"It's me who should be thanking you, you have saved me from living with those three on my own," she smirked.

Just then Luca came in with my luggage.

"Do you want these on the bed Angel?"

"Please."

Angel. I hadn't heard that in a while. We heard Alex dragging Jazz's bags, "what the hell have you got in this sis?"

Jazz turned to me, "We'll let you unpack and get settled. I'll get Sonja to bring us some tea up."

Sonja was the housekeeper, a real lovely lady, a mother figure I'd always liked.

"That sounds wonderful." I watched Luca and her leave.

I stood looking round for a moment, taking it all in; I had never had such a huge room before. Near the window were two big comfy arm chairs that I could picture myself snuggling down in and reading a good book. In between them was a small table that had a vase full of fresh cream coloured roses, the scent permeated the room.

The bed had a 42" plasma TV built into the foot board, a quick flick of a button and it extended or retracted, "wow!" I said to myself, don't you just love modern technology. There were two doors that were closed, one lead into a walk in closet, *love it!* The other was my very own fabulous en suite bathroom, an oval tub that just begged for bubbles and a shower cubical, all in amazing sandy coloured tiles, which gave it a European feel.

All my favourite shampoos and soap, even toothpaste and the mouthwash I used, Jazz had hit every nail on the head. Smiling to myself I thought I would never ever want to leave.

I'd just unlocked my case when Sonja knocked and walked in, bringing me a much needed drink.

"Welcome home Izzy," she lovingly cuddled me.

"Thank you. How have you been Sonja?"

"Oh I can't complain. Anything you want, just holler OK? I'll leave you to it then, dinner will be ready at six."

I loved her thick Russian accent.

"I'll be down then and thanks Sonja."

I finished unpacking my clothes, the rest of our things were being shipped out by road, which included my baby powder blue Fiat 500i. The minute I saw it on the showroom forecourt I had to have him, yes him, I'd named him Bertie. They would be arriving by truck on Sunday. I still had a few ornaments and bits and pieces I had brought with me so the room did start to look like mine. I was so excited to beginning this new era of my life.

I called Gran everyday and all seemed to be well on her end; unbeknown to her I also called Rita once a week, just to check in just to make sure. It seemed like the medication was doing its job for now. I had told her I would come and visit as soon as I got settled into my new job and she was looking forward to it, she made me promise to call on Monday after my first day.

It was Friday and Mika was due back in town late afternoon, he had been in New York handling business. I had asked Jazz what the brotherhood was. She'd said she thought it was some Russian form of the Masons. Savas her dad had been head of it,

Mika had inherited the role now.

"You know how secretive the Masons are, well Russian's are even more so."

"Are Luca and Alex in it?"

"Yeah, it's some sort of male thing, not many females are allowed in it thank God."

That night Jazz and I decided to paint the town red, a last blow out before our new responsible adult lives began on Monday. We planned to have dinner with the guys before heading out; my tummy was full of butterflies about seeing Mika again.

While sprawling on my bed watching some reality crap TV Jazz was addicted to, she casually informed me that Mika was home. I tried to hide my stupid girly smile.

"I know you have a thing for him I always have!"

"What? No, don't be silly I don't – NO."

By now she was giggling at my bumbling awkwardness.

"Ermm, yeah, I do have eyes."

"Oh shut up!" Talk about being mortified.

"I could have a word with him?"

I knew she was winding me up but I still bit.

"Fuck Jazz don't you dare, I swear to God I'll move out, leave the State!"

She loved it, "Chill, I'm just teasing, and I promise I won't."

She crossed her heart as I slumped onto the pillows.

"Anyway, in his eyes I will always be a little girl."

I sounded defeated and that somehow was like I'd given Jazz a sign.

"Izzy my aim tonight is to change that, Mika will see you tonight as the new, sexy, drop dead gorgeous woman you have become."

I liked the sound of that, "OK, you are on," let the challenge begin.

Jazz leapt off the bed and into the closet, all I could decipher was "No, no, no, ERM-mm what were you thinking, AHA!," she emerged with a black lace over dark green satin dress, it had off the shoulder capped sleeves a sculpted bodice and it figure hugged the hips, it stopped just above the knees and wearing it with killer 5 inch spikes made me feel sexy as hell. She did my make-up, making my eyes real smoky, the colours made my blue eyes sparkle and really stand right out.

"Oh babe, you have those come to bed eyes down to a fine art."

She made me blush, "Do you think it's too much?"

"Never," she winked as she went to get ready while I straightened my hair.

"You ready?" she shouted while I was in the bathroom.

"Nearly, I'll meet you downstairs," I said as I walked into the bedroom.

Jazz was standing there and her jaw dropped.

"Wow Izzy, the full get up is so much better than I had envisioned, you look so different, the boys are gonna be fighting for your attention tonight girl. Mika will definitely not be seeing a little girl any more, trust me; I can't wait to see his face."

"I'll be down in five; I've just got to find my earrings."

"OK, see you down there."

As I approached the lounge I heard them all chatting, Mika was standing leaning with one arm on the mantle by the fireplace. I had forgotten just how tall he was, the power and confidence radiated from him, he was the ultimate alpha. His designer suit was simply perfection, defining his muscular body and eye popping assets. But something had changed, his once warm, caramel eyes seemed darker, colder and he had an air around him, one of caution and danger, but that could just be my nerves getting the better of me. When I moved I caught his eye, he turned giving me his full, undivided attention as I stepped into the room the light gave him an unobstructed view.

His eyes widened in disbelief, taking me all in as they travelled the full length of my body. I could feel them burning into me as it sent a tingling sensation throughout my body, it was like he was actually touching me.

His eyes softened to the warm sexy ones I remembered.

"Isabelle, I didn't recognise you; my God you are a vision and half!"

"Why thank you, it's wonderful to see you

I walked into his open arms. Holy cow it felt like heaven in his embrace, I could have kicked myself when I let slip a low, husky moan, and I quickly walked to Jazz who was grinning like the Cheshire cat.

Alex piped up in Russian again.

"Didn't I tell you she was fucking stunning? God what I would give to...."

Mika cut him off.

"Touch her and I'll bleed you, brother or not."

Thank God I had my back to them as I silently mouthed "WOW!" to Jazz, before speaking in Swedish, "What was all that about?"

"Who knows, but I think we accomplished our quest – Mika noticed you."

Giggling we turned round and realised all three men were staring at us.

"Care to explain what that was little sister?" Mika asked.

"It's rude to speak in Russian around Izzy, so now you know

what that feels like."

Mika looked impressed, "Touché Princess, what language is it?"

"Now that's for us to know," Jazz teased him.

We watched his brows fuse together, his posture stiffened he really didn't like that at all. We loved it.

Throughout dinner I felt Mika's eyes on me.

"Where are you two going tonight?" Luca asked.

"Wherever our feet take us," Jazz replied.

"You will have Viktor drive you and bring you home!"

That wasn't a request but a statement from Mika.

"OK, yeah," Jazz moaned.

Luca spoke again.

"Alex and I are going to the new club tonight, why don't you call in, it might give you some ideas for your bar Jazz."

"Oh that sounds great, what's the club called?" she sounded excited.

"The Vanguard."

"Cool name, sounds like a plan."

Mika just sat and listened, taking it all in. We called Viktor after we said our goodbyes, and by the time we'd walked out-side he was already waiting for us.

"Thanks Vik," we both said.

"Buckle up ladies and lets blow this place," he chuckled.

Mika's world had gone into slow motion the moment he saw her, all the air left his lungs, it felt like he'd been punched in the gut and winded. She was a total beauty with a figure to be kissed and worshipped forever, he couldn't believe his eyes, Izzy had always been a sweet cutie, but holy mother of God how had she changed. She certainly wasn't a chubby, freckly kid any more but the most strikingly, hypnotic woman he'd seen in a very long time, maybe even ever. When he held her she fit perfectly into him, like she was made to measure and it had felt good, that damn sexy groan had caused his lower region to respond, what kind of spell had she cast on him?

After they left, Mika went into Boss-mode, bellowing to Luca, "Get Vik to call us as soon as he drops them off, I want eyes on them every fucking second!"

"On it."

"Alex you stay here, I'm going with Luca to Vanguard."

Alex looked down trodden, this was punishment from the comment he'd said earlier, he knew it.

"OK," he muttered. Even he knew better than to argue with the Pakhan. Mika went and quickly showered, changing into something more casual, this was going to be a whole new experience.

CHAPTER FIVE

Since taking over as Pakhan after his father's untimely death, Mika had carried on with his Papa's wishes. Savas had changed the brotherhood, bringing it into the 21st century and from being a total criminal organisation. The Bratva still caused feared just by the mere mentioning of its name and today anyone who threatened it never lived to tell the tale.

But now 75% of its business was legitimate and making millions of dollars, 25% was still old school, dealing in prostitution, gambling and loan sharking but even those had been modernized and brought up to date. No one woman was forced into the sex trade, none walked the streets and no money was ever exchanged from client to escort. All the ladies had monthly health checks by their own medical staff.

This was achieved by paying a membership and joining an exclusive high-class gentleman's club called *The Mansion*. All the clubs were kind of like a five star hotel that catered for every taste imaginable. If any member marked one of the ladies intentionally, well I can leave that to your own imagination.

On the books were some of the top brass and well known high ranking officials, it was safe to say they were well and truly left alone.

The Remizov's' had a chain of hotels, bars and clubs, all strictly above board and legal. The Head offices were situated down town and the conference room was state of the art sound proofed, monitored and scanned for bugs 24-7. Meetings held there were highly secretive and sensitive and not always kosher.

Mika's office was on the top floor, next to the conference

room. It housed just himself and his PA, Katia, who knew 100% of both sides of the business and she was the only female to be initiated into the Michigan brotherhood.

He had chosen Luca as his 2nd, the under boss, they were very much alike and the brotherhood accepted and respected him. Alex on the other hand was still learning and liked being a player too much; Mika wished he'd just grow out of it soon.

But who could blame him? He was handsome, rich and ripped, women threw themselves at him and Mika remembered what that had felt like. He trusted Alex with his life but the brotherhood still had to be convinced before giving him a seat on the board.

Instead Alex worked as a director in the hotel chain based in the Majestic Hotel, just a few blocks away from the head offices.

On the next floor down was Luca's and Sergi Polzin's offices. Sergi was Mika's *Kassir*, like he'd been his fathers before him, a trusted and respected friend.

The rest of the building consisted of Administration, Marketing, and HR, Reservations for the *Redline Corporation* and of course a staff canteen. Mika was proud of what his father had accomplished and always tried to walk in his footsteps without disrespecting him.

The office in *Vanguard* looked directly out onto the dance floor, the club was thumping and thankfully it was sound-proofed so the pounding music stayed out on the dance floor where it belonged. Mika stood watching, surveying the crowd below. Vik had called letting him know the girls had just entered the club. He was lovingly cradling a glass of aged bourbon as he waited patiently.

"What are you doing Mika? Jazz and Izzy will be fine you know that."

"Yes I do but I just want to make sure," he sounded so unconvincing.

Luca laughed, "Has she got to you brother?"

"Who, Izzy? She will always be just little Isabelle, another sister to me."

"Keep telling yourself that, you're not kidding anyone."

Mika turned and glared at Luca, who just tilted his head to the bar area and said, "So that won't bother you then?"

Spinning back round Mika watched as some stranger pawed at Izzy, rubbing his hand up and down her back. He felt the rage firing up inside him, his pulse raced as his eyes locked onto the target. The grip on the glass he was holding tightened so much it shattered the glass into a thousand shards.

"Oh yeah, just a sister, admit it Mika you are attracted to her."

Without another word he turned back round to watch her.

"Who is that prick?" Mika asked.

"Just some punk trying his luck I think."

Luca couldn't stop teasing him; he could sense Mika was close to bolting out of the door and kicking several tons of shit out of the poor schlep.

"Kick him out of the club," Mika ordered.

"What! No why?"

"Just do it Luca or trust me I will and you won't want that." Mika's tone was deadly.

"Christ, OK, but Mika get a fucking grip man."

With that Luca rang down to the front door and told them to remove the problem. Mika stood and enjoyed the scene that played out in front of him, he felt smug for a while but that was to be short lived.

Jazz and I were having a scream, the bars had been packed, the music fantastic and to top it off in *Vanguard* we meet up with some guys we went to school with who we hadn't seen in years. That was until a fight broke out and everyone got kicked out including Jazz and I.

"Jazz, tell the bouncers who you are."

"Balls to that, they're total dicks, lets go with the guys come on."

I had to agree that the door men were dicks.

Craig shouted, "Izzy, Jazz come on lets hit Club XS," and about fifteen of us marched up to the club.

Once all the commotion had died down Mika searched the sea of faces for her and Jazz, maybe they had gone to the ladies but after ten minutes still nothing. He had a female member of staff go check all the female restrooms, by now he and Luca were on the floor. When the staff member returned and said they weren't in any of them, panic bubbled in his gut. The pair walked to the entrance.

Luca asked, "How many did you kick out?"

The asshole puffed out like a proud peacock, "About fifteen, boss."

Mika erupted, "What! I said four guys; how the fuck did you translate that in to fifteen?"

Luca interjected, "Be precise, how many were women?"

"About four."

"You fucking idiot, two of them were family, where the fuck did they go?"

"Boss, no one said anything, we're sorry; I think they're headed east."

Mika boomed, "Luca, fucking find them.....now!"

I was quite tipsy and still enjoying myself, but after taking two more sips of my drink I was totally wasted, the room began to spin, I swear I was going to pass out. That's when Jazz got to me.

"Shit Izzy, lets get you home."

I could hardly form any words. Jazz hailed a cab and that was the last thing I remember until being shaken.

"Izzy we're home."

I fell out of the cab and scuffed my hands and knees, then the fresh air hit me and it turned my stomach, I managed to crawl to the bushes before puking my guts up.

"Izzy you are such a light weight," I heard her giggle.

The front door suddenly flew open, "Yeah, yeah they're home, well Izzy's in the bushes."

I could hear Alex speaking on his cell, by now all I wanted to do was die.

"That's what I said, in the bushes puking and flashing her ass off."

Jazz egged me on, "Get it all up girl."

I hated her at that precise moment, what the hell was happening to me.

"OK, see you guys soon," and he hung up.

"Jazz, that was a pissed off Mika; I suggest you go to bed before he and Luca get back."

Jazz wasn't laughing now, "Why's he mad?"

"You both got kicked out of *Vanguard* and disappeared, they have been looking everywhere for you."

"Shit, thanks for the heads up, what about Izzy?"

"I'll carry her, you just go," he warned her again.

Alex walked over to where I had collapsed, "Come on Angel, let's get you to bed."

I was completely out of it after that and I remember nothing else.

Alex laid her on the bed, still fully dressed, he just removed her shoes, before throwing a blanket over her, he propped pillows down her back so she wouldn't roll over on to it before he went to get a bucket, leaving just the bedside lamp on. When he returned he sat next to her on the bed and waited for Mika and Luca to come home, fearing leaving her alone.

Mika had every available man out searching, he had been so worried. All the Bratva's enemies knew who Jazz was, and the pair unknowingly had huge targets on their backs. It was two hours later, at three a.m. when Alex called.

Hanging up his phone Mika said, "They're at home. Thank fuck, turn the car round lets go."

"You'd better call the search off," Luca told him as he drove.

Ten minutes later they were home.

"So where the hell were they?" Luca asked.

"No idea, Alex said Izzy was off her head and puking in the bushes and he'd sent Jazz to bed."

"Oh the joy of having them home," Luca sighed.

Stepping out the car all seemed quiet and peaceful, inside the only lights on were the staircase and the hallway to Jazz and Izzy's rooms. Mika followed the light to his old room where he found Alex sitting on the bed beside her. She was still fully dressed; Mika would have beaten the crap out of him otherwise. Alex had placed the bucket at the side of the bed, just in case. Luca had gone to check on Jazz.

"She's snoring away like a drunken sailor," he smiled as he returned.

"You two go to bed, I'll stay with her," Mika told them.

"She's puking like the kid off the exorcist; surely she can't have anything left?" Alex graphically informed him.

"Nice," Mika grinned as he patted Alex's back, "thanks for looking after them," and ushered them both out of the room.

Mika slept with one eye open in the armchairs by the window, every time she made a noise he was awake. He'd only had one close call at around five, since then she hadn't stirred so just after eight he decided to chance it and left her, he needed coffee desperately as well as bringing her Advil and his own hangover cure he knew she'd need.

He had just sat down at the breakfast bar when Jazz crept in cautiously looking fragile.

"Morning Jasmine." The stern voice of Mika had rattled her delicate head.

"Hi." She sat next to him, hugging her coffee mug like a life preserver, waiting for the inevitable lecture.

"Where the hell did you go when you left *Vanguard*?" he asked.

"Left, more like kicked out, by that dick on the door," she huffed.

"Tell me what happened?"

Jazz replayed the nights events, "Then some ass threw a punch and whacked Craig, that's when all hell broke loose."

"Who's Craig?"

"Izzy and I met up with the old school gang we hadn't seen in years, it had been wonderful till that dick and ass threw us all out."

Mika felt a twinge of guilt; it had been his fault after all.

"So where did you end up?"

"Club XS, but I think someone was messing with our drinks, one minute Izzy was fine, the next I'd never seen her so drunk," she frowned sounding upset.

Mika could feel his rage building again, if that was true he would find and kill the person who had done it.

"What about the one thing I insisted on Jazz, calling Vik?"

"I'm sorry; I was too worried about Izzy and wanted to just get her home, please Mika don't be mad."

"The best thing you did last night was taking Alex's advice and going to bed, trust me it would have been a whole different story had you not."

He gave Jazz one of his stern glares, which made her squirm in her seat.

"And to top the night off I had to baby-sit Isabelle to make sure she didn't choke on her own vomit all night."

Jazz had never been so grateful that she had such an over protective brother. "Thank you for that and I'm truly sorry, I really am."

"Do not do it again, I can promise you this, next time I will not be quite so forgiving." Feeling ashamed, she lowered her head, "We won't I swear."

"Luca, Alex and I have to go out soon on business, make sure to check on Izzy, get her to drink some water, we'll be home later." Just then the other two walked in dressed and ready to go, he walked over to Jazz, and kissed the top of her head, then the three left, leaving her and Izzy to suffer together and that alone would be punishment enough.

CHAPTER SIX

Jazz walked into Izzy's room, the drapes were closed, and the only light was coming from the bedside lamp. The air was heavy and oppressive so she went and opened the window, letting fresh air in. Izzy looked so pale and she still had last nights clothes on, her dress splattered with vomit, which Jazz unzipped and managed to remove without ripping the fabric, leaving her in her bra and panties. She tried to wake her but the only reaction she got was a muffled groan, so decided to leave her for a while and went to shower and change.

Jazz was so concerned that Izzy wasn't a big drinker but she'd never seen her like this before. Thirty minutes later she returned with Advil and a glass of fresh cold water, and touched Izzy's clammy cheek.

"Izzy please wake up!" After trying for what seemed like an age, her eyes flickered and eventually opened a little. Helping lift her head she asked, "Can you please drink some water Iz," and held the glass to her mouth. She was relieved when Izzy sipped it but seconds later was placing the glass down and reaching quickly for the bucket, as it came back up. This went on for over an hour, by now Jazz was worried sick.

Izzy couldn't keep anything down and she was not coming round.

She ran to her room and called Mika; it went straight to voicemail, "Call me ASAP," she then rang Luca.

"Hey piss-head, how are you feeling?"

"Where's Mika?" Jazz snapped

"Whoa, whoa, what's wrong, he's in a meeting?" Jazz was becoming hysterical and Luca was getting worried.

"It's Izzy; I think she was roofied last night!"

"Roofied, what the fuck are you talking about Jazz?"

"Izzy is so sick, she keeps throwing up and passing out and she is so disoriented, Luca I'm scared, I've never seen her like this before, should I call 911?"

"Princess we're on our way, just stay with her."

"Hurry," she pleaded.

"I'll call when we are nearly home." After she hung up she returned to Izzy.

Luca stepped out of the elevator just as Mika and Tomaz Krupin rounded the corner, Tom had been placed in charge of *The Mansion* clubs.

"Luca I thought you would've been in on the meeting today?" Tom said as he held out his hand.

"I had other business to attend to but I will next time," Luca answered as he shook his hand.

"You must drop by the club soon, it's been a while."

Smiling, Luca nodded and bid farewell, "Till next time Tom."

The instant the elevator doors shut Mika was on Luca.

"What's up?" knowing something was wrong just by his unexpected arrival.

He quickly explained what Jazz had said causing Mika to change right in front of him. No longer was he the loving brother, but the fearsome lethal Pakhan whose rage and anger had deadly consequences, even Luca knew to fear him.

On route in the car, Mika called Reg Duffy, the owner of Club XS and issued demands, Reg had the common sense to not refuse, agreeing to go through the surveillance footage with Alex, then he rang Alex.

"Find me the fucker who spiked Izzy's drink and bring the cunt to me."

Luca asked him to ring Jazz and let her know they were two minutes out; he did this in his calm, loving, brotherly voice. When they pulled into the drive way, Jazz was stood anxiously waiting for them and as soon as Mika had the door open she ran into his arms, eager for his comfort. With his arms around her they walked into the house.

"Princess, go and put a fresh pot of coffee on its going to be needed." Giving her a quest to do would keep her mind occupied, he pecked her cheek then left her with Luca.

Mika opened Izzy's door and was greeted with a cool breeze, the drapes were slightly ajar and the window open. The lamp still on lit the room, subtly shining on her pale face, making the dark circles around her eyes more prominent. He sat on the bed taking hold of one of her hands, turning it and gently nipping the skin on the back of it together, it took far too long to return to normal, a sure sign she was dangerously dehydrated, which concerned him. Reaching for his cell he called their doctor, who worked for them strictly off the books of course, and explaining the situation the doctor said he'd be there in twenty minutes. Mika left Izzy sleeping and walked back to the kitchen where Jazz handed him a coffee.

"Well?"

"I've called the doc. She's really dehydrated from all the puking and as for being drugged I'd say definitely, I'm going back up to wait with her. Send the doc straight up when he arrives," he said as he turned and left.

Dr Terence (Terry) Morton arrived within the fifteen minutes. He was a plastic/cosmetic surgeon with an affluent clinic down town; he also had a taste for the ladies and panache for Texas hold'em. The brotherhood had made a real sweet deal with the doc under Savas' rein, free membership to all *The Man-*

sion clubs and a one off, two million dollar line of credit to one of the back-room high stakes games, for his medical services and facilities with no questions asked, it worked well and both parties were very satisfied.

"So Mika, what do we have here?" Terry asked.

"We think she was drugged last night, when she's not passing out she's vomiting, Jazz said one second she was fine, the next she was out of it," Mika explained while Terry examined her.

"I think you are right, but the good news is whatever she was spiked with is out of her system now, this is just the after affects. I'll give her something to stop the vomiting and put an IV line in to get fluids into her." Mika nodded.

"I think it's wise for you to wake her, she knows who you are, I'll probably scare her."

He agreed.

"Izzy, Izzy, wake up, come on Angel wakeup for me." He spoke softly and gently, as he stroked her cheek. It took a few moments but she finally opened her eyes, giving him the sweetest little smile.

"Izzy the doc here is going to give you something to settle your tummy and make you better, so you'll feel a little scratch." He held her hand, "You can squeeze my hand babe," then he nodded to Terry to proceed.

With the drip in place, Izzy was soon sleeping again, Terry and Mika stepped to the far side of the room.

"She should pick up pretty quickly once the fluids have been replaced. Give her plenty of glucose based drinks and as for food, just small and light for the next 24 hours, I'll be back in the next few hours to remove the IV, any problems just call me."

Mika walked him out. "Thanks Terry."

Jazz and Luca were waiting at the foot of the staircase, "Can we see her?" Jazz asked. Mika nodded, all three walked back up to her room.

"When will she come round?"

"As soon as that drip has put some fluid back in her." She looked relieved to hear that.

"Do we have Gatorade or something like that in the fridge?" Mika queried.

"I don't think so, why?"

"Izzy will need plenty of it." Luca suggested he'd go get all the necessities and by the time Jazz had finished, he had a huge shopping list.

"Gee thanks Jazz, are you sure there isn't anything else!" Luca's reply was saturated in sarcasm.

I woke up feeling like Michael Flatley was doing the Riverdance in my head and it hurt to open my eyes. I could hear Jazz and Mika talking, my throat was raw and dry.

"Oh God kill me now." I sounded like a two pack a day smoker.

"Izzy you are awake!" I felt the bed dip, "How are you feeling?"

"Rough, and thirsty, can I have some water please, what time is it?"

"Of course you can, and it's seven p.m." Holy shit, I'd been out of it all day.

"Hello Angel, you have had us all worried," Mika said and then went on to explain what had happened, filling in all the gaps. An hour later I felt almost human again.

"I really need a shower and to brush my teeth," I had practically begged, but Mika warned me.

"Not until the doc says so, he'll be back soon." Thankfully that was only ten minutes later.

Dr Morton removed my IV, he was extremely pleased by my recovery.

"Yes my dear you can take a shower, but just take it easy and don't push it for the next few days." He then gave Mika a list of do's and don'ts instead of me and that really peeved me off. As soon as he left I was up out of bed, asking Jazz to grab me some clean sheets while I went to wash the last 24 hours from my body.

"OK, but be sure to leave the door open just in case." She was deadly serious.

"I will, I promise." Carefully I made my way to the bathroom on very jelly legs, sitting on the toilet I was beginning to doubt my decision, but the need out weighed the risk and once the water hit my skin it was worth it.

Luca stumbled into the kitchen laden down with grocery bags, and Mika helped him put everything away.

"Hey has Alex called yet?" he asked.

"Yes, he'd only say it looks promising." Mika sounded annoyed, but Alex had been right not to say to much until he knew for sure what they were dealing with.

"He's going to call back when he knows more."

"OK."

Luca lightened the mood. "I need a shower and then do you fancy watching the game I recorded earlier?"

Mika actually smiled. "Sounds good to me, I could do with an ice cold beer after today."

"Cool I won't be long, I'll take Izzy a drink up on my way, get it all set up," he shouted on his way out.

Luca knocked on her door and walked straight in, only to be greeted by Isabelle with just a towel wrapped around her waist; her hair was wet, dripping down her exquisite body, freshly clean from her recent shower. His eyes popped out on stalks as he took his mistake in, what a body!

"Shit Luca, what the hell!"

"Fuck Izzy, I'm sorry." He turned and bolted for the door just as Jazz came down the hallway.

"What's wrong?"

Luca was blushing like a teenage girl as Mika arrived.

"I accidentally walked in on her while she was half naked, and Wow!"

"What?" Mika sounded furious, wanting to skin Luca alive and basically kill him in the most painful way possible? He was so jealous Luca had got to see what he could only imagine. Jazz snapped him out of it by giggling.

"Oh well accidents happen, I'll go talk to her." She took the bottle from him and left the two of them standing there. Mika felt his blood pressure boiling,

"I think I'll pass on the game, I need sleep more." It was either that or punch Luca.

"OK, see you in the morning, I'm sorry Mika it was an honest mistake." Luca felt he had to say something, he knew even if Mika didn't want to admit it; Izzy was someone special to him.

CHAPTER SEVEN

I woke up with the larks, feeling thankfully like myself again with only a slight headache. Showering had proved the best way to get rid of the annoying throb and blow the proverbial cobwebs away.

Pulling on my dressing gown I made my way into the deserted kitchen, as the coffee machine brewed its life saving elixir, I opened the French doors, it was going to be a beautiful day, the sun had just begun to rise, casting a golden glow on everything it kissed.

I filled a mug and walked out onto the decked patio area with its comfy cushioned seats and round table, sitting listening to the dawn chorus and feeling the cool breeze blowing gently on my skin; deeply inhaling fresh air had always been the best medicine.

I sat quietly, thinking about what the day ahead had install, all our things from California would be arriving sometime this afternoon.

Movement in the kitchen caught my eye and it was far too early for it to be Jazz, then Luca appeared, still looking mortified from last nights incident, which now I found highly amusing. The way he had tried to get out of my room by looking anywhere but at me, until he eventually found an escape.

"Ermm, hi Izzy." I could feel his awkwardness. "I'm really sorry about last night." His cheeks were taking on a rosy hint.

"Don't worry about it, but you do know the rule don't you?" I asked him.

Stony faced he looked confused. "No what?"

"Well you have seen me naked, now I get to see you. We can do it here and now or later in your room," I teased but letting him think I was serious.

Poor Luca didn't know how to respond; he was tripping over words and mumbling, I simply had to put him out of his misery.

"Luca I'm messing with you."

"That's just not funny." We both ended up laughing and decided to bury the mishap. We sat chatting and reminiscing about the past, I hadn't realised just how much I had missed the guys. Soon Jazz and Alex joined us, the last to grace us with his presence was Mika, looking even hotter in jeans and tight t-shirt that strained against his bulging biceps, even more than in his designer suits did. Wow he was the sexiest man alive, well in my eyes anyway.

"How are you feeling today," he asked.

"100% better thanks, sorry for causing so much trouble." I felt really guilty for that.

"You were no trouble, it wasn't your fault, you just had us all worried." He turned his attention to Luca and Alex speaking in Russian "Be ready in ten, we got shit to clean up!"

The pair just stood and left without a word. "Jazz, Izzy, we'll be back soon, if you need me just ring." He then left as well.

The little prick that caused all the worry and stress was Lenny O'Keefe, a skid mark of a man, he was a suspect in a few sexual assaults around the city but the police had no solid proof, now thanks to Alex and Reg, Mika did. Mika had watched the playback that showed Lenny dropping something into Izzy's drink when her back was turned, and then he stepped into the shadows and discreetly waited for the drug to take affect before swooping in.

Luckily for Izzy, Jazz had walked up to her as she took a sip from the laced drink and five minutes later Jazz was holding her up and helping her out of the club, the rest Mika knew.

"Gotcha!" he had hissed after watching the link Alex had sent him. He had men searching the streets for this piece of shit all night, and just before nine a.m. this morning Ivan had called informing him the package had arrived and was ready to talk.

Mika's blood was already at boiling point before they pulled into the warehouses on Industrial, there would definitely be no mercy on the cards today. Before reaching the storage room where their guest was waiting for them, Mika heard the cowardly cries and pleas begging for his worthless life.

Walking in, he took one look at this sexual predator, a pathetic, sniveling opportunist who prayed on the vulnerable.

Now it was time to settle a score by removing this sick parasite from the face of the earth.

"You messed with the wrong fucking lady Lenny...........MY LADY!" Lenny's face drained of the last bit of colour, Mika was really going to enjoy every fucking minute of this.

Mika stepped back and looked at the total carnage he'd created by his hands alone. Lenny was no longer a threat to the female population of Detroit or anywhere else for that matter.

Covered in the disgusting pervert's blood, he headed for the staff locker room showers, "Get rid of that garbage and scrub the room," he ordered as he walked out.

While he scrubbed himself raw, Alex collected the blood stained clothes and went to incinerate them, shoes and all before returning with fresh clean ones. Once again Mika had proved to the brotherhood he was one lethal Pakhan who should never be crossed.

It took me a few weeks to settle into my new job role, I honestly didn't realise just how many businesses the Remizov's were involved in, thankfully I was a quick learner.

There were six of us in the Administration department; the office manager was Margo Clark, a nice approachable lady.

Amanda Neal (Mandy) was my co worker and we took care of the hotel side. Mandy was just like me but about two years older, I was the baby of the office. Then there was Peter Craig and Joe Averin who see to all the imports and exports.

The only one I didn't like was Ruth Gowan, she was a striking looking woman in her early thirties and a royal bitch to boot, she had taken an instant dislike to me, and her job was to deal with all the bars and clubs.

Nobody knew about my connection to the Remizov's and I was eternally grateful to Mika and Luca for keeping that quiet, I was treated just like everyone else, even bullied a little by Ruth, which I took for a while but trust me her time will come.

At the end of my working day I would drive to *Red Square* and meet up with Jazz, watching the place turn from a building site into her dream bar over the course of a month was exciting. She had picked out all the fixtures and fittings, it all looked fantastic. The bar area was styled like a traditional English pub, with stools around the bar for hopefully the regular customers it would eventually attract, blackboards adorned the walls with chalk written specials and guest beers. By the window was the designated eating area and around the dance floor there were high tables for people to stand resting their drinks on whilst watching whatever band was playing on the stage or whoever would be entertaining the crowds with karaoke, it already had a real welcoming feel.

Jazz had already hired a chef, Danny Major and the pair had the menu planned out, which by the way sounded delicious and was very reasonably priced. She'd also had a banner made, which had been put up outside, displaying the re-launch date and advertisements had been published in the papers, announcing that the local favorite band Retro 73 would be playing; they had a pretty big fan base here.

With just over three weeks to go, she had all her staff employed. Three bartenders and four waitresses that Mika had arranged and was managing the door staff as well so that he would be kept in the loop of any un-savories that may want to cause trouble. Jazz was on a permanent high lately and I loved her enthusiasm.

She had over spent on budget, I only found that out by the snide remarks Ruth kept coming out with, saying things like:

"I see the Princess is home," and, "if it was anyone other than little Jasmine they would have been fired."

I was getting close to ripping her throat out, my patience wearing very thin; no one spoke about Jazz like that and got away with it.

At the start of the following week, Mandy and I were sat in our offices small break room, chatting and putting the world to rights, and bitching.

"Ruth is really threatened by you Izzy."

"What, me no." Shocked was a mild understatement.

"Yeah look at you! You've taken her crown, you're bubbly,

sweet and drop dead gorgeous with youth on your side," she giggled. "She's usually the one Pete and Joe hit on, but not any more...I love it."

"I don't encourage them, but why is she so territorial?" I asked. "Shit, she really is I never thought of it like that, she has a huge crush on Mr. Remizov and I mean big time." Mandy was still giggling. "You should see the way she preens herself when he summons her to his office."

I had to know. "Which one?"

"Mika."

I felt my insides tighten. "Has anything ever happened between them?" Hoping to God the answer was no.

"I don't think so and it's not from the lack of trying on her part." Then she looked at me. "Have you met Luca yet?" She sounded all dreamy and I just stared at her. "Oh Wow, he is so fucking hot, he could take me right here and now on this table." And as she slapped her palm on it, I nearly spat out my coffee.

"Mandy!" I howled, "So you have a thing for Luca?"

"God yeah, wait till you see him, but Hey! Hands off he's mine," she joked, she had me in stitches.

After lunch Margo came to me, "Izzy, Mr. Remizov would like to see this quarter's figures and a quick briefing, would you mind taking it?"

"Sure if Mandy doesn't mind." Mandy actually looked relieved.

"Good, just go to the top floor, Katia will direct you from there." Margo smiled as she returned to her office.

Mandy leaned forward. "Did you see Ruth perk up when she

heard top floor?'"

Before I had a chance to reply, Ruth had sauntered over, "Isabelle, if you are busy I can give him the briefing, I need to see him anyway?"

"No, no I'll do it; it's only fair, the hotel and hospitality is our area, but thank you." I was so sweet I'd made myself feel sick, but watching her face change was worth it.

"Fine, but remember Mr. Remizov is an extremely busy man and has no time for small talk, he certainly does not like time wasters." She stropped off back to her corner.

Turning to look at Mandy I silently mouthed "WOW!" then smiled as I watched Mandy biting her lip trying not to laugh.

Gathering up all the paperwork I needed, I asked Mandy, "How long do these usually take?"

"Usually twenty minutes, give or take five, good luck." I grabbed my thermos cup and set off for the elevators.

"Isabelle, surely you are not taking that with you, are you?" Ruth snapped at me.

"Yeah, why not?"

"Well it doesn't send out a very good impression now, does it?" she sniped.

"It's coffee not vodka in disguise, anyway it's a briefing not an AGM in front of all the directors now is it!" Choosing not to listen to her answer, I walked out gracefully.

I actually felt nervous, this would be the first time I'd see Mika as my employer. Checking my appearance in the elevators' mirror, I was quite pleased with my wardrobe choice this morning, a pale grey skirt suit with a cream silk blouse combo, which

I had to put a camisole underneath to hide my bra. On my feet were 3 inch nude heels.

I smoothed my skirt with my free hand and tucking a stray strand of hair behind my ear that had escaped the chignon, I chastised myself just before the doors slid open, "stop fidgeting you look fine."

I followed the sound of typing and announced myself.

"Hi, I'm Izzy, here to see Mr. Remizov," trying to sound confident.

"Oh hi Izzy, I'm Katia, he won't be long take a seat."

Instead, I walked over to the window and looked out, it was raining heavy now with the sky a dark steely grey and I just hoped this wasn't an omen and would be reflecting Mika's mood.

Hearing Katia announcing me on the phone, she smiled.

"You can go in, he's ready for you, just follow the hallway to the end."

Thanking her, I walked up to the huge double doors and knocked. Mika's deep husky voice answered. "Come on in Izzy." God this man made my whole body react something wicked and that was just his voice.

It had been a few days since he'd seen her or Jazz, they had been working late at *Red Square* nearly every night and for the past week he had been in Florida on business with Alex.

The company was looking to expand the hotel chain into the South Eastern Seaboard State and it was looking promising, but it had still been a very long seven days. He'd also wanted to give Izzy time to find her feet here first, but that had been a lot harder than he'd expected, just seeing glimpses of her at work caused his mind to wander and drift.

She didn't even notice that men were taking second glances at her, she was a vision to behold and the best thing about this breathtaking beauty was she didn't even realise it. This however was just an informal meeting to see how she was doing.

Mika couldn't believe this was the same 'little Angel' his father had loved and protected all his life and he'd finally gotten the truth out of him why he did, just a year before he was killed.

Every year, one day in March Savas would shut himself in his home office and get drunk, his mother had told them all never to disturb him. That year Mika had forgotten and had entered, finding Savas passed out on the couch with an empty bottle of vodka laying on the floor, and on his chest was a photo frame clutched tightly over his heart. Mika picked up the bottle and removed the photo just as Savas' eyes opened.

"Mikhail what are you doing?"

"Sorry Papa, I needed some paperwork, I can come back later." He tried to leave but Savas called him back.

"Please sit son, that photo you are holding." As Mika sat he took a good look at it, his father must have been nineteen or twenty and there was another guy about the same age and Izzy, no wait that couldn't be right. Mika's face must have spoken volumes.

"That my son is my best friend and 2nd, Nikolai Bazin, his sister and I." Savas' breath caught. "Natasha. She was the love of my life. We were to be married but she was taken from me, gunned down in the street just before her eighteenth birthday." He was silent for a moment, so Mika just sat waiting.

"Once I became Pakhan I decided that we needed someone inside the DPD, so Nikolai became Nicholas Bays and for ten years he led a double life. He did an exceptional job for both the brotherhood and police. He feared the last time we met would be the last time, he made me promise, swear on my life to take care and protect his wife Jess and their unborn child. To make sure they would want for nothing and to never find out who he really was. He was killed in the line of duty the next day, bringing down fucking Albanian scum, that was nineteen years ago today. It gets harder every year when I see Isabelle growing up, she is her Aunt's double, my Natasha, now you know, you must swear to keep the secret, no matter how hard the desire to tell the truth becomes. Always protect her, she is so very special."

"I promise I will Papa."

"Thank you son now go, I need to be with the ghosts of my past."

All the questions Mika had wanted to ask his father for years had unwittingly been answered, and he left his father to mourn the past in peace.

Growing up Mika, Luca and Alex had always looked at Izzy like another sister and loved her just as much as Jazz, they were the families' Princess and Angel, the only difference was the DNA gene pool.

The Remizov's were tall dark and not boasting but very handsome, Izzy was the total opposite, short with long, curly, honey blond hair, freckles and piercing blue eyes, her moniker suited her perfectly, 'Angel' that was then, but now she had shed that childhood cuteness look. The freckles had been replaced with flawless skin and now her figure was something to drool over, curves in all the right places, a perfect ass and breasts that begged to be kissed and caressed.

Every red blooded male noticed her and none more than him. She took his breath away, made him hard as steel without even trying and no woman had ever done that to him before.

As he watched her walk into his domain, he couldn't kerb the smile that was plastered across his face, he really should have stood up and greeted her, but his dick had decided to stand to attention making that impossible, shit it was like being a teen again, having no control over his horny hormones, God how he wanted her.

He asked me to take a seat and I had to clench my thighs together, trying in vain to stop the pulsing throb between them. Sat behind his huge desk he looked the typical powerful CEO and I saw him in this new light and had a whole new respect for him.

We talked for an hour and as I stood up to leave with Mika's seal of approval and high praise for a job well done, I felt a surge of pride, I was really chuffed for Mandy and I.

"Will I see you at dinner tonight?" he asked.

"No, I'm heading to *Red Square* to help Jazz with some finishing touches."

"Ah yes, the grand opening is soon, I'm looking forward to seeing what she has done to the place since she has barred us all from it," he smiled.

"It's fantastic. I'm so proud of her."

"OK then I'll see you later, can you send Ruth up?"

I felt like he had just dowsed me in ice cold water. "Sure," I said forcing myself not to sound to annoyed.

Walking back into our office I saw Ruth glaring at me, "Oh, Mika would like to see you now," giving her a well practiced fake smile, and loving the way her eyes bulged when I had called him Mika.

As I sat down at my desk Mandy looked fit to burst.

"You've been gone so long I started to think we'd done something wrong!"

I reassured her, "No, no, no he was really pleased with us, he just wanted to know how I was settling in and we generally chatted for a while."

Mandy seemed impressed, "Seriously you sat and small talked with the big bad-boss man about things other than work, and you got to call him Mika!"

"Yeah, what am I suppose to call him?"

"Err...Mr. Remizov, like everyone else," she laughed.

"You should have seen Ruth, she has been pacing around the office like crazy, it was really rather entertaining, I nearly pee'd myself when you said Mika's ready for you, did you see her face it was priceless." Chuckling to myself, if only she knew. Fifteen minutes later Ruth walked back in, I could feel the daggers being thrown into my back by her, but hey that was her problem and nothing new for me.

CHAPTER EIGHT

The Monday before Jazz's re-launch party, I was once again summoned to the Gods and instantly Ruth was in my personal space.

"Why does Mr. Remizov want to see you?"

"How would I know, I haven't spoken to him yet."

It was killing her and childish as it maybe, I loved it. She had gotten even worse since Friday, when Mandy had booked a personnel day, I decided to go to the diner across from the office for lunch on my own. Mika had come in and asked if I was eating alone and just as I nodded Ruth and her catty friends from marketing walked in and spotted us straight away. The way her mouth fell open was comical and I could actually lip read what she said to her friends, 'what the fuck do you think is going on there?' Her friends turned to see what she was talking about and all I could do was smirk.

Picking up my club sandwich I spoke to Mika who had his back to them.

"Mika, do you know you have an admirer in the office?" His eyebrows lifted, "Who?"

"Ruth."

"Oh I know and no thank you."

By now I was giggling, "You knew?"

"I'm not blind Izzy; she couldn't make it more obvious if she tried." I had to restrain myself from launching across the table to kiss him, and since then Ruth has watched me like a hawk. I just kept giving her more fuel to hate me even more.

Jazz was having a complete melt-down on an epic scale, a Defcon 1 scenario. Five days before the grand opening, the band Retro 73 had called her with a major problem that threatened everything, their female singer Lisa had been hospitalized after falling and fracturing her femur, she'd had to have surgery since it had been such a bad break. Paul Gandi, the male singer was so apologetic.

"I don't know what else to do Jazz?" Then jokingly said, "If you know of any available woman who can sing?"

"I DO, I really do! Can you come here and rehearse if I get her on board?"

He was astounded. "Yeah sure, we can be there around five, Tony Adams our lead guitarist finishes work at four."

"That's great I'll see you guys then."

After hanging up with Paul she rang Mika. "Mika! I need you to let me have Izzy till Saturday?" she pleaded.

"Whoa, whoa, why?"

"It's a matter of life or death, I'll either sink or swim and Izzy is the only one who can save me." She was on the verge of a hysterical break down.

"Tell me what has happened?"

"I can't, but it will all become apparent on Saturday and I swear you will not be disappointed, Please Mika?" she was begging now.

Mika could never refuse her and the worst part was Jazz knew it too. "OK, give me an hour and I'll send her, but so help me God Jazz this had better be worth it."

"Oh believe me it will be, you are the best brother in the world, I love you." She sounded alleviated.

"Yeah and don't you forget it."

I announced myself to Katia, "Hi, I've been summoned," my tone made her smile.

"Yeah; he's waiting for you, just go on in."

I knocked and got no reply so I opened the door slowly.

"Helloo!" still nothing, the office was empty, then I heard the private toilet flush and my inner child took over, pressing my back to the wall next to the door I waited for him to walk out.

"Boo!" His feet left the floor. It would have been hilarious if it hadn't been for the expression on his face.

"Oh shit Mika, I'm sorry," realising that had not been one of my best ideas, especially since Mika was my boss who could fire me.

By now he had hold of my arms. "Izzy, I should throw you over my knee and spank you!" I couldn't tell if he was being serious or not.

Raising my eyebrows, "You want to spank me?" I asked, intrigued. It was fun watching him back peddling.

"Ha, ha, I'm only joking with you." Was he actually blushing? "Err anyway, Jazz has problems and needs your help," he quickly changed the subject.

"What's wrong?"

"She won't say but only you can save her apparently, if you're OK with that I'll let Margo know?"

"Yes of course."

"Good, you can get off now if that's alright?"

I took that as my cue to leave. I don't know what came over me but as my hand held the door handle, "Mika if you wanted to spank me you could have," I winked, leaving him sitting behind his desk speechless and catching flies.

As usual at this time of day, the doors to *Red Square* were unlocked. Looking round I saw Suzi and Jamie, two of Jazz's waitresses.

"Hey, where is she?" I asked.

"Oh hey Izzy, she's in the kitchen," Suzi smiled. Thanking her I headed towards it.

"Jazz," I shouted.

"You made it, praise be," she sang.

"What's going on, you've got me worried?"

She pulled me into a hug, "I have a major disaster on my hands and only you can help me."

Talk about being put under pressure. "For Christ sake Jazz tell me?" I was starting to get pissed at her.

"The female singer from Retro 73 has had an accident and is in hospital. Paul the other singer rang to cancel the gig, unless we knew another female singer," she looked at me with anticipation.

That's when the penny dropped. "Me?"

"Izzy you are a fantastic singer, please?" she was coercing me.

"Shit Jazz, I have never sung with a band like that before."

"I know, I know, that's why the band for the next five days will be rehearsing here with you."

I was stunned into silence.

"They will be arriving at five, please Izzy, please say yes?"

I was scared shitless but at the same time excited as hell.

She squeezed my hand, "I'm begging Iz, please."

I smiled. "OK, but don't blame me if I'm awful."

Jazz squealed so loudly she nearly burst my eardrums.

"Suzi, Jamie, she said yes, my life saver, God I love this woman!" We were all laughing at her while I crossed my fingers and prayed silently, hoping that I wouldn't be a failure.

A van pulled up outside the bar around 16:30 p.m. It held

all the bands' instruments and equipment. I never realised just how much gear was involved. Jazz and I stayed out of the way, we had absolutely no idea what to do to help, we did offer but it was thankfully declined and after twenty minutes they had everything set up.

We were waiting for Paul and Tony to arrive, so Andy Taylor, the drummer did the initial introductions over coffee while we waited. When Paul and Tony showed up, Paul shook my hand.

"Izzy we can't thank you enough."

"Hold your thanks till after you hear me sing," I joked outwardly but inwardly I was deadly serious.

Jazz left us so we could get started; it was a daunting feeling having to get up onstage with an experienced band, something I'd never felt before. Paul and the guy's must have sensed my apprehension because Paul placed a supportive hand on my shoulder.

"Izzy, we are gonna just sit on the dance floor with Tony and Lee," Lee Eastman was the keyboard player, "and just jam, break you in gently OK?" he winked.

It was amazing and after just a few songs my nerves vanished. All the guy's had a really calming persona.

"Tell us what genre you prefer?" Paul asked.

"My taste is very eclectic, I like everything from the 60's to now, I do love classic rock and you can't beat a little AC/DC and Def Leppard or the husky voice of Alison Moyet. But nothing from Whitney or Celine, that's far too high and I would only massacre them."

He chuckled. "What do you want to sing now so we can hear you for ourselves?" he asked encouragingly.

"Mmm, well one of my go to songs is Paul McCartney's 'Live and let Die'."

Tony got all excited. "I love that song." He began to play, well here goes I thought.

As the song finished I looked at them for feedback, it felt like I was on X-factor.

"Fuck me!" Lee shouted out laughing. Paul was clapping and the rest cheered.

"That is so going on the play list," Paul said.

Lee was already climbing on stage, "Let's see what it sounds like with all of us playing?"

My head swelled, I was loving this; hopefully I'd still feel the same way on Saturday.

By Friday we had our set list, everything from Simon and Garfunkel to Lady Gaga.

"OK guy's, after lunch we'll do a full run through," Paul had just said when Jazz walked out of the kitchen followed by Suzi and Jamie carrying lunch for all of us. We had tried everything on the menu over the past four days, since we were there from ten in the morning till late, Jazz had provided all our meals, and all six of us gave the thumbs up to every dish.

"Jazz, since we have been your unofficial tasting panel and for that we thank you, will you and your staff be our first official audience and give us your honest reviews?" Paul so eloquently asked.

Jazz could not hide her pride. "Can I be Simon Cowell?" she giggled.

"Only if you can speak in an English accent?"

She pouted. "Oh pooh."

I just chuckled.

Two hours later I was singing the last song that would unofficially end the gig, Paul had said 'you always have a few more for the encore; hopefully the fans will cheer for more if we have put on a great show.' So singing my last solo, 'Bridge over troubled water' I sang my heart out and the last note was met with cheers and whistles from Jazz and her staff.

Paul winked, "A sign of things to come."

Jazz was clapping like mad with tears in her eyes. The last two songs were duets.

"Always end on a love song," Lee laughed, "I wonder just how many passion filled nights we are responsible for?" He had a dirty chuckle.

I picked, 'I've had the time of my life,' it seemed pretty appropriate because it had been five crazy filled days and I had made five good friends. I even met poor Lisa; she gave me her blessing to stand in for her on the night, since she was literally in traction. Paul had chosen, in my opinion, the worlds ultimate love song, 'Up where we belong,' it was perfect to end the gig.

Placing the mic back on to the stand, I was startled by the band crushing me in a testosterone filled bear hug. We could hear Jazz and the gang clapping and screaming, I was on such a high.

All of us jumped off the stage and joined our audience for a group hug on the empty dance floor.

Jazz was now fully sobbing. "You were amazing, better than I had imagined, you're all gonna bring the house down."

I had never been as excited and happy as I was now.

"OK guys, I think that's a wrap, we're ready and all I can say is bring it on, have a good rest and we'll meet back here tomorrow at six for final checks." Paul sounded thrilled as we had one last group hug before we left.

I needed a hot bath and a good night's sleep; I had never worked so hard or given so much effort in my life, ever. As I soaked in my tub, Jazz came in and sat on the floor.

"Have you picked out what your gonna wear yet?"

For the first time I actually shocked her. "Yep, for the first set I'm wearing a black leather mini skirt with a matching waistcoat that flashes my naval ring and just enough boobage, with 5 inch black, knee high boots. Then for the second set, a 60's black and white mini dress, again with 5 inch black spikes, though I really need you to do my hair and make-up, I have to look sexy as hell, a real hot chick." I waited for her answer.

"That sounds fucking awesome and as for making you look sexy, well that's easy, you are anyway." Lying on my bed we watched reruns of Friends, just like old times, until I yawned.

"That is it, sleep time," Jazz said as she cuddled me, "I'm heading in early tomorrow to do final touches so I'll see you at the bar. I cannot believe it's here already, I owe you big time, and how can I ever thank you?" she said, sounding so emotional.

"Enough already!" I was firm with her.

"OK, OK, sleep tight," and she stood there with her hands on her face like the kid off *Home alone* and screamed, making me laugh.

It took ages for sleep to claim me but when it finally did I slept like the dead. The next morning I had the whole house to myself, it was peaceful and relaxing, "Ahh bliss," I thought as I sank back into bed with my kindle and coffee, my perfect day, I had nothing to do until four o'clock.

CHAPTER NINE

Jazz and her crew were hanging balloons and banners, the finishing touches, everything looked perfect. Danny had the buffet food sorted and stored in the refrigerators, the bar was fully stocked and the cases of champagne were chilling in the cellar, waiting to be popped tonight for the toast. No expense was spared.

Mika had called letting her know that he and the rest of the family would be arriving by around seven. There would be about ten people from the head office coming, including Ruth, the one Izzy hated. Jazz decided to keep that tidbit to herself for now, no need to stir the proverbial pot. Nobody at the office knew just how close Izzy was to the family but after tonight she had a feeling they would.

Freshly showered, waxed, plucked and buffed to within an inch of my life, I loaded Bertie up with everything I needed and drove to the bar. I was going to get ready in the dressing room, which was next to the stage, thankfully it was pretty big so the guys could quickly change and then mingle with the fans leaving me with my entourage to get sorted.

Jazz had wisely decided to make tonight a ticket only event to control numbers, the last thing she needed was the fire officer coming in and shutting her down. Every ticket had been sold, even with the $10 cover charge, which she planned on giving to the band as well as her check.

I walked in and the place looked spectacular.

"Izzy you're here, well what do you think?"

"Wow Jazz, it looks fantastic, no, more than that, sensational." Her excitement oozed out, it was contagious.

"I need help bringing in my things," I said and she turned to the bar.

"Max, will you give Izzy a hand?" she asked the bartender.

"Sure, no problem." She was practically drooling.

"You naughty girl Jazz!"

"Oh shut up you," she laughed.

We headed to where I'd parked Bertie. Max grabbed the heavy things while I carried my clothes.

"Thanks Max, you're a star." I let my eyes glide over his very nice body and tight ass, Jazz had a type and Max fit it to a T.

Inside the dressing room I asked her, "Are you going home to change?"

"No, my dress and things are in my office, I've asked Suzi to do your hair and make-up, she's nearly finished a beauty course at college. I hope you don't mind?" I knew she would be busy and worried about tonight and the idea of her coming at me with eye liner was frankly quite a bad one.

"No I don't mind and I love the way Suzi does her own make-up."

She sighed. "Good, well I'm gonna go get ready myself, I'll send down some drinks for you guys."

"Just water for me please."

She blew a kiss and left just as Suzi walked in, then the guys all piled in, just as Suzi was getting her work station set up.

"Hey Izzy, how you doing?" Paul beamed as he handed me a bottle of water.

"Fine and I'll be even better when I get my alter ego on."

Tony whistled. "Can't wait to see that," as the rest of the band nodded in agreement. They all changed into T shirts and black leathers, the typical rock band attire and then left to go socialize.

In the dressing room, Suzi and I could hear the place starting to fill up, music playing from the jukebox, the sounds of glasses clinking and people's laughter filtered in. I was a little gutted to be missing out on the festivities. The door opened and in walked Summer, one of the waitresses carrying two flutes of champagne.

"Jazz sent these down for the toast, she didn't want you missing out."

"That's my girl," I smiled.

"Wow Izzy, you look amazing, I hardly recognized you!"

I knew what she meant. "Thanks, Suzi's made me into a mega Diva," as I looked into the mirror nearly speechless

"You're really good, I don't even look like me." I felt like a cross between a young Madonna and Christina Aguilera, uber sexy and now it was show time.

The guys walked in and all stared at me dumbstruck.

"Hellooo! What's wrong, is it too much?" now I was panicking.

"Fuck no! You look amazing," Tony said.

"I will second that, Jesus Izzy you're gonna blow men's minds when you get on stage," Paul laughed. That was what I needed, a confidence boost and now I was totally ready to get this show on the road, so in the bands words, 'bring it on.'

Mika and his entourage walked in, each man on their own was pretty intimidating but when twelve of them walk in together, everyone just stopped talking and stared, as if something serious was about to happen. When a waitress approached them and Mika smiled, people realised the men were just here for the opening of the new bar.

It was the first time Jazz had allowed any them into the place. The waitress carrying a tray of champagne offered them drinks, Mika graciously accepted and as he sipped his drink he took in everything. Looking around at the newly refurbished bar he was thoroughly impressed, the air inside was warm and welcoming and he was filled with pride for his baby sisters' accomplishments.

Jazz could tell the moment her brothers and family had entered the place by the lull in conversations around the bar and she ran to them. "Mika what do you think?"

He pulled her to him, "You have blown me away," he hugged her tight, "Princess it's magnificent, I'm so proud of you." Everyone praised and congratulated her, kisses reined down on her cheeks.

Alex whistled, "Look at you all dressed to impress." Jazz jokingly curtseyed.

Mika leaned in. "Where is Izzy, I thought she'd be with you?"

"She's here and you'll see her in about fifteen minutes."

That just simply confused him.

Jazz stepped onto the stage, and Andy gave her a drum roll to get peoples' attention. She held the mic to her lips.

"Ladies and Gentlemen I am so thrilled to see all of you here tonight, to celebrate with me on the opening of my dream bar. Firstly, before Retro 73 take the stage, I'd like to say a few thank you's to some very special people in my life, because if it wasn't for them I wouldn't be standing here. First to my wonderful brothers,' especially Mika," she blew him a kiss, "and secondly to my fantastic staff who have for the past few weeks helped me get it ready and looking so fabulous. Last, but by no means least, my best friend Izzy, who has well and truly saved the night, I love you Iz. Now has everyone got champagne?"

The crowd yelled 'YES' making Jazz laugh. "Right then, please raise your glasses to *Red Square,* for the fun filled nights to all who enter her doors." Everyone cheered '*RED SQUARE!*' and chinked glasses together. "Please welcome to the stage RETRO

73."

Suzi and I raised our glasses. I was really touched by what Jazz had said in her heart felt toast, then the guys and I all huddled together like a pre-football ritual with fist pumping and enthusiasm bubbling.

"You're gonna knock em dead Izzy." Paul hugged me before they all exited out on to the stage, leaving me in the wings until my grand entrance. Their Fans went nuts when they saw the band, you could feel the vibrations, the atmosphere was electric.

Paul addressed the crowd. "What a privilege it is to be the first band to play here at such a fantastic venue, hopefully we will get to come back. I'd like to thank you guys for all the cards and well wishes you sent for Lisa, who is doing really well and determined to be back soon. But have we got a treat for you install tonight – for one night only we have an amazing guest singer and new songs to boot. Let the count down begin."

The band begun with Robbie Williams 'Let me entertain you' and holy shit they sure did, it was completely different when the bar was packed full of people cheering and singing with them, it was addictive, I was itching to get out there. One more song and I would be, Paul had said let the count down begin and now Europe's 'the final countdown' began to play, my tummy was doing somersaults, I could feel the stage bouncing with Paul and Tony jumping up and down on it from here. This was it Paul looked at me standing in the wings and winked. "Please give a real warm welcome for the amazing IZZY!"

Jazz was stood with her family, watching Mika closely noting he had not once taken his eyes off the stage as he was eagerly waiting for the first glimpse of her, just like everyone else. When Paul introduced her the place erupted and went ballistic, even though Jazz had a good idea what to expect, even she was blown away when she saw her step out on to the stage. Suzi had made her look like the star she was and Izzy's wardrobe choice was perfect. Jazz looked at Mika, he was totally mesmerized, transfixed.

"Fuck me, is that really Izzy?" Alex gasped.

"Holy mother of God," added Luca. Mika still hadn't said a word or even blinked, he was spell bound, and Jazz sung to herself, 'Nailed it.'

Mika watched her come alive on stage, she was something else, the way her body moved to the beat and that voice, it was hypnotic. The flashing lights illuminated those sexy blue eyes he'd been dreaming about, and that amazing as fuck ass had every man in the place undressing her with their eyes. He fantasized about running his lips all over that body. He had to restrain himself from jumping up on stage and covering her up before killing every cocksucker in the bar for defiling her with their eyes. Mika felt an arm tugging on him, bringing him back to reality.

"What do you think?" Jazz asked.

"She is amazing, the band is. I didn't even know she could sing like this, or fucking look like that!"

Jazz laughed, "Oh boy, I wonder just how many cell numbers she'll get tonight?" Mika frowned and that only made Jazz want to laugh more.

After about an hour Paul announced to the crowd, "Time for a well earned drink, we'll be back in twenty." Jazz had bottles of ice cold beers waiting for us, and God it was pure nectar. Time for a quick wardrobe change in front of the guys, with Suzi's help she topped up my make-up and for this set curled my hair into ringlets. This time I looked more elegant than hardcore and in a blink of an eye, twenty minutes had flown.

"Time guys," Paul announced.

All the jitters and stage fright I had first time going on had totally vanished and was replaced with sheer excitement and pure ecstasy. I loved every minute of it. Paul sang The Who's

'Pinball wizard' with me backing him. It was the first time I actually looked round at the bar scanning the sea of faces.

I tried to find Jazz and it wasn't that hard really, I just followed the direction most women were looking and saw Mika, Luca and Alex with at least five other huge guys and standing in front of them in a protective arc was Jazz. Giving her my biggest smile I blew her a kiss, which she pretended to grab. My eyes then focused on Mika, he could make my heart race by doing nothing, I could feel his eyes on me, giving me his full attention and I loved it.

In rehearsals it had taken three hours from start to finish. On the night it was closer to four and a half, but sadly it had come to an end, the crowd had begged for more, even after two encores.

Paul announced, "Thank you and Good night, we hope to see you all real soon, enjoy the rest of the night, and Jazz, Good luck to *RED SQUARE*," as the whole place cheered. The guys came up front with Paul and I, we all bowed and clapped at the crowd.

"Izzy you'll have to do another guest spot they love you," Tony smiled.

"Maybe," but I knew once was enough, I could happily tick another thing off my bucket list and doing it a second time would never feel as good as this. I was itching to go to Jazz, we all left the stage with Paul tucking me under his arm as we made our way to the bar.

"I'm gonna see Jazz."

"We'll bring you a cold one," Tony winked.

"God I could kiss you!" I chuckled.

Jazz was hopping up and down like a cat on a hot tin roof; "You blow my mind away every time, you simply just get better and better," as she strangled me, literally strangled me.

Everyone kept coming over to us congratulating the guys and I, my ego was as tall as the Empire State Building. Tony handed me a beer just as Paul cupped my cheeks and kissed me.

"Thank you for the last six days Izzy, it's been a pleasure getting to know you."

I hugged him, "I've had a total blast."

Out of the corner of my eye I saw Mika puff out and stiffen as he watched us intensely. Luca sensed it too because he placed a hand on his shoulder.

"Guy's, come sit," Luca said, speaking to the band, leaving Jazz and I, she raised an eyebrow at my unasked question.

Mika wanted her all to himself, he wanted to break that fucking arm that was around her shoulder, he wanted to beat the living daylights out of Paul when he kissed her cheek, it was seriously about to become ugly until Luca's warning touch. Christ he had to get grip, get some self control, what was this person he'd always looked at as a sister now doing to him? The time had come to either admit his feelings or he had to bite the bullet and let her go live her life; the latter in his head wasn't even an option. Izzy was chatting with Jazz and Suzi when he approached.

"Excuse me ladies but can I have a quick word with Izzy?"

Izzy smiled at him, "Sure," then she walked just far enough away from eves droppers before turning.

"No, in private." His tone was slightly more harsh than he intended it to be.

"Oh, are you alright Mika?" she asked, now looking concerned. He simply nodded before placing his hand on the lower part of her back and escorting her into Jazz's office. He opened the door and gestured for her to enter, which she did without hesitation. He closed and then locked the door. That action caused her to spin around, her eye's questioning the act. He stalked over to her and with every step he took she took one backwards until the desk stopped her retreat. Mika looked into those wide blue eyes and could see the fear in them as well as excitement.

Sara A Miller

They were so close to one another that her sweet breath hit his face; he could see the pulse in her throat beating rapidly, matching his own heart rate. As he wrapped an arm around her, he pushed his other hand under her hair feeling the heat of her neck. She opened her lips to speak but instead he consumed the words with his mouth as he kissed her hard, nothing gentle, just raw and hungry.

He parted her lips with his tongue, searching for hers, it was pure animalistic and she did nothing to stop him. She pulled him in tighter, his hard cock firmly pressed against her stomach; she was just as aroused as he was. He whispered in Russian, telling her how much he wanted her, to taste her while she came in his mouth, to fuck her so hard she'd be begging for more, all the time thinking he could say what he liked because she didn't understand him. When he spoke in English he was softer and gentler.

"Isabelle, do you know what you are doing to me?"

If it hadn't been for the knock at the door he would have claimed her there and then on the desk.

"WHAT!" he bellowed.

"Don't you shout at me mister, it's my office now open the door!" He did and Jazz stood there with her hands on her hips.

"People want to meet Izzy so stop hogging her." He just grunted and left.

"What the fuck just happened in here?" she asked, like she didn't know, her dirty smirk giving her away.

"I don't know but he sure rocked my world and left me wanting more," I smiled.

"You've smudged your lip stick," she laughed.

"Oh shit."

Looking in the mirror, I quickly tidied myself up.

"Mika's lips were a lovely shade of pink, which strangely

enough is the same shade as your lippy." I blushed. "Come on, lets meet your fans, they're asking for you."

It was twelve thirty and the crowds had thinned a little, some still on the dance floor, dancing to the jukebox. That was when I spotted a group from work, Luca and Alex were standing with them, and Mandy left her seat as soon as she saw me.

"Hey you! You are a seriously dark horse lady," she giggled.

"I know and I'm sorry I didn't say anything but if people knew I was a family friend of the bosses they'd have treated me differently, do you forgive me?"

"Of course I do and by the way you fucking ROCK!"

Once again she had me howling. Jazz came over and joined us, I was thrilled when the two of them hit it off. Mandy being Mandy couldn't help herself.

"So, you are Luca's sister?" Again I was in stitches.

"Mandy what are you like?"

"What?" she said, all innocently.

Jazz chuckled, "So you got a thing for Luca?"

"Duhh, I'm a single hot blooded, damn horny female. What do you think? God just look at him!" Mandy sounded out, all dreamy.

Jazz grabbed her hand, "Come on, I'll properly introduce you to him."

"Fuck, no way, I work for him; I'd rather keep the things the way they are and not registering on his radar as the pathetic woman who drools every time he walks passed. I mean, come on look at him then look at me; he is so far out of my league I'm practically in another State." I get so annoyed with her when she puts herself down like that.

"Mandy, don't say things like that, you are so pretty with a killer figure and boobs to die for, you are so bubbly and full of life not to mention funny as hell, what's not to like?"

Mandy gave us a coy smile. I could tell by the look on Jazz's face she would be doing a little meddling, putting the feelers out and getting some Intel. I winked at her to go ahead and do it.

Alex came over to join us. "Can I get you ladies a drink?" Jazz declined, I asked for a bottle of water, "driving" I answered the questioning look, and Mandy asked for a beer.

While they chatted, I scanned around, trying not to be obvious, and my heart stopped the second I saw him and Ruth looking all cozy in the far corner. She was constantly touching him, batting her false eye lashes, totally fawning over him, and Mika seemed to be relishing in it. She caught me staring, which only seemed to encourage her even more, giving me the evils as she moved in closer. God I hated that bitch, he was laughing at something she had said and he had obviously completely forgotten about our little interlude already. What the hell had that kiss been all about or the things he had said, even if he didn't realise I'd understood them, had he thought he'd made a mistake, was that it? I was a mistake. I was mad as hell, maybe even more hurt than angry and I had to turn away.

I strolled over to the band, the guys had already dismantled all the equipment and most of the gear was in the van outside.

"Hey Izzy, I have some money for you," Paul snuck up behind me.

"I don't want any; I did it for Jazz and had a great time doing it. Split my share between you all."

"Are you sure, it's yours, you earned it fair and square. What's wrong?"

"Oh nothing, I'm on a downer after that high," I lied.

"The band is going to Mickie's diner for our post gig ritual cherry pie, you wanna join us?" I didn't think twice.

"Sure I'd love to, let me grab my things and change quickly." That cheered me up, I needed to get away from the bitch and Mika before I did or said something I'd later regret.

Pulling on the jeans and T-shirt I'd arrived in, my feet sighed as I slipped on my comfy sneakers. Lee came into the dressing room to grab his jacket.

"Give me your keys and I'll put your stuff in your car."

"Thanks, you guys are the best."

Andy picked up my screwed up clothes while Lee carried my bags.

"We'll see you outside Izzy."

"I'll just say bye to Jazz," and luckily she was standing by the door, talking to the door staff so I didn't need to go and find her.

"Hey I'm heading home, I'm beat and I need a shower."

"Oh! OK I'll see you at home." I kissed her and left her standing there stunned by my sudden departure.

CHAPTER TEN

Jazz watched confused, what the fuck had just happened, she was determined to find out what she had missed. As she walked over to where her family was she bumped into Mandy.

"Hey have you seen Izzy?"

"She left." Even Mandy looked perplexed. Then Jazz saw Mika chatting away with a woman, "who's that with Mika?" she asked, somehow she knew this was ground zero.

"Oh that prize peach is the cow bag Ruth, the ultimate office bitch," Mandy hissed a reply. No love lost there Jazz thought. Leaving Mandy, she walked up behind Mika. Ruth gave her a warning glare, which roughly translated into 'interrupt at your risk,' which Jazz blatantly ignored and tapped Mika on the shoulder.

"Hey Princess."

"Who's this?" she asked without a hint of warmth.

"Jazz this is Ruth from work, Ruth this is my wonderful sister." Ruth gave Jazz a smile.

"Oh so you are Jasmine, it's a pleasure to finally meet you." Her voice was sickly sweet.

"Jazz, only my Dad called me Jasmine." Mika stiffened at the animosity seeping from his sister.

"I honestly thought she was your date by the way you two are all cosy and touchy feely over here in the corner." She didn't even try to hide the sarcasm. Mika pulled back, putting some distance between him and Ruth, which made her begrudgingly remove her hand from his arm.

"No we were just talking shop," he adamantly told Jazz and caught the hurt look that crossed Ruth's face. "I'm sorry Ruth if I gave you that impression, but that will never happen."

She tried to laugh it off, "no, no, of course not. We can never mix business with pleasure." Jazz couldn't help but smile smugly at how the cow was blushing before turning around and walking away, "mission accomplished," she said to herself.

Max shouted to her, "Jazz, we're out of Bombay Sapphire and Jim Beam," causing her to change direction and head to the stock room.

Mika left Ruth, "where's Izzy?" he asked Luca.

"Dunno, last I saw she was mingling with the crowd."

Mika at just over 6'5, towered over the most of the patrons in the bar and he scanned around but he still couldn't see her. He glanced over to the stage area, which was now completely stripped, where the fuck was she? Returning from the very empty and vacated dressing room he saw Jazz behind the bar.

"Princess do you know where Izzy is?"

"She's gone home, said she needed a shower and her bed."

"What, when?"

"Oh I'd say when she saw Ruth's hands all over you!" Jazz was amazed just how clueless all her brothers were about women, anything else they were strategic and lethal but when it came to the female sex not a damn clue.

"I'll see you at home then," he quickly said as he kissed her.

"Make sure you go home with Luca!" he shouted. Facing away from him she raised a hand with a "Yeah, yeah."

Luca and Alex were both on alert as soon as they saw Mika bolt out of the door and set off to follow. Jazz caught them on the way out, "Whoa, stop!" she yelled.

"Where the hell's he going in such a rush?" Luca asked.

"Probably home to beg for forgiveness?" She explained what

had gone on.

"I hope to God she forgives him, I'm sick of him being grumpy and moody all the time these days."

Alex sighed, "I can't believe it, he's so dumb, poor schmuck," Luca laughed.

Jazz instantly turned on him, "You are all stupid, not just him, don't even get me started on you! You blind dick!"

Luca's mouth dropped open, "What the hell have I done?"

"It doesn't matter."

"No, you called me a dick now spill."

"OK, a little advice. Open your eyes and see what's right in front of your nose because you could really miss something special."

"Jazz stop being fucking cryptic and tell me what your talking about." Luca was getting frustrated by her but that's all Jazz would say.

I followed the two car convoy to Mickie's diner, it was all the way over the other side of town. It only took fifteen minutes to get there at this time of night with hardly any traffic on the roads, and I can safely say it was well worth the trek.

I was sat squished in between Paul and Lee, eating the best cherry pie I had have ever tasted. "Mmmmm," was all I managed to say, my taste buds were in orgasmic heaven.

"Told you didn't I, we've been coming here after every gig for years to wind down and refuel; it's the jewel in the crown."

Lee laughed at Paul's statement, everyone else was too busy shoving pie into their mouths.

It was just what I needed and the first time I'd ever regretted not having my own place. I knew Mika wouldn't bring her back home but still, if I'd had my own place I wouldn't have to see him doing the walk of shame in the morning, it's probably a walk of glory for men. I could not get that fucking smug look

Ruth had spread across her face out of my head.

We'd been sat in the diner for over an hour, it was close to two thirty.

"It's been one hell of a crazy ride Izzy," Paul said when we were all stood by the cars.

"Promise you will keep in touch."

Tony hugged me goodbye, all the guys followed suit, Paul held on to me the longest, "Stay safe kiddo and thanks again. Do what Tony said and stay in touch."

We all drove out of the parking lot and headed in two different directions, it would take me at least twenty minutes to drive home, oh the joy!

Mika must have been speeding like crazy to make it home in less than ten minutes; he slammed the brakes on and skidded to a halt. Jazz had knocked him sideways by what she'd insinuated, the more he thought about it, the more it annoyed him. He replayed the night's events, quickly realising he'd missed all the fucking signs and he cursed himself. Ruth had been practically throwing herself at him, how could he have missed it?

He honestly thought that Ruth knew that nothing would ever happen between them. They would only ever have an employer, employee relationship, you could bet your bottom dollar she does now. Then he thought about Izzy, how could she think there was something going on, especially after what had just happened between them, that he'd just go in search of another woman, how little did she think of him?

In the past he had been a womaniser, he'd fucked one woman and gone home with another on the same night, but Izzy didn't know that side of him. Never before had a woman got to him like she did. He had to talk to her, lay it on the line and make her understand; she is the only one now and forever.

He nearly took the door off its hinges, he flew up the stairs and down to his old room, "Isabelle." He switched on the light, but she wasn't there. "Isabelle," he boomed out as he searched the house yet he was answered with silence. He rang her cell, "Where are you, call me?" After a few more messages each one angrier than the last, he threw his cell on the counter top, luckily this time it didn't break, he'd lost more than one cell phone like that.

Just before two thirty, Jazz, Alex and Luca walked in, "Have you heard from her?" he growled at them.

"No," Luca told him.

"She might have gone for a drink with the band; they all left at the same time?" Jazz added, thinking she was being helpful but only adding fuel to the fire.

"Find her!" he spat at Luca.

"Mika calm down, I'll ring her, stay Luca!" Jazz shouted.

"Hey! I'm not a damn dog Jazz."

She simply ignored him and switched the coffee machine on before walking into the garden and calling Izzy. With three pairs of ears listening, it was time for a little Swedish!

"Hey," Izzy answered sounding miserable.

"Where are you?"

"Why the Swedish?" Izzy asked.

"I have earwigs," Jazz sniggered.

"I've been for pie with the band, I'm on my way home now, should be about ten minutes."

"Good."

"Why?"

"The big bad wolf is after blood." Jazz turned and looked at the three angry faces.

"What have I done?" Izzy asked.

"Nothing, but Mika came home just after you left and has been looking for you ever since, and I'm giving you a heads up, you got it all wrong about Ruth, I saw him put her in her place." Jazz could swear she heard Izzy smile, "See you soon," and she hung up.

"Will you stop speaking in that shit, what did she say?" Mika yelled.

"She had pie with the band and now she's on her way, she'll be here in ten minutes, so be nice to her," she warned him.

Alex and Luca looked at each other, "Well that's enough for one night, we're off to bed," not wanting to be there when Izzy got home.

"Me too." Jazz had read their minds and agreed, so all three left him waiting alone.

I sighed, wondering what the hell I was about to walk into. I seriously didn't want to leave the safety of Bertie. The house looked quiet, oh well it was time to face the music and I couldn't put it off any longer.

The door was unlocked; so I crept inside and locked it quietly and then was met by the aroma of fresh brewed coffee. I entered the kitchen expecting to find a welcoming party, but no one. There sat a still warm half drank coffee cup on the counter, this was my lucky break and high tailed it upstairs. When I reached the top I heard the toilet flush downstairs and it made me sprint quickly to my room. Once inside I leant against the door feeling like the worlds biggest coward, but the wrath of Mika could wait until tomorrow.

Mika paced the kitchen, finishing his coffee he checked his watch, it was well passed the ten minutes and she should have been home by now. Mixed with annoyance and a little worry, he decided to wait outside for her, and hoping the fresh air would clear his head. Pulling on the door handle he found it locked, and it hadn't been when he checked ten minutes ago.

His irritation level began to rise; he stepped outside and saw her car parked next to Luca's Range Rover, "Oh no, she didn't!"

he hissed through clenched teeth. Slamming the door he marched in and stormed upstairs, leaving all the lights on and doors unlocked, nobody in their right minds would attempt to sneak into the Remizov's house.

Opening her door without knocking, once again she wasn't there, but the lamps were on this time and he heard the shower running and the bathroom door was shut. He walked to the window where the drapes were open and he looked out on to the moon lit garden, as he waited he began to calm down.

It was utter bliss, washing all the make-up off my face and about a gallon of hairspray out of my hair, after brushing my teeth I wrapped a fluffy white towel around me and walked into my bedroom.

"Fucking hell Mika you scared the shit out of me," I yelled, nearly waking the whole house up.

"Where the hell were you, I've been going out of my mind, do you realise how God damn dangerous it is out there?" He stood in the bay of the window like a giant grizzly bear, ready to tear me a new one.

"Dangerous! That's a bit much; I was with the guys at a diner, what is your problem?"

"You have no fucking idea Isabelle! But trust me, it is."

He was speaking in riddles and I had no clue what he meant.

"Why do you want to know anyway?" I spat back.

"Because I DO!" He was enraged, I had never seen him so mad.

"Well I want to know about Ruth, and what the hell was that kiss about?" Now I sounded petty. He moved so quickly he took my breath away.

"Ruth means fuck all to me, and that kiss means you are mine."

Mika's eyes seemed to penetrate my soul, he was so intense. I actually kept my mouth shut for once, not daring to speak.

My breathing grew faster and I could hear the blood rushing through my ears. I was terrified but at the same time exhilarated, like the feeling you get from being at Six Flags and about to ride 'Zumanjaro' the drop of doom.

Pure nervous excitement was building in anticipation, knowing something mind blowing was coming; I bit my lip to stay focused. He was beautiful, not a word usually used to describe a ripped Alpha male, but he was.

Raising his hand, he tugged at the barrier that stood between him and his ultimate goal, his prized possession. He let the towel slide down and pool at her feet before letting go of it, taking in her naked sculpted body.

"You are even more fucking perfect than I had imagined," he said, his voice so low and husky it vibrated through her.

Dropping to his knees, he kissed her stomach as he descended. His hands roamed all over her silky, smooth back and delectable derrière, pulling her harder on to his lips. His tongue going straight in for the kill zone. He traced the creases of her thighs from one side to the other, stopping just above her neatly waxed triangle, hearing her gasping at his expert touch.

"You smell divine," as he inhaled deeply. "I can't get enough."

She pulled his hair tight as she ran her fingers through it, wanting so desperately to feel him work his magic with his mouth and he loved it. He loved driving her crazy with desire, bringing her close to the edge, wanting to claim her first orgasm with his tongue and feeling her juices run down his chin as he lapped her to completion.

He looked up at his goddess while his tongue stimulated her clitoris as she watched with unblinking eyes. He pushed two fingers into her tight, wet hole, finger fucking her deeply, and just hearing the sounds of her aroused, soaking wet pussy was making, nearly had him blowing his load, she was so receptive to his touch.

Pulling out his nectar covered fingers from her snug hole, he held them to her mouth, "Taste how exquisite you are Angel."

He could feel his own underwear dampening with precum leaking out of his pulsating cock as he watched her lick and suck his fingers clean. He couldn't wait any longer his cock hurt from being so hard, he picked her up and gently placed her in the centre of the bed. As he stripped, her eyes never left his body, seeing his hard phallus peeking over the top of his boxers eager to play, caused her to gasp slightly at the size of him, praying it wouldn't hurt too much. No man had ever been worthy of taking her virginity, but this was no ordinary man, this was Mika.

She watched him slip on a condom, latex covered his impressive shaft, all the while never taking his eyes off her. Climbing on the bed he pushed her legs apart, crawling up her body, stopping over her quivering pussy for one more teasing lick, "it should be a sin to taste that good," and she quivered under his touch again. Making his way to her mouth, he slipped a hand around the back of her neck pulling her up onto his lips. His other hand held his cock and gently rubbed the tip of it on her already stimulated clit, making her moan as she dug her nails hard into his shoulders. He couldn't hold back anymore. He slid into her feeling her muscles contracting, it was like she was pulling him in, consuming him. She was so tight he had to thrust hard to get all of him inside her, burying himself deep. He immediately stopped when he felt a barrier snap, pushing up on to his arms but still inside her trying his damnedest not to move.

"Izzy?" he looked at her, she had her eyes scrunched shut, sucking air in through clenched teeth. "Angel, Christ you should have told me, Fuck! I would have been so much gentler." He spoke so soft it was like a whisper.

She looked at him and smiled. "Don't you dare stop!"

He began to move at a snails pace, seriously not wanting to hurt her.

"Mika I swear I'm OK really....Please for the love of God just

Fuck me!" she practically begged him.

He had made her so wet it had eased the discomfort somewhat and for him it felt so fucking good. Increasing his speed and force he felt the tell tale signs of her climax building.

"I'm gonna cum, God don't stop!"

The way she gasped caused his fingers and toes to curl. "Cum with me Angel." That's all it took, those words in that husky tone to push her over the precipice, giving her the best electrifying, mind-blowing orgasm she'd ever had, Mika was apparently on the same wave length as he released his seed and he called her name.

Mika embraced me lovingly in his arms, so protectively shielding me from the world. He kissed my lips ever so softly it was as if I was made of fine China, so fragile, he seemed scared, as though he would break me. I couldn't hide the smile on my face, this monster of a man was my very own gentle giant, and I didn't want this to end.

"Izzy, I need to ask, how and why?"

I was totally confused.

"Angel how in Gods name were you still a virgin? You are beautiful and sexy as hell and sweeter than honey."

I felt my cheeks heating up through embarrassment.

"How in the world have men not killed over you?"

Little did she know he already had.

"What you gave me was the most precious gift ever."

I tried to avert my gaze but he captured my chin and made me look into his warm caramel eyes.

"I've had boyfriends; I'm not all that innocent... they, just weren't you."

Mika felt his heart explode with sheer joy; he whispered, "You waited for me?"

He knew there and then that he would never let her go; no

other man will ever touch her body or kiss those wonderful lips but his.

"Oh Izzy I have always loved you, but now I am head over heels in love with you." He spoke with so much passion that I was lost for words; I swear I was having an out of body experience. He is in love with me! I felt a sly tear slip down my cheek.

"I have loved you for as long as I can remember, it's only ever been you."

"Sleep Angel, tomorrow we will move your things into my room, I want to fall asleep and wake up with you in my arms, every night and day."

He pulled me in tight as he turned me over and spooned me; we fit perfectly together, like we'd been made to measure. Sleep came quickly, closing my heavy lids just as the sun broke the horizon, and the last thing I heard was, "I love you."

CHAPTER ELEVEN

Jazz dragged herself downstairs in search of caffeine and as she walked into the kitchen Alex and Luca were sat at the breakfast bar, looking all bright eyed and bushy tailed, she silently cursed them.

"Morning Princess."

"Coffee," was all she muttered, shuffling towards her target, the coffee machine.

"Ahh," she sighed, it was just what the doctor ordered. "It's like liquid gold," she said, finally stringing her words together.

"Did you hear anything last night?" Luca asked.

"No, once my head hit the pillow I was out, you?"

"I heard Izzy's car pull up but nothing after that."

Neither bothered to ask Alex, he could sleep through the out break of world war III.

"After I finish this I'll go see her and find out what went down." She raised her cup to her lips, "Have you seen Mika yet?" she enquired.

"No but his car is still there and his room door is shut, maybe he's having a lay in?" Alex answered.

"That's strange, Mika is usually always the first up."

Feeling more human, Jazz poured a mug of coffee for Izzy, "If you see Mika before I get back, find out the gossip!" she instructed them as she walked out.

The sun was streaming into Izzy's room, Jazz was grateful she had left the drapes open, well at first, until her eyes focused on her brothers naked body, thankfully the sheet covered his modesty and he had Izzy sleeping soundly in his arms. She backed out as quietly as possible, softly closing the door before running downstairs giggling, trying desperately not to spill the coffee.

"Back so soon, she kicked you out!" Luca laughed.

"Erm, no," she said, with the cheekiest grin on her face.

"OK sis out with it."

"Ha, ha, it's safe to say they made up," she burst out laughing.

"Fuck…

I woke up still in Mika's arms, and tried to move without disturbing him.

"Where are you going Angel?" His sleepy voice was just as sexy.

"Bathroom before I have an accident." Looking for my robe, I was feeling the need to cover up my nakedness.

"Shy now eh, after what we did last night?"

I smiled sheepishly.

"Never hide your gorgeous body from me," and he pulled me back on the bed to him and kissed me.

"How are you, sore?" he asked.

"Mmm, a little."

"How about a hot, soothing soak in the tub?"

"Now that sounds like a plan and a coffee would make that perfect," I winked.

He reached for his boxers, "I'll get the drinks while you run the bath."

As he left the bed I saw the blood stain on the sheets, evidence of my lost virginity.

"Don't worry about that, be proud of it," he smiled, "because Izzy, I am." He kissed me again before leaving.

Once inside the bathroom on my own, I had time to reflect on what had happened, my whole life had changed and it would never be the same ever again, we could never go back to the way it used to be. My world had turned on its axis, for years I had fantasized what it would be like with Mika, what he looked like naked, how his touch would feel. Nothing had quite prepared me for the real thing, and I was still waiting to wake up from this amazing dream.

The tub was full when Mika returned, "Angel, coffee," he called out as he entered.

I had a flimsy silk robe on and my hair tied was tied in a loose bun.

"God you are fucking beautiful," he sighed, making me blush. The smile on his face put to rest any doubts I'd had that we'd made a mistake.

"If you weren't so sore I'd fuck you till the sun went down."

That made me laugh, "Maybe tomorrow," I winked at him.

The scent of coffee was making my taste buds water, "Here," he passed me the cup as if he'd read my mind, "Oh and be prepared for an inquisition, I've just been ambushed." Now that didn't surprise me at all.

By the time Jazz had finished her interrogation it was dark. Mika had been called away on business just after lunch when Luca came in like a freight train speaking in Russian.

"Trouble is brewing; Tomaz has a prick tied down after finding him downloading shit from his computer in his office."

"Who?" asked Mika.

"That's why he called, it's one of Delushi's."

Mika stood up pissed as hell. "Let's go," he ordered. He looked at me and smiled, "Angel we have to go to the office, business calls, we won't be long." He kissed my nose and quickly left.

Something wasn't right, this felt so wrong. I found Jazz in the kitchen, "Who are Delushi and Tomaz?" I asked.

She turned to me, "Delushi, I have no idea, Tomaz was my Dad's friend, why?"

"The guys got a call and went to see Tomaz, something they didn't want me to know because they spoke in Russian."

"Who the hell knows ..?Men!" she sighed.

It was now dark and late, "Where are they?" I moaned, feeling a little concerned.

"Stop it, you sound like an old married woman already," she teased. I tried to laugh it off but I couldn't shake this bad feeling.

"That's it, I'm beat and I've got work early tomorrow." I kissed her goodnight.

"Night sweetie, I'll be at the bar tomorrow if you fancy a drink after?"

"You're on."

I was woken by Mika climbing into my bed, "Sorry Angel, business went on longer than I expected," he whispered, as he kissed the back of my neck.

"What happened?" I quizzed.

"Nothing for you to worry about, now sleep its late."

I was dying to ask questions but I knew I shouldn't, though I was determined to do some digging later.

A month into our relationship I was thoroughly loving my newly found sex life, it's a wonder I'm not bow legged. Mika kept insisting I moved into his side of the house and honestly I was dragging my feet, saying it was way too soon and that just seemed to piss him off. Then one day I came home from work and walked into my room for a shower and was stopped dead in my tracks, my room was void of all my things, "Where's my stuff," I shouted, asking no one since I was alone.

"In my room."

I leapt out of my skin, "Jesus, Fuck, Mika, stop doing that!" I screamed at him, which he thought was highly amusing.

"I had Sonja move everything, I was getting tired of waiting for you. Are you mad?"

"No, no, I'm not mad." How could I be mad at him for wanting me!

He did agree with me when I suggested we keep our relationship at work a secret. It was already going to be weird now everyone knew I was friends with the family. Mandy and Margo acted liked normal and Pete and Joe still kept flirting with me.

Ruth on the other hand kept herself to herself; personally I think she was still licking her wounds. I also insisted on driving myself to and from work, he did not like that at all but there was no way in hell I was going in at seven when he did. That was way too early and it was hard enough keeping my hands off him at home, let alone at work in his made to measure suits.

Over the last few months I'd visited Gran as often as I could and sadly I had to admit she had gotten worse every time. She was a constant worry to me, Rita called telling me she was forgetting to take her medication and the icing on the cake was when Gran had left her house to go visit friends and got completely lost and confused. She didn't know where she lived and couldn't remember anyone's names or phone numbers who she could ring to help when the police had found her. Luckily she had Rita's phone number in her purse for the police to call.

Poor Rita was in her eighties herself and didn't need all of this stress, "Sorry honey to be the bearer of bad news but I thought you should know, she was quite lucid when I finally got her home." I knew it was time to discuss moving her into a facility that had 24 hours monitoring, thankfully Gran had already mentioned it so it hadn't been my decision to make, that night I had sobbed in Mika's arms. It was time for me to go to Milwaukee.

The next morning Mika had said he wanted to come with me, even though he was really busy at work, some big problems were arising but he would not share the details.

"No. I have to do this on my own and it will only confuse Gran, but thanks."

"Call me every hour!"

"That's impossible and you know it Mika, but I will ring as often as I can."

"Fine. When will you be home?"

Sighing, "Hopefully Sunday," and I held on to him not wanting to go at all.

"Drive safely Angel and I love you." As I pulled away in Bertie, I blew him a kiss.

As I pulled under the car port on Gran's drive, I saw her and Rita waiting for me, Gran looked so old and fragile.

Rita hugged me, "Coffee honey?"

"Oh yes please." I turned to Gran. "Hi Gran."

She smiled then I saw the confused look lift. "Oh my Izzy."

My heart broke every time, I was losing her even quicker than I had expected to. Walking in to the once homely house, it was my turn to be confused, it was practically empty, just boxes piled high, packed with most of her things. Gran and Rita had already made all the arrangements, she had a place at Sunset Gardens, a facility that cared for people with dementia and Alzheimer's in varying stages of the dreadful disease. Gran had been quite happy about moving there, she had been going twice weekly to the day centre and had enjoyed it.

The house was ready to be put up for sale; it just needed my signature to finalize it. I knew I would eventually end up moving her into a care home but I certainly didn't think it would be on this visit, but she told me a room had become available and she wanted to go. Once again Gran had done all she could, not wanting to burden me with anything. I called Jazz and Mika to tell them what was going on. Jazz cried with me and Mika wanted to drop everything and drive out, it was the saddest few days I'd had in a long time.

By late Friday afternoon we had just about finished unpacking Gran's new home and getting her settled in, it was bright and cosy.

"Izzy come sit by me." She patted the small sofa, I smiled and sat next to her and she held my hand.

"Tell me how Savas is?" She asked.

"Gran, Savas and Petra died about three years ago now."

She frowned, "Oh my dear I'm so sorry, he did a lot for you and your momma, he was so kind and had a real big heart for a mob boss." She turned and looked out of the window leaving me with my mouth on the floor.

"Gran, what do you mean, Mob?" I shook her arm trying to get her attention back.

"Oh Izzy, when did you come?" she had that glazed look and I knew it was pointless. I took her to the dining hall for dinner.

"I'll see you tomorrow Gran." I kissed her.

"Bye Jessica, I love you."

I sat in Bertie and let the flood defences break and I cried my heart out. Alzheimer's was the worst disease and to be honest, it was hardest of all on the family. I would end up losing her twice, once when her mind went and then when I'd bury her next to Mom.

Back in her house, no longer her home, I went through all the paperwork I needed, and the rest I would just shred. After an hour I came across a box file with my name on it. Inside were photo's I'd never seen before of Mom and Dad, and one of me and Dad. No wait, that can't be right, he looked about twenty and the girl maybe sixteen. I couldn't believe the resemblance, it was like looking at me in this photo. There was another person stood with them that had been cut out, all that remained was an arm, and written on the back in Cyrillic *Natasha and Nikolai*.

There were newspaper clippings about the death of my Dad I'd never seen before. It explained about the drug bust that the DPD had executed against the Albanian warlords, most of them had been killed, and the rest had been arrested. My father and two other officers had also been killed. It also went on to hint that the tip off had come from the Russian mob but they had no proof. The box file also had documents of a trust fund in my name that had close to half a million dollars and on my twenty fifth birthday I would be allowed access to it. It had been opened by Savas Remizov before I was even born; this had my eyes popping out and caused even more questions.

Why had Savas opened a trust fund for me, was Gran telling the truth? Was Savas a mob boss? What was that photo about, why was he called Nikolai, who was Natasha and why the hell was it all written in Russian? Was my Dad a mole for the Russian mob and was that what had gotten him killed? Holy mother of God what was going on, I could feel my world start to crumble, had I been lied to my whole life? The more I thought about things the more questions it raised. I needed to talk to Jazz and find out what she knew, and I prayed she was as much in the dark as I was because if she knew I honestly didn't know if I could ever forgive her.

The next day I decided to go home after visiting Gran and by two p.m. I was on the highway. I had to figure out what I was going to say, I couldn't just come out with, 'hey Jazz was your Dad the godfather of the Russian mob?' That's when another bomb dropped, was Mika the new head? Is that why he is always so secretive about work and always speaking in Russian? Was I sleeping with fucking, *Don Corleone?*

The six hour drive back was flying by, I'd hit the outskirts of Detroit just after seven and decided to head straight to *Red Square.* Zac and Grant were on the door.

"Hey Izzy, you OK?" I smiled, "Yeah, I will be once I have a cold one." Grant held the door open and The Rolling Stones cover band that was playing 'Paint it black' boomed out, they were pretty good.

Max waved from behind the bar, "Hey Izzy, what's your poison tonight?" he asked with a friendly grin.

"An ice cold beer would be great thanks."

"From the tap or a bottle?"

"Bottle always." I'd learnt my lesson the hard way and as I watched him pop the cap I asked, "Where's Jazz?"

"Boss lady's in her office."

"Cheers Max."

I knocked on her door not wanting to barge in and heard a welcoming "come in." I poked my head around the door.

"Hey, you busy?"

"Izzy." She jumped up and came running to me. "I thought you weren't home till tomorrow," she squeezed all the air out of me and it was just what I needed.

"Well Gran's in her new home and I was alone in her empty house and she thinks I'm my Mom and keeps calling me Jess!" Once again I had tears filling my eyes.

Once we had both composed ourselves I told her nearly everything, leaving out the part about the trust fund. I watched her reactions closely, looking for any signs of recognition but there was none and I hated myself for ever doubting her.

"Izzy, I have heard that all my life, it used to really upset me when I was younger. Momma told me once that people are narrow minded and prejudice, because we came from a wealthy Russian family in a predominant Russian community. People assumed we were mob affiliated, just like the rich Italian families are with the Mafia."

What she said made sense. Again I asked about the brotherhood.

"It's a Russian tradition, my family has been part of it for generations, it's definitely a male thing and a real honour to be part of, it's very selective and secretive. But they help out the community keeping it safe, sort of like a neighbourhood watch, like the Masons, it has a hierarchy and my Dad held a high position, which Mika inherited. I hope that explains it more."

"It does, but is that all you know?"

"My Mom did say she would tell me more when I was old enough, but sadly now she can't so you know as much as I do. Izzy, I don't want to sound unsympathetic but Gran's mind is really messed up, she could just simply be confused."

"Yeah I know, you're right but it was just a shock." I still had a niggling feeling but I decided to keep that to myself for now.

"Thanks Jazz, I feel a lot better, but please don't say anything, especially to Mika, he'll think I'm nuts."

She crossed her heart, "Sister swear." We hugged and she asked, "How about a stiff drink?" Half a bottle of vodka later we were sat watching the band.

"They're really good." Jazz said as I sipped another cold beer, "Can't beat the Stones," I slurred.

Max leaned over the bar, "Izzy, keys please."

"What, I'm not gonna drive."

"Keys now, I know your not." He wasn't taking no for an answer, and I watched him place Bertie's keys in the cash register before I turned back to watching the band.

CHAPTER TWELVE

Mika had called a summit, which included Delushi. The brotherhood and the Italians had agreed to a compromise decades ago to share the State and not interfere with one another's business. Delushi's main income came from the drug trade and money laundering, while the Bratva dealt with imports and exports of arms and of course, the high class entertainment businesses. Like the brotherhood, the Italians had legitimate companies, although theirs were not as profitable as the *Redline Corp.* The tension in the conference room was palatable but both syndicates knew they needed one another.

The once wiped out Albanians had been slowly re-growing in stature, gaining more power and a foot hold in Detroit but were still fairly quiet in the rest of the Michigan area. Yet these new breeds of Albanians were even more ruthless, even to the Bratva they were barbaric, praying on the vulnerable and weak. Usually Delushi and the Brotherhood wouldn't be bothered about such a small group but they were gaining in strength and numbers. This is what made Delushi agree to the impromptu meeting, not only the loss of his own personnel but the Albanians had been encroaching on his turf, taking over more of his drug empire bit by bit. It wasn't just the Italians who'd lost soldiers, the Brotherhood had too and over the last two months they had buried six good men, the last being Gregor on Friday, a close and good friend of Luca's and now he was after blood.

Both sides had tried, but to no avail, to find out who was calling the shots, they needed to know who the Boss was and deal with him permanently, no compromising, just elimination like the old days. The prick Tomaz had found downloading files was one of Delushi's schleps that had been when everything came to light. Delushi had thought Mika was behind all the shit that was going on, and Mika had thought the same thing about delushi. It had taken a lot of persuasion on both sides to believe the other was telling the truth. Now they were working together with one aim in mind, to rid the City of that scum once and for all, to basically divide and conquer.

Once Delushi had left, Mika still had his men around the table, "I want back-up, call Mark in Chicago?" Mark was his Uncle, their mother's brother and he was Pakhan of Illinois, he told Luca.

"There is a threat to my family and I want minders on Jazz and Izzy all the time until this is over!" Nobody disagreed.

Tomaz stepped in, "I have two of the best, Illa and Gavril, and I shall post them now."

"I do not want Jazz or Izzy to know, it will only have them asking questions so just keep them safe. Leave Izzy for now, she's in Milwaukee till Sunday, but Jazz is in *Red Square*." Tomaz nodded.

Mika had guards posted on all of the high ranking members families, he knew the Albanians wouldn't give a shit about the contract to keep all the children safe, that had been forced into action all those years ago and he wasn't about to risk it. By seven Mika was exhausted, but the plan of attack had been formulated and set in motion. Mark was sending him reinforcements, making Detroit's manpower triple in numbers. War had been well and truly declared.

Jazz slipped back into her office to call Mika.

"Hey Princess, everything OK?" he sounded tired.

"Yeah but I thought you should know I have a pretty drunk Izzy here."

"What?"

"She turned up about two hours ago, really upset."

"Why the fuck has it taken you so long to call me?" He was so mad, Jazz could feel his rage seeping down the line.

"Hey Buddy don't you shout at me, I'm her best friend and she needed to talk to me. Everything is not always a fucking vendetta against you, just be grateful I'm calling you now!" She matched his anger as she spat her reply back at him.

"Why didn't she call me, what did she say?"

Jazz relented a little and told him all about Izzy's Gran but left out the 'mob' bit.

"I'm sorry Jazz, I'm on my way, don't let her leave."

"Max has confiscated her keys."

"Thanks Princess, I'll see you soon."

Jazz returned to the bar but couldn't find her, "Shit!" she cried, "Where is she Max?"

"Getting her groove on." Smiling, he pointed to the dance floor, where Izzy was dancing away in her own little world. Jazz sat back down on the stool she had vacated earlier and Max placed a drink in front of her and handed her Izzy's bottle he had kept safe behind the bar.

Mika pulled up outside the bar, "I'll drive Izzy home, you drive her car," he said to Luca.

"Fine but after a day like today I need a drink first."

"Have one at home!" Mika snapped.

Luca huffed, "Fine," but not amused at all.

Entering, he spotted Jazz straight away, she waved and pointed to the dance floor where Izzy was dancing all by herself, getting lost in the music, he couldn't help but smile a little and decided to let her be for a while.

"Luca get me a drink when you get yourself one," he conceded.

"That's more like it," Luca smiled.

Mika went to sit with Jazz, "I'm sorry for shouting at you."

"I know."

"I was just concerned."

"I know," and she threw her arms around him, "she's pretty wasted," she said and his reply, "I know," made her chuckle.

The music might have stopped but my legs didn't they were so drunk. I wobbled my way back to the bar, that's when I saw Mika; he was a sight for sore eyes.

"Hi," I slurred.

"Hi, you, you're drunk."

"Only my legs!"

I expected a mad Mika but instead I got the loving one.

"How about I drive you home and put you to bed?"

"Now that sounds like a great plan." I remember sitting in Mika's SUV feeling warm and content but to be honest nothing much after that.

I woke up the next morning naked and alone, feeling pretty good considering how much alcohol I'd consumed. Showering and dressing, it was time to bite the bullet and face the masses.

Sonja was in the kitchen, "Good afternoon sleepy head, you hungry?"

"Hi, no thanks, just coffee please, where is everyone?"

"Jazz went to the bar, and Mr Remizov is in his office with Luca I think?"

Just then Luca came down the stairs at speed, "You OK Iz?" he was a blur as he ran past.

"Yeah fine thanks."

"Gotta go, back later," he yelled as the door slammed.

"What the hell was that all about?"

"Who knows in his house," Sonja chuckled, "I'm going to the

store. I'll see you soon."

With everyone gone apart from Mika, I had a brain wave on how to get back into his good graces. Knowing exactly what to do, I walked upstairs with my coffee and set 'operation forgiveness' into action. Stripping out of my sweats I selected the most revealing, sexy lingerie I owned, a flawless sheer black and midnight blue Basque with an intricate design. The barely bra left little to the imagination and matching thong, slipping on 5 inch black porn star heels that lifted everything perfectly, the finishing touch was a black silk kimono, which I left untied, giving me a sultry look. Un-clipping my hair I let it fall into natural wavy curls. One last look at the end result, I must say I can pull off sexy pretty well, lets hope Mika thinks so too.

Instead of knocking I just let the door open tantalizingly slow before provocatively sauntering in, letting Mika experience the full x-rated risqué entrance. I reached one hand high up on the door letting the robe open even more giving him a totally unobstructive view while I posed seductively. I was stopped dead in my tracks by the look of horror on his face; his mouth dropped wide open like something off a cartoon. This was not the look I was hoping for, and then my spidery sense tingled before my blood froze in my veins. Not only were Mika's eyes on me but so were two other pairs as well. You could have cut the tension in the room with a knife; this was bad, so very, very bad!

Standing up ridged I wrapped my robe around me. "Shit I'm so sorry," before retreating quickly and slammed the door. Dying from embarrassment I ran to my old room, begging the floor to open up and swallow me. I ran to the bathroom and hid behind the open door, sliding down the wall, humiliated beyond belief and planned to remain here till I died, praying for God to take me soon, preferably this very minute.

I kept seeing that shock and horror look on Mika's face, it looked like he was about to stroke out, or more likely commit murder – on me! I swear he must be regretting ever starting a relationship with me, I had, unbeknown to him, accused him of being in the mob and now embarrassed him in a business meeting looking like a high-class hooker, what the hell had I done?

Thirty minutes later I heard my name being bellowed, commanding me to come out. No fucking way! His terrifying tone scared the very life out of me, and then the bedroom door opened, "ISABELLE!" Holding my breath I stayed statue still, in the perfect hiding spot behind the open bathroom door, tucked in to a small ball. Thank God he never saw me, I sighed in relief as he closed the bedroom door, his shouts fading as he walked away.

An hour had passed and I was still cowardly cowered in a ball behind the door undiscovered, listening to raised voices, the only thing I could make out was my name when Mika boomed it. I was slowly regretting my decision because the longer I stayed the worse I was making it and the madder Mika was getting. This was the first time in my life I was afraid of him; silent tears ran down my cheeks, not from humiliation any more but fear.

Outside the door I heard Sonja's voice, "Mr Remizov she didn't come downstairs, she must be up here somewhere?"

"I've looked every fucking where," he growled.

They entered Jazz's room and their voices became muffled. When my door opened again the noise made me jump, I was physically shaking as the footsteps approached.

"Izzy, where the hell are you?" Mika spoke softly.

I sniffed and gave my position away; the door closed slowly leaving me exposed. I was sitting with my arms wrapped around my knees huddled in a tight ball with my head buried. His knees cracked as he squatted down to me.

"Angel," he lifted my chin, forcing me to look up at him, "You're trembling."

"I'm so sorry." My voice was thick with fear and I whimpered. He swept me up in one fluid motion and carried me into the bedroom before sitting me on the bed.

"You had me scared to death, I couldn't find you." He pressed his lips to my forehead then walked to the door.

"Sonja I've found her, take the rest of the day off," he yelled.

"Thank the Lord, see you tomorrow."

He came back to me.

"I am so sorry Mika, I didn't mean to cause you trouble I thought you were alone," I sobbed.

"Sssh now, I know," he lovingly embraced me, then he actually chuckled, "I think Tomaz nearly had a heart attack, and as for Illa, well he thinks I'm the worlds luckiest Bastard walking."

I couldn't believe it, I pushed myself up to look into his face, "You're not mad at me?"

He smiled, "Mad at you, never, but with them I'd happily gouge their eyes out, your body is for my eyes only."

I actually sighed with relief. All the stress and tension had eased, and he picked me up and carried me to our room.

"Now Angel, show me what you had in mind?"

Suddenly I was hot, flustered and had totally lost my nerve. "Sorry I can't," I said, sounding all shy and timid, "But please Mika, make love to me, show me you have forgiven me."

He traced her lips with his thumb. "You are too beautiful for a monster like me," his deep voice reverberated through her, biting her bottom lip, pulling it ever so softly before running his tongue over them teasingly slow, dipping it inside her mouth. The kiss became more intense, he devoured her greedily as his arms snaked around that sculpted body, tracing the contours of her ass, finally finding that sweet spot between her legs, gently but forcefully pushing them apart. She was holding her breath.

"Breathe Angel, enjoy it, let yourself go."

He swiftly disposed of the thong as his fingers expertly pulled apart her plush lips, exposing her sensitive clit to the cool air as his thumb skilfully ran circles over the swollen nub with just the right amount of pressure, while his fingers penetrated her tight, wet little hole. He captured her groan with his mouth, her body aching for his touch. Sliding his fingers in faster she struggled to fill her lungs, he was sending her spinning out of control.

The heat their bodies' were creating threatened to ignite, her moans echoing off the walls as he continued pushing in harder.

"I want you to soak my palm with your cum," he growled low into her ear. "Cum for me baby, let me feel your body come apart."

This sent a charge through her, causing her back to arch and her muscles to spasm around his fingers, her pleasure receptors exploding into a million pieces.

"Oh God.......Yes!" She came in pure ecstasy and he latched on to her dripping pussy and drank the orgasm he had inspired. Feeling her honey coating his tongue as he lapped greedily at her, making her pleasure last longer, she screamed through too much stimulation.

"Fuck, you're killing me."

"I want to watch you ride my cock."

She straddled him, feeling his thick shaft stretching her wide to accommodate his girth. The feeling of total fullness was a sensation she loved as he glided smoothly into her, she had the power, she had the control and how she loved it, watching him struggle to relinquish his hold, his need to possess her. She rode him hard, feeling every inch of him, with each thrust she clenched around him, bringing him close to completion. When he moaned her name it seemed to spur her on even more. With his hands on her hips he tried to dictate the pace but failed so he used his thumb to graze over her clit, flooding her with heat, which brought him closer to utter annihilation, she was relentless, he grasped her hips and drove deep inside her, she cried out as he spilt his seed into her, a feeling that felt never-ending, which brought her to her own climax.

Dropping onto his chest completely exhausted, she whispered, "Oh baby, I got you."

He held her close, both spent they collapsed in each others arms and dozed off; the feeling of contentment was bliss and made for the perfect sleep.

CHAPTER THIRTEEN

The winter was closing in fast with long dark nights and bitter cold days. Today the sky threatened to drop its first snow fall of the year. I loved Mika more each day but lately his mood matched the weather, cold, grey and ominous and I was worried. He growled at everyone with the exception of me but that changed on Friday night.

After leaving work I decided to get some early Christmas shopping done, since Jazz was busy at *Red Square* and Mandy was heading up to Roger City to visit her family, I went alone. I pulled into the shopping malls' car park ready for some well needed retail therapy. After a pleasurable two hour spending spree, Bertie's trunk was full of bags and gifts. I was feeling pretty proud of what I had accomplished and patted myself on the back for getting a head start. I blasted out Dusty Springfield, singing at the top of my voice 'I only want to be with you' but turning into the driveway I was surprised by the amount of vehicles parked up and the house was lit up like Rockefeller Plaza, I had to wonder what was going on?

I struggled to open the door with my hands full and literally fell in when it gave. Two men I had not seen before greeted me, scaring me half to death. One shouted in Russian "Boss, she's here." The pair towered over me, scowling through their vexed eyes.

"What's going on?" I snapped.

"ISABELLE! Where the fuck have you been?" Mika yelled. "Why didn't you answer your fucking phone, I've had men searching the damn City looking for you?" I stood shocked into silence. "WELL! Answer me, NOW." His tone was lethal.

"I've been Christmas shopping and didn't realise my phone had gone flat till I got to the car." I hadn't done anything wrong and my eyes now burned with angry tears.

"You should have told me where you were going. You do not go anywhere without letting me know, ever! Do you fucking understand me Isabelle?"

I was white hot with rage, "Fuck you Mika! You are not my father, you do not own me, nobody does, do you fucking understand ME!" I yelled, bringing complete silence to the house; you could have heard a pin drop, even with the house being filled with giant men who were looking anywhere but at me or Mika.

"Get out of my sight," he hissed, turning and walking away from me.

"Fucking gladly...Dick!"

He turned on a dime and was nose to nose with me. "Do not push me." He spoke in a deadly calm.

I ran upstairs crying my heart out; dumping the bags in our room I locked myself in the bathroom. Standing so long in the shower trying to calm down had pruned my skin. I was all cried out but still fuming, how dare he speak to me like that? Who the hell does he think he is? Dressing in my PJ's I walked into Jazz's room and called her from the land line in the room. When she answered I couldn't hold back.

"Mika has just gone completely mental on me!" I told her everything that had happened in between sobs.

"The bar is quiet tonight with the weather being so shit, I'll get Max to lock up, I'm on my way home, stay in my room, and I won't be long."

I heard her angry voice as she arrived home, yelling and then it all went quiet, fifteen minutes later she walked in to her room.

"What's happened?" I asked.

"Well I started off by giving him a piece of my mind." She came over and sat next to me. "He is so worried but will not go into detail about what or why, but what he did say is someone has threatened the family and he just wants to keep us all safe." Jazz sounded sorry for him.

"Why didn't he just say that instead of going crazy, I would have understood, I'm not stupid."

She smiled, "He wants to talk to you."

My anger had dissipated somewhat, "I'm still mad at him for speaking to me like that and in front of all those goons."

Jazz sniggered, "Apparently those 'goons' have been watching you and me for weeks, we have fucking sexy as fuck body guards and we didn't even know it!"

"What? Never mind body guards what have the police said?"

"Mika doesn't want the police involved."

That didn't make any sense, "Why not?"

"You'll have to ask him, but look on the bright side, we have some serious eye candy watching over us," she jiggled her eye brows trying to make light of the situation.

I stood up, "Where is he?"

"In the den waiting for you."

As I walked to the door I saw my reflection in the mirror, my hair was in a high pony tail, I had on fluffy pink PJ's, furry slippers and a face like thunder, I looked just like a petulant child.

My defence wall was up and nothing was going to penetrate it anytime soon. The two goons I had seen earlier were standing on point outside the den doors, I didn't speak a word but gave them my filthiest look that dared them to stop me, they didn't and I walked into the den. I stood rigid behind the closed door with my arms crossed, "What do you want?" I couldn't stop the snide tone of my voice.

"I'm sorry I yelled at you the way I did," he said, still sounding mad at me. "Izzy you added years to my life tonight." His voice now had a worried edge to it.

"Why?" To which he basically repeated what Jazz had said. "If you are so worried why haven't you called the police?" He stared at me, silently debating whether or not to tell me. "Well?" I was losing my patience.

"Because that is not how we handle things," he snarled. Once again Mika rattled me by the way he spoke and what he was insinuating, I tried yet again to get him to clarify more but again I failed.

"Izzy do you trust me?" he asked, did I? I used to, but things were changing and I had questions. He looked hurt when I didn't reply, "Well, do you?"

"Yes," I said, trying to sound convincing.

"I will never let anyone hurt you or my family, promise to do what I say until this problem is eliminated?" Giving him an icy glare, "Fine, whatever."

He gave me a small smile and walked towards me, and I held out my hand, "stop! I need you to stay away from me, I need time to think, this is all too much." Opening the door I walked out, not looking back at him. I went to my old room and thankfully no one disturbed me, not even Jazz, it was one of the longest and darkest nights of my life.

Over the next few days the tension in the house heightened, everyone seemed on edge, as if waiting for a bomb to go off. I was still in my old room, which only added to the stress and I simply couldn't let it drop it, it was horrendous. Sitting in Jazz's room one night, I suggested it might be better if I found my own place and moved out since it was partly my fault that the atmosphere here at home was so bad. You'd honestly have thought I'd told her I was leaving the country; she lost it big time, so consequently I didn't bring the subject up again.

The fracture between Mika and I grew, he became distant

and quite cold towards me, causing pain I'd never felt before and something had to give soon before we reached a point of no return. I had moved most of my things back into my old room and Mika hadn't stopped me, saying "it's probably for the best for now." That caused more emotional turmoil and it felt like he'd plunged a dagger into my already shattered heart. I simply didn't know what to do, six months ago I was happy and oblivious, and now my world was disintegrating around me on a daily basis and I had absolutely no control over it. The most hurtful thing was Mika had stopped calling me 'Angel'.

Work strangely enough was my only salvation and thankfully I never saw Mika. Mandy and I would deal with Margo or Luca; even Luca looked stressed out and told me to be patient, whatever that meant. The start of the following week we had just finished the quarter's figures and needed Luca's signature to close the files.

I rang him, "Come up to the conference room, we are about to have a meeting but no-one has arrived yet." I quickly grabbed all the necessary paperwork that needed his authorization and headed upstairs. Katia met me at the lift, "Hurry," and she quickly ushered me inside.

There were two men inside besides Mika and Luca. "Morning." I spoke politely and the older man looked at me like I was a freak, he just starred.

"I can't believe my eyes." He sounded like he was a heavy smoker even as he spoke in Russian. "Seeing her makes me believe in reincarnation – she is the embodiment of Natasha." He turned to Mika, "You my son have your Papa's taste in beautiful women."

I could feel Mika's eyes burning into me, my ears picked up at the mention of Natasha's name but my face stayed neutral from years of practice. The older man continued.

"Look at her, Nikolai would have been so proud of his little girl. I never understood why he didn't want her to know her heritage, it is such a shame Nikolai was such a good brother."

My body tensed up internally, my head began to spin. "Thanks," I said softly to Luca as he handed me the paperwork back, then I looked at the man and Mika, "Goodbye." It sounded so final…and it was.

CHAPTER FOURTEEN

I managed to walk out of the conference room calmly, even though my mind was racing, and by the time I stepped inside the elevator I was nearly hyperventilating. My whole life has been a fucking lie, my father wasn't the law abiding man I thought he was, he had been a Russian mole inside the police department, working for the fucking mob, and that's what had gotten him killed. Did my Mom know? Because sure as shit, my Gran did. So Natasha was my Fathers sister and my Aunt, that's who was in the photo, I'd bet my last dollar the other person who'd been cut out was Savas. I had been born and raised inside the 'Bratva' and I never knew. Mika did, I could tell by the look on his face and that was the final nail in the coffin, the point of no return had been reached, and I would never forgive him for that.

The sheer urgency to escape the building and the goon who was assigned to follow me was consuming. Mandy was working away at her desk.

"Hey, can I have a quick word in private?" I asked.

"Sure, let's go grab a coffee." I walked behind her into the small break room, "What's up?" she asked, as she handed me a cup.

"I need a huge favour?"

"Anything, what?"

"I need to borrow your car for awhile."

She looked perplexed, "What's wrong with yours?"

"Nothing, you can use mine while I borrow yours." That only

caused her more confusion.

"Why?"

"Promise me you won't breathe a word to anyone?" The look on her face was becoming ever more worrying. "Mandy I swear it's nothing illegal, I just need to get away." She wasn't buying any of it. "Listen, I'm being followed and he knows my car, Mandy I'm begging you, please."

"Are you being stalked? Shit, tell Mika or Luca."

"I can't, trust me; I wouldn't ask you if I wasn't desperate, I really need your help." Tears were in my eyes.

"OK, OK I will."

Thankfully it was lunch time so when we left, nobody even noticed. We went to the parking garage and exchanged keys.

"Izzy please be safe, don't do anything stupid and please call me."

"I will, I promise, but swear you will not say a word." She nodded unconvincingly. "Look, see that black SUV parked down the street, that's him, now drive around for ten minutes then come back here."

"OK but why don't you call the police?"

"I'm dealing with it, and you are helping me more than you realise."

Sitting inside Mandy's car, I watched her pull out on to the street and then once the SUV had passed by the entrance I drove out in the opposite direction, heading God knows where. With my phone connected to the cars Bluetooth I called Jazz.

"Hey Izzy Wizzy, you heading down for lunch?" she sounded so happy but that was about to change.

"TELL ME YOU DIDN'T KNOW?" I exploded venomously, "TELL ME YOU DIDN'T FUCKING KNOW?"

"Whoa, Whoa, Whoa. What the hell are you talking about Iz?"

"My family, Nikolai my Father and his sister Natasha!" I yelled.

"I have no idea what you are talking about, what the hell is going on Izzy?"

"I told you it was the fucking Mob; your dad was my Fathers best friend..." She cut me off mid rant.

"Izzy I don't know anything I swear on my life, please you're scaring me."

I could hear the raw emotion in her voice, "Jazz my life has been one fucking lie," I cried.

"Izzy where are you, tell me please?"

"I'm so sorry Jazz, I can't stay anymore, I love you." I disconnected the call before she had chance to respond. I had lost everything I loved in the last two hours and all I could do was drive in a daze.

Jazz still had hold of her cell, listening to the disconnected tone, she was beyond shocked. She ran from her office and out to the car, shaking with anger she pulled her keys out and screamed in frustration as she watched them fall down the storm drain as if in slow motion. Looking around for help, she spotted her shadow who was sat watching her in his car, and by the time Jazz reached him he was stood outside.

"What's wrong Jazz?"

"Illa I need you to take me to Mika now?"

"Sure, hop in."

The elevator opened on the top floor and Jazz ran towards Mika's office, only to be abruptly stopped.

"Mr Remizov is in a meeting."

"Where?" Jazz snarled.

"Jazz is that you?"

"Where the fuck is my Brother?" Even Katia knew when she

was beaten and simply pointed, "Conference room."

Jazz banged on the door, looking at Mika through the glass panelling with deadly eyes; if looks could kill he'd be dead ten times over. Luca excused himself from the table and went to the door, before he had chance to close it he roared, "What the fuck Jazz?"

But she matched his tone. "Tell me what the fuck you know about Izzy's family, Nikolai and Natasha? Tell me about the fucking Mob and the Brotherhood?" Luca's face was a picture.

"Oh my God, Izzy was telling the fucking truth." She turned to run but Luca's reactions were quicker and he grabbed her.

"JAZZ!" but she was fighting him like a feral cat, kicking, punching and even biting.

"Get the fuck off me you lying asshole!"

By now Mika was there pulling her off Luca, "JAZZ! What the hell has gotten into you?" he yelled.

She scowled at him with pure hatred, "YOU! You son of a bitch, you did this, you drove her away, get your fucking hands off me," she screamed, fighting once more. Illa and Luca held on to her pinning her to the ground.

"Take her to my office, now!" Mika growled just as Gavril came running down towards them. Mika froze, "What the hell are you doing here?"

"Boss she tricked me... I, I, I lost her."

"FUCKING FIND HER NOW!" This could not be happening. Mika instructed Tomaz to finish off the meeting and literally ran to his office.

Inside stood over Jazz were Luca and Alex, while Illa and Gavril were back on the street searching. Slamming the door his voice was toxic, "Tell me everything now," Jazz stared out of the window ignoring him. "JASMINE, so help me God."

"What...What the fuck do you care?"

Luca looked at her, "That's not helping Jazz."

"Oh fuck you too Luca," she spat. Mika was losing it.

"TELL ME!" he bellowed, the power and wrath in his voice making Jazz jump.

"She heard you talking about her father and Natasha."

His brows fused together, "How could she, she doesn't understand Russian?" With the bemused look on Mika's face Jazz realised their secret was well and truly out of the bag. "Fuck Jazz how long has she known?" Mika asked with deadly calm.

Jazz was starting to sob, "Since we were kids, she's as fluent as you and I." Her brothers simply looked at her in disbelief. She told them everything, including what Gran had said that started the catalyst; Mika's legs wouldn't take his weight anymore and slumped into his chair.

Mika finally told Jazz the truth and she took it far better than he gave her credit for.

"We have to find her and bring her home," she pleaded.

Mika rang Gavril, "Who was driving Izzy's car?"

"Some woman called Mandy from her office." His voice echoed from the speaker. Mika hung up without any pleasantries and ordered Luca to bring Mandy up to them.

"Mika, if you still love Izzy why have you been so mean to her?" Jazz asked, teary eyed.

"I thought I was keeping her safe, if they knew what she really meant to me the target on her back would have been enormous. So putting distance between us was the right decision, or so I thought."

"So you do still love her?"

He looked so down trodden, "I love her more than life itself, it has been killing me to see her hurt and in pain, the sorrow in her beautiful eyes, and knowing it was me who put it there. I hate myself for it, but I had to do it."

Jazz pitied him, "Mika I'm sorry, but this is beyond fucked up."

"Do you have any idea where she would go?"

"No not now, if her Gran was still all there I would have said there, honestly I have no clue." She rang Izzy's cell for what seemed like the hundredth time, voicemail again.

Luca walked into the Admin department where Mandy's desk was empty. Margo popped out, "Luca can I help you?"

"I need to see Mandy?"

"She's in the break room, she said Izzy has gone home sick, I hope she's alright?" she asked, genuinely concerned, knowing about Izzy's relationship with the Remizov's.

"I'll let you know when I find out," he winked at her before walking into the small staff room. Mandy was sat nursing her cup.

"Mandy," he spoke gently.

"Mr Remizov."

"Please Mandy, call me Luca, do you mind if I join you?" She looked scared, "No, not at all." Even with her face all puffy and her eyes bloodshot she was still a stunning woman.

"Where's Izzy?"

One stray tear ran down her face dropping on to the table, "I really do not know."

"Why were you driving her car?"

"She made me promise not to tell," she said looking into Luca's eyes and he could see the fear in them. If she had been a man Luca wouldn't have thought twice about beating the truth out of him, but this was sweet and lovely Mandy. He held her hand, cupping it in the palm of his own and gently traced his thumb over the top of her fingers, "Please Mandy, she is in danger?"

That made her break down, "I know she told me, I do not

want him to hurt her."

"Who?" Luca asked.

"Her stalker."

Luca was now confused and worried, "Her stalker?"

"That guy, outside in the black SUV."

Now it clicked, "Mandy that's Gavril, her minder not a stalker."

"What?"

"Tell me everything that happened." He prompted her.

"She took my car, telling me she had to get away quick." She composed herself once more. "She was so upset Luca, I'm sorry."

Luca's cold heart had warmed to this sweet woman, "Mandy honey, it's not your fault," he reassuringly stroked the top of her hand with his thumb. "What make and model is your car?"

She stared at him, "Are you going to help her, bring her home safe?"

"I will, I give you my word."

"It's a black and white Mini Cooper, CFA 7261," she sounded defeated.

"Thank you sweetie, I also need Izzy's keys and your cell number."

"Why my number?"

"So I can call you and take you home later," he kissed her hand and left her speechless.

I was still in Detroit and I pulled into a shopping mall on the South side of town. I needed money and some essentials, and clothes since I'd left everything behind, including my big padded winter coat. There was a bank inside the mall and I pulled as much as I could over the counter, and pulled the card limit out on three cards at the ATM machine, giving me nearly $7,000 in cash, I bought all my shopping on my card, that would be the last paper trail for a while. I also bought a new prepaid cell phone and transferred Jazz and Mandy's number to it before switching my smart phone off and removing the battery, I had seen enough CSI to know about GPS.

I left the mall with a suitcase filled with cheap, warm winter clothes and toiletries, before wheeling it to the road and hailing a cab.

I decided to go to Bay City, North Michigan, it had been the last place my Mom had taken me before she got sick, and it held some wonderful memories. I instructed the cab driver to take me to Michigan Central station. Outside the station I called Mandy from the payphone.

"Hello?"

"Mandy listen it's me?"

"Izzy where are you?"

"Listen I don't have long, your car is at Brookfield parking structure, the keys are on the drivers' side rear tyre and under the sun visor is $100 bill for parking, thank you."

"Wait, wait, wait, where are you going?"

I felt guilty, "I'll call you when I know, bye."

Mandy rang Luca's extension straight away but he didn't pick up, she then called Mika's PA.

"Katia its Mandy, is Luca with Mika?"

"Yes they're in a meeting and do not want to be disturbed."

That really annoyed her, "OK then just let him know Izzy just called me?"

"Hold on."

The next voice she heard was male. "Mandy this is Mika, what did she say?" She repeated word for word what Izzy had said. "Luca is on his way down; he will drive you to pick up your car, and Mandy, thank you."

Luca was at Mandy's desk in a flash. "Ready sweetie?" Ruth

watched intrigued from her desk, she had listened to Mandy's conversation with Mika, something big was happening. The atmosphere inside the building was on high alert and now chubby little Mandy was being taken out by Luca. It all seemed to revolve around precious little Isabelle, and she only hoped it was something very, very fucking painful. Leaving her desk she walked into Margo's office.

"I need to nip out for ten minutes."

"Shit Ruth don't be long, I'm already two staff down."

Ruth feigned sympathy, "Who?"

"Izzy has gone home sick and now Luca has taken Mandy. It's all really strange, I over heard Luca on his cell saying Izzy has Mandy's car."

Ruth put her concerned mask on. "I'll make it five then, OK?"

Margo grinned, "Thank you."

Outside Ruth pulled her cell out and hit the call button. "Hi I thought you'd like to know, the lovely Isabelle by what I can gather, has flown the coup and ditched her tail. She is all alone somewhere in the city in a mini cooper, this is your opening."

CHAPTER FIFTEEN

Luca and Mandy reached the Brookfield parking structure and on the fourth floor they found her Mini Cooper, Mandy got out of Luca's Range Rover and checked the back tyre and just where Izzy said there would be were the keys, she shook them at Luca. She stared out of the building and looked down at the traffic.

"What is it Mandy?"

"When she called, I swear I could hear trains, I'm just surprised we're not near a train station."

Luca's tone changed, "Give me your cell," and she handed it over with no question asked. He scanned the incoming call history, "This number is from a payphone," he informed her.

"I'm sorry, I had no idea."

Luca rang Mika and gave him the number to trace and by the time Mandy was safely at home Mika called him back, "It's a payphone outside MCS."

I simply couldn't bring myself to board the train and leave Detroit; I had my ticket in hand and just couldn't do it. I had questions and the only way I was going to get them answered was to ask the one person I despised most at this moment in time, Mika. I left the station pulling my case behind me and walked around until I found the first inconspicuous hotel, the Holiday Inn and I booked myself in for three nights under the alias Linda Smith.

Sitting in the room I felt so alone, a total out cast, like poor little orphan Annie, at least the room was warm and clean. I felt frozen to the bone and hoped a hot bath would remedy that, so while soaking in the tub I replayed the day's events. I decided to call Jazz tomorrow; I just couldn't face that tonight. Drying off, I put on my new fleecy PJ's and sat on the bed watching TV, and waiting for room service to bring me the food I'd ordered.

Mika had his computer wiz's working round the clock, running Izzy's cards and cell records. As of three p.m. she'd gone dark, they had surveillance footage from MCS and the surrounding areas, which showed her leaving the station and heading West until she turned a corner into a black spot and they lost her. At least Mika knew she had not left the City. He had them checking every hotel reservations in a four mile radius of her last known whereabouts, even though he suspected she wouldn't be using her own name. By four in the morning he was exhausted, strolling into the den he found Jazz sleeping on the couch, so he picked up a blanket and covered her up. She stirred, "Have you found her?" she asked sleepily.

"No, not yet Princess, go back to sleep." Luca had stayed at Mandy's just in case Izzy called her, Alex slept on the other couch, which left Mika the armchair and foot stool; all three had their cells close at hand, all waiting to hear something.

I actually slept, not stirring once until waking up mid morning, feeling disorientated, basically I felt like shit with a blocked nose and sore throat. Then I remembered the previous day's events and it caused my stomach to knot. I dressed and walked to the store just a few doors down, buying junk food and some fruit; as well as decongestants and Advil to get my temperature down. Arriving back I picked up my cell and made that ominous call. I couldn't put it off any longer, I was missing her and the sound of her voice dreadfully, and so keeping my number blocked I hit the call button.

"Hello?" She sounded suspicious and I couldn't blame her.

"Hi." My own voice was croaky and very hoarse.

"Izzy, fuck where are you, please come home?"

"I can't, not yet, if ever after what has happened?"

"Izzy, what you said it's all true, but there is so much more you need to know. Come back and Mika will explain everything?" I could tell she was struggling to hold it together.

"I just need time Jazz, please understand?"

"I do, I really do, but Izzy you are in real danger, tell me where you are so I can come and get you?" I started to cough. "You sound sick, what's wrong?"

Eventually after a coughing fit "It's just a touch of the flu, I'll call you soon I promise."

"Izzy don't go!"

"I have to, I love you," and I hit end.

"Mika," Jazz yelled at the top of her lungs, which caused him, Alex and Illa to come running.

"What, did she call?" He asked and saw tears running down her sad face.

"Yes, she's safe but she sounds pretty ill."

"Did she use her cell?"

"No, her number was withheld," A small twitch on his face was the closest to a smile in days, "but we can still trace it."

Knock; knock "Room service." It took all of my energy to just get off the bed and walk to the door. As soon as I pulled the handle down and unlocked it, it was forced open, smashing me in the face and knocking me on my butt, totally dazed and bewildered.

The pain from my forehead was excruciating and I could hardly see through my left eye, it had swollen that quickly, and then I could feel the blood dripping down my face. My hair was pulled hard by the roots dragging me back into the room, throwing me hard on to the bed. I spun around and that's when my eyes saw the gun.

"Now my sweet, not a peep," he spoke really softly.

"Hello Isabelle, we finally get to meet in person at last, do you know how excited I was when I discovered you really did exist. It was like a gift from God. I was quite happy just to eradicate and destroy the fucking Remizov's one by one and everything associated with them, but you, sweet, little Isabelle, you are the game breaker!" Then this freak just stared at me with dead eyes.

"What, who are you, what do you want with me?"

He gave me a bone chilling smile, "I'm Adair Nano. I am the last Nano because that cunt who fathered you and that fucking scum Remizov had my family killed, every last one of them, leaving just me. So my '*Angel*' revenge is going to be very, very sweet." He walked towards me and I was unable to move through fear, he grabbed roughly at my chin, "I can really see what Mikhail sees in you, and that will make this so much more delightful."

Pulling away from his grasp I spat, "I mean nothing to him!" but it only seemed to tickle him.

"Oh you stupid, blind, naïve little girl, it seems the only one fooled by his pathetic charade is you."

My head was swimming and I was finding it difficult to process what was coming out of this pricks mouth.

"You mean everything to him, how can I explain this so you will understand? Aha, have you read the Harry Potter books?"

What was this fucking psycho talking about? "Erm yes."

"Good, then this is like a game of Quidditch and you my dear are the golden snitch, you are the key, and who ever has you wins the game and I have you, so I win." He removed a syringe from his pocket, "Don't look so worried Isabelle, I'm not going to kill you, not yet anyway, you are far too valuable at this moment and I so want to play with you for a while."

I fought with all I had but he over powered me, stabbing me in the thigh with the needle and as I began to lose consciousness he cradled me in his arms.

"Sleep tight *Angel*," and I felt him kiss my forehead.

Adair called in his extraction team and five minutes later paramedics came into the room followed by the hotel manageress. The medics worked on Isabelle and strapped her to a gurney while the manageress consoled him.

"My wife collapsed and hit her head on the table," Adair said with added panic to his voice.

"Sir I'm so sorry, I hope your wife will be OK," she comforted him.

"Thank you, I'll stay at the hospital with her so we won't need the room anymore."

As the paramedics wheeled her out, Adair collected her belongings and followed them in his car. Arriving at a pre designated meeting place, he had Isabelle moved into his car. "Destroy the ambulance then return to base," he ordered before driving off with her.

The call that Mika had been waiting for finally came. Izzy's cell signal had come from within a mile radius of MCS. With further research it was narrowed down to a few streets and in that catchment area there were only three hotels. After an hour of skimming hotel security cameras they found her.

"Sir she is in room 407 at The Holiday Inn, under Linda Smith."

He issued his orders, "Illa stay with Jazz and do not let her out of your sight."

Illa nodded. "Of course, I got this covered."

Mika had four men guarding the perimeter and while Alex drove he called Luca and his reinforcements. When they pulled up outside, Luca, Vik, Sergi and Gavril were all waiting. Mika climbed out, "Luca, you're with me and the rest of you cover all the exits and be vigilant."

When she didn't answer the door, Luca forced it open with hardly any effort. The room was a mess, the bed had been pushed aside and there was medical waste and trash strewn across the floor.

"What the fuck has gone down in here?" Luca asked, scanning the room for any clues. Then he spotted a blood trail that lead to the door, a clump of bloody, blond hair and skin was stuck to the woodwork around the door frame. Leaving the room, the pair headed to the front desk.

"Hello Sir, how can I help you?" the manageress asked.

Mika gave her a small sterile smile, "I'm looking for the lady that's in room 407, Linda Smith?"

Her face fell and she looked at him upset, "Oh yes, Mrs Smith was taken ill and her husband called for an ambulance, they're at the hospital now, I'm ever so sorry."

The colour instantly drained from Mika's face.

"When was this?" Luca asked, taking over the questioning.

"About forty five minutes ago."

Luca thanked her and they both walked outside.

"Fuck Luca, they have her, they fucking have her."

CHAPTER SIXTEEN

Adair sat in his chair, sipping an aged whiskey, contemplating the recent events. The war between the Russians and Italians he had tried to start had backfired and instead of killing and blaming each other they had formed a fucking alliance, which had made things a little more difficult. The two biggest criminal organisations were now solely fixated on eradicating the Albanian threat once and for all, raising his glass Adair chuckled "Good luck with that you mother fuckers."

Mika had been in touch with his uncle Mark and he'd held a summit with the head of the Albanian syndicate in Illinois, to discuss the matter brewing in Michigan. The Albanians were still relatively small compared to the brotherhood and they had felt the wrath of the Bratva on numerous occasions but were still growing in numbers. What had emerged from the meeting was eye opening and surprising to say the least. The disappearance of Isabelle Bays had nothing to do with them. Ever since Savas had expelled them from the State they hadn't tried to re-establish there again, but they had heard chatter amongst the ranks of a small group of Albanian descendants gaining a reputation and forming a personal vendetta against the Remizov's. They had promised Mark to look into it and having a favour owed to you by the Bratva was always a good thing to have and even the Albanians knew that.

The next morning, Mika received an encrypted Email and when he opened it, his heart stopped. His Angel lay unconscious in only her underwear, handcuffed to a bed, her beautiful eyes swollen black and blue, her face smeared with blood from the deep gash on her forehead, and all that was written was *Tick,*

Tock. Mika erupted and his blood boiled, he went on a rampage, destroying everything in his office, anything that wasn't screwed down.

"Jesus Christ Mika!" Luca yelled, as Mika launched his computer monitor across the room. Katia and Alex ran in just as the rest of his computer crashed to the floor.

"I want that fucker found now…Alive!"

Luca grabbed him by the arms, "Tell me what the fuck has happened?" he shouted, trying to get Mika to focus.

"I opened an Email, fuck Luca, it was Izzy, she looks in really bad shape," his eyes glassy from unshed tears he refused to let fall.

"Show me," Luca said, but Alex pointed to the broken monitor.

"Use mine," Katia said from behind Luca. She retreated back to her desk and opened Mika's private Emails then stood back to let him input his password. All four looked in horror at the photo. "Holy cow," Katia gasped.

"Get I.T. on to it and find out who sent it?" Mika instructed Alex.

Luca placed a hand on Mika's shoulder, "I was just coming to tell you Delushi called, his guys found two men trying to burn an ambulance, they have them at Club Trevi and he thought you might like a chat with them?"

"Get the car," Mika ordered.

While driving to Delushi Alex rang Mika and he answered it on speaker-phone.

"You will never believe where that Email was sent from, it was Izzy's computer, here at the office!"

Both Mika and Luca sat dumbstruck for a second. "Did you hear me?"

"Yeah, yeah, we heard you," Luca answered.

Mika's fury was rebuilding, "We've got a God damn fucking mole! Alex find out who was in this morning, and do it discreetly I don't want to tip them off that we are on to them, we'll be back soon but if you hear anything call me immediately?"

Adair stood with one of his henchmen looking at her; as soon as Ruth had called him he'd had men posted at every bus and train terminal in the city and it had definitely paid off. She was now all his to do with what ever the hell he wanted. She was still out of it and burning up with a fever, "Why isn't the bitch coming round?" Adair demanded.

"Krye," he replied, the Albanian word for Boss, "You gave her enough to knock out an elephant, plus she is sick, it's lucky we didn't overdose her. It's just gonna take longer to get out of her system than normal."

"Keep a close eye on her, I do not want her dead yet, that would just be a waste."

Delushi was sat in the empty club with three of his trusted men waiting for them to arrive, "Mika, Luca, welcome to my humble abode," he greeted them.

"Where are the fucking pricks?" Mika's rage was evident and the smile dropped from Delushi's face.

He stood up, "Follow me," and he led the way down into the bowels of the building to what looked like a medieval dungeon.

"We so need one of these," Luca said, totally serious.

Two beaten and bloodied men were collar chained to the concrete floor, unable to stand.

"You're barbaric Delushi!" Luca said with admiration, "and you started without us."

Delushi looked up at them, "I wanted answers too; I lost ten good men to these fuckers."

"So what did you find out?" Mika asked, kicking the closest of the men in the head, knocking him unconscious.

"Not much, I guess these two are just shit shifters but they do know something about Isabelle, so I'll let you find out more."

Mika crouched down to the one still conscious, "Tell me what you know?" he snarled.

"Fuck you, asshole," then spat blood filled saliva into Mika's face.

Mika never flinched, he just grabbed one of his hands and began to slowly twist it, causing the once hard faced dick to scream like a bitch. The sound echoed, reverberating around the cell walls and then a loud sickening crack as his wrist bone snapped. Still the idiot didn't talk, he just whimpered. Mika took hold of the unbroken hand before pulling out a pair of pliers, clamping the pincers to the thumb nail and then he began to pull painfully slow and watched as the nail ripped from the skin as it became detached.

The gaping empty nail bed now oozed with blood, "One down, nine to go," Mika laughed sadistically. After the third nail had been extracted, the pain on the man's face was evident and he passed out.

Delushi turned to Mika, "You are one sick mother fucker!"

"I know, now throw some water on this prick so I can carry on?"

Delushi obliged and the guy came to, coughing and spluttering.

"Ready to talk yet?" he asked with the pliers gripping the fourth nail ready and waiting. Finally he could stand no more and he caved, telling everything he knew.

"Do you want us to dispose of the trash?" Luca asked but Delushi had already pulled a Sig from inside his jacket and had the muzzle pressed against the forehead of his prisoner. The now whimpering man opened his mouth to speak but before a sound came out the gunshot exploded his brains all over the cell walls. Walking towards the door he fired again, putting a bullet in the brain of the other man and yelled, "Hey Massimo, fire up the furnace, we're burning tonight." He laughed as he escorted Mika and Luca out, "Mika I hope you find her, I really do." Mika nodded and they exited the club.

They had the fuckers name, Adair Nano; he was the only son of an Albanian mobster who was killed twenty four years ago by Nikolai in the drug bust that had also claimed his life. This wasn't a turf war or power play, it was simple vengeance. Adair had been planning and scheming for years and over the past eighteen months had set it all in motion, he'd recruited a small army with one aim in mind, to torture and destroy the Remizov's. Whoever the mole was inside had been siphoning money and arms, funding Adair's plot. Mika had known about the missing shipments, as well as the books not adding up and had people looking into it but they had found nothing until thirty minutes ago. The prick had told them about the headquarters, a run down crappy old club house on the Eastside of town, a place normal people would avoid like the plague, but Izzy had not been taken there. Adair had her hauled up some place unknown.

Back at home, Mika gathered his troops; with Jazz safely in her room and Illa keeping a watchful eye over her, he addressed his men. He lay down the mission ahead and a plan of attack was set. Go to their base, gather as much Intel as they could and then exterminate the vermin and remove it, no one was to survive! At three a.m. Mika received the call. There had been one hell of a gun fight but all Adair's stooges there were dead, two of their own had been injured but were still alive. Inside the ramshackle club house was very little information. In all the commotion they had started removing evidence and torching the building when Mika's troops arrived and the only legible piece of information found was a name, Andrew Channing.

"Fuckers," Mika had yelled. Tomorrow they had to find the mole, and hope that would lead to finding Izzy, it was their only chance.

CHAPTER SEVENTEEN

I was awoken by the constant pounding in my skull and even on the soft pillow, turning my head sent a stinging pain through my whole body; I really struggled to open my eyes and gave up on the left one since it was now completely swollen shut. The skin on my face was tight with dried blood and mucus; all I wanted to do was rub my face but couldn't move my hands as I was shackled to the headboard.

I was finding it hard to breathe, it felt like a heavy weight had been placed on my chest and my lungs crackled every time I breathed in and it burned deep when coughed. When my vision focused I saw a man watching over me.

"Please help me?" I croaked but he just walked out of the room without saying a word.

I heard footsteps approaching and then the door opened.

"Aha, sleeping beauty has finally woken up."

Fear gripped me causing me to lose my voice, and when he produced a large pair of scissors my heart rate spiked.

"Please, please don't," I begged.

"Isabelle, we need to send Mika a gift, it's only right."

He pulled hard on my ponytail making me wince and then I heard him slice through my hair. He handed my long lock to the silent man.

"Place this in a box and tie it with a ribbon, then hand deliver it to the Remizov's residence. I want you to take three men with you and pay the spoilt Princess a visit; she is at home today and only being guarded by two." He looked at me, "I'm guessing they are low on man power after last night?" he smirked.

What had happened, how long had I been out? Adair returned his attention to the silent man again.

"Kill them all!"

"NO!" I screamed, "Kill me not Jazz, you have me!"

"If I was going to kill you don't you think I would have done so already? You are worth more to me alive, it will be torturing Mika knowing you are my pet, imagining what I'm doing to you everyday."

When the silent man left, Adair turned his full attention to me, "You smell repulsive, I think I'll bathe you!" This freak was a total nut job, 100% certifiable. While I lay there listening to the tub fill, I prayed to God, 'please protect Jazz and please don't let him drown me.' He strolled back into the room and unhooked the restraints from the headboard, still keeping me cuffed, and then he slung me over his shoulder and walked into the bathroom.

"Do your business," he pointed to the toilet, and before I could even pull down my panties he tore them off. "I hope you're not shy because I'm not leaving."

I was so desperate I had no choice, never in my life had my privacy been so invaded.

"Spread your legs wide open and let me see."

The disgusting pervert's eyes never left my intimate area as he watched me urinate, he was actually getting off, and it made me feel so dirty. I stood up and he unclipped my bra leaving me totally naked.

"What a body, perfectly trimmed and flawless skin, it will be a shame to mark it," and he trailed a rough finger round my breasts before twisting my nipple, hard making me cry out in pain.

"Scream as loud as you want, nobody can hear you."

He was a sadistic son of a bitch. I cried silent, invisible tears and switched my brain off, closing my eyes I blocked him out.

"Mika you need sleep," Luca said, knowing full well it would just fall on deaf ears. Over the past forty eight hours everyone had survived on caffeine and power naps, and by six a.m. all three brothers were walking into the down town office with one aim in mind, to catch a mole. Mika was certain it had to be someone from the administration department, any stranger hanging around would have raised too many questions, so it had to be someone who worked there. Alex brought up the rota from the day before, every member of the admin team had been in at least sometime during the day, but only three people had been in when the Email was posted, Mandy, Joe and Ruth.

Luca was sure Mandy wasn't involved; she had left his office just seconds before all hell had broken loose in Mika's. Joe had been born and raised within the brotherhood and like all the Remizov men he was following in his fathers footsteps. He had red Russian blood running through his veins, so that left only one, Ruth! Alex sat at Mika's desk working away on his new PC and pulled up Ruth's file.

"Ruth Channing, thirty years old has been with the company three and a half years...."

"Wait, what was her surname?" Luca stopped Alex.

"Channing!" Luca and Mika looked at one another.

"When that bitch gets in, escort her up here," Mika demanded.

"Don't you want to go to her place now?" Luca asked surprised.

"No, let her think we're still in the dark, the slightest hint and she'll tip that fucker Adair off."

"Good thinking," Luca agreed.

"What time is she due in?" Mika asked Alex who was still sat at the computer scrolling through her files.

"It says nine on her rota."

At eight fifty Mika sat watching the plasma tv in his office, he had the foyer on live feed, and it was killing him having to be this patient. Then he saw her enter, looking like she didn't have a care in the world and he felt like she was laughing at them all. He intensely observed the scene as it played out, Luca and Gavril approached her and although he couldn't make out what was being said the smug look on her face suddenly disappeared and he watched her go pale instantly in front of the camera. The game was up, Mika watched her hand her bag over to Alex and all three men marched her to the elevator brining her to him.

As the office door opened, Gavril literally threw her in and she stumbled, trying to keep her balance.

"SIT," Mika hissed, but like a deer caught in headlights she just stood, paralyzed.

Luca pulled a chair out and forced her into it. Ruth looked down at her lap and fidgeted with the hem of her skirt, the once cool, calm and collected Ruth was now worried, with perspiration forming on her brow. It's always the confident and cocky ones that are the weakest link and the first to cave when they are caught, they would sell their own mother to save their own ass. Mika glared at this woeful, pathetic excuse for a woman and could not hide his contempt for her.

"Ruth, you do realise you are a dead woman walking don't you? The only thing you have control over now is whether it is painless, or slow and excruciating, it's your choice?" he stated venomously.

Ruth was turning green and was visibly trembling.

"Tell me where she is?" Mika demanded.

"I don't know!"

Luca squeezed hard on her shoulder, "That's not a very good start."

Mika watched her flinch at Luca's touch. "How do you know

Adair Nano?" he asked, not taking his eyes off her. He could see the cogs of her brain working overtime.

"He kidnapped my Father."

Mika had not expected that, "Andrew is your Father?"

Ruth's face looked shocked, how did he know her Fathers name? "Yes... yes, he took him three years ago and said if I didn't do what he wanted he'd kill him."

Mika wasn't in the mood to believe a single word that was spewing from her mouth. "I know you have been funding his little vendetta with my money and stock.... MINE!" he yelled. "Now Ruth, tell me everything?"

She crumbled, telling the whole story. The aim was to work for and gain the trust and respect of the Remizov's, getting Mika to fall for her, and then lead him to the lions den. No matter how hard she tried to seduce him he never took the bait, then Izzy came into play and after some digging and research Adair had found out exactly who she was, and that changed everything. The four men listened to her story, intrigued and disgusted.

Katia came flying in to the office, "There's trouble at your house!"

Mika stood bolt upright, catching the slight smirk on Ruth's face. He turned to Katia, "Do your thing and get what we need quickly, Gavril will help."

Katia smiled, "With pleasure," then she walked over to Ruth and touched a spot in the crook of her neck so delicately but it made Ruth scream out in pain. "You will talk." And that is why she had become the only sister in the brotherhood.

CHAPTER EIGHTEEN

Jazz was staring out of the kitchen window looking at the freshly laid snow that covered the garden; it was so tranquil and beautifully untouched like a picture postcard. She felt like all this was a dream or just the affects of sleep depravation, the last three days had been a nightmare but looking outside you'd never believe it. Jazz feared for Izzy and could only hope to God she would get to see her again, but with each hour that passed it seemed less and less likely.

When Mika had finally confessed their families dark secret she really hadn't been shocked, for the past twenty years she had practically buried her head in the sand like an ostrich and denied it, and she had found that easy since nobody had actually confessed anything to her, so it simply wasn't true.

Once again, Jazz found herself speaking to God, asking him for a chance to confess and to beg Izzy for forgiveness. Jazz didn't hear Illa walk up behind her.

"Are you OK?" He knew it was a stupid question, but still he had to ask. They had grown really close over the past few weeks and she found him easy to talk to.

"No," she replied, "why is this all happening?" He couldn't answer her, so he just kissed the top of her head.

The sound of fire crackers went off in the distance, which caused Jazz to spin around. Illa was immediately on alert and went straight into action mode, taking her hand he opened the small cleaners' cupboard and pushed her inside.

"Stay, and do not make a sound."

The noise was obviously gun fire and it was getting louder, "I'll come back for you I swear," he said, locking her inside.

It sounded like a war zone outside and Jazz curled up into a tight ball and listened to gunshots ricochet and voices yelling. She pulled out her cell and rang Mika, only for it to go to his voicemail, she wanted to scream. Then she called his office number and Katia picked up, hearing the sounds of gunfire rattling down the line.

"Jazz, Jazz, what's wrong, where are you?"

Panic filled, she spoke as loud as she dare, "Home, I'm at home."

"Stay safe. I'll tell Mika and get help, just stay safe."

As quickly as it had started, it was over, all went quiet, a deathly silence. Jazz didn't move, she couldn't even if she wanted to. The door opened and light streamed in blinding her for a moment. Illa stood in the door way.

"Illa, you're bleeding!" She rushed to him, catching him as he slumped to the ground, "Don't you die on me, don't you dare fucking die on me," she yelled. She put pressure on the wound and her eyes scanned around at the carnage, it looked like a scene from a gangster movie. Two men she did not recognise lay dead but the other one still moving she did, it was Ivan, he looked like he'd been shot in the leg.

"Jazz!" she heard Mika's voice boom through the house.

"I'm in here," she called out as her brothers' came running.

"What the hell?" Mika gasped.

"Boss we were ambushed," Ivan answered while Alex tended to his wound.

Mika looked at him, "You did your job, Jazz is safe and all the scum are dead." That was high praise coming from the Pakhan.

"Boss, that ugly fucker had a box," he said pointing.

Mika picked up the now blood splattered box with its fancy

bow and dread filled his soul; he knew something of Izzy was inside. He lifted the lid and for a second he closed his eyes. Inside was a piece of tissue paper with a hand written missive on top.

To Mika

Just a small gift for you, I hope you enjoy it!

Adair.

He removed the tissue to reveal her long blond hair tied with a ribbon and he breathed out a huge sigh in relief, "Hair will grow back."

Four dead goons and two of his own men lay injured. "Call for the clean up and get Illa and Ivan to the Doc." Mika issued his commands just as his cell rang.

It was Gavril, "He's in a cabin near Battle Creek!"

Mika smirked at the irony of the name.

"It was purchased by Ruth's grandfather years ago, a hunting cabin and it's well off the grid and away from prying eyes; it's a good 125 miles away."

"Call in everyone, this ends today," he ordered.

Adair had left the useless bitch unconscious again, lying on her stomach struggling to breathe. He had planned on ripping her wide open as he fucked her hard in every orifice, but even a sick bastard like him couldn't get a hard on by the sight and stench of her. Snot and drool oozing out of her nose and mouth, and the sound she made as she puked all over him had made him lose it and he'd brought his fist down so hard on her jaw he'd felt it break under the impact, knocking her out cold. At least now he didn't have to listen to her gagging any more. He did however enjoy carving his initials deep into the pristine skin on her back and watched the deep gouges fill as the blood oozed out of them, highlighting the A and N, his laugh was pure evil.

With no word or contact from anyone for hours, Adair knew the Remizov's were coming, he also knew Isabelle would be long dead before they arrived. He knew he should have listened to Ruth, she had warned him, she told him he was rushing things, and ruining the plan he had worked so hard on, making silly mistakes.

As soon as he'd found out who Isabelle was and that she'd left the Remizov's fold, he'd been obsessed on capturing her, she was his golden goose. Nothing else but her mattered and that's when the fissures that had started forming began to crack open wide. He'd been so wrapped up in her he hadn't given the Russian scum enough credit and that would be his ultimate downfall.

Adair had wanted to destroy the Remizov's piece by piece but that wasn't going to happen now, he still managed to smile smugly, at least he'd killed their precious fucking Princess, and soon the bastard spawn of the cunt that had killed his father too. He knew how much Mika and his fucking worthless siblings loved the only two females in that family, and it was satisfying to know that they would suffer forever, until they drew their last breath. Now anger filled him, it was all that bitches fault, she'd been his curse from the minute he'd learnt about her existence, her genetic DNA seemed to be programmed to wipe his out, and she was his kryptonite. He was going to kill her before she killed him and he marched into the bedroom to finish what he had started.

A convoy of six black SUV's sped down the I-94, all filled with guys and guns. It was as if the police knew not to intervene and the few squad cars they over took simply chose to ignore them. The miles passed by quickly, but not quick enough, and Mika's only thought was, '*Please let me find her in time, let her be alive.*'

CHAPTER NINETEEN

I had never felt such extreme harrowing pain like this before in my life, any movement was sheer agony. My body was completely wrecked inside and out, and I was left with two choices, One: simply give up and die in this festering hell hole, or Two: I had to face some home truths and accept my fate, I was Bratva, I was my Fathers Daughter and I had to fight, fight until I could fight no more.

He had left my hands untied and that would prove to be the biggest mistake the prick had made, that and under estimating me, I wasn't just going to die quietly. He had left the knife he'd used on me, lying on top of the fire place, the stained tip peeping over the edge of the mantle. Using every ounce of strength I had left to remain quiet, I silently screamed inside with each and every step I took. Managing to retrieve the blade, I shuffled back to the bed and stuffed the knife under the pillow, clenching the handle tight. As I lay down on my stomach, I made a promise to myself that I was going to enjoy watching the life drain from that fucker's eyes and smile every second of it.

It wasn't long before I heard him walk back into the room.

"Well Isabelle, you have served your purpose, it's time to meet your maker."

I lay statue still, my heart drumming in my ears, the copious amounts of adrenalin running through my veins was thankfully numbing the pain for now. My fingers grasped tight around the blade, and I waited, not knowing what he was going to do, shoot me or smother me? That's when I felt his hand on my shoulder, forcing me to roll over on to my back, he stroked my hair as he whispered in my ear, "Say hello to daddy!" He slipped his hands around my throat and I opened my eyes as wide as I could, and without so much as a whimper I stared straight back into his cold evil eyes. His grip loosened slightly at the shock, which gave me my chance and I did not hesitate, plunging the knife in and slicing his neck wide open, slashing his carotid artery that sent arterial blood to spray out with force. It covered me like the scene from Carrie and it was now my turn to wear the psychotic smile he'd worn earlier. It was truly satisfying watching the evil diminish from the fuckers eyes as his life force drained out through his throat and on to me.

"Burn in hell you sick son of a bitch," I growled painfully through my smashed jaw.

His lifeless body rolled over and slumped to the floor. My own body was beyond exhausted and giving up on me fast as the knife slipped from my fingers, at least now I could die in peace knowing he would never hurt the Remizov's again. I just prayed I wouldn't see Jazz on the other side, not just yet anyway. My eyes closed as the blackness surrounded me and the coldness began to fill my soul.

Inside the first car in the convoy were Mika, Stephen and Andre with Gavril driving, they left the highway and were now travelling down a country road, just then the GPS instructed them to turn at the next left on to a dirt track.

Mika asked, "Are you sure this is right?"

"That's where his cell signal is coming from; it should be just over that rise," Gavril confidently told him.

"Pull over at the bottom of that hill; we'll go by foot from there?"

Gavril did as he was asked and he watched through the rear view mirror as the rest of the cars followed suit.

As Mika stepped out, Luca was already by his side.

"We lost?"

"No, the cabin should be just over the hill," he pointed to the wisps of smoke rising in the distance. Mika addressed the group, "Split up and surround the cabin, no one is to escape. Stephen, stay with the cars." Stephen was just twenty, the youngest and still a little too trigger happy for Mika's liking.

There was just a Lexus parked up outside the cabin, nobody patrolling the perimeter and the only sign of life was the smoke that billowed out of the chimney. With guns drawn ready for action they swiftly moved into position, stalking the building like a covert op's team. The door was unlocked and Gavril and Mika entered from the front, just as Alex and Luca came in from the back. The place was deserted, like the Mary Celeste. A coffee machine still switched on had half a pot of coffee still warm sitting on it, the TV was on and the fire was blazing away, but no signs of life.

Alex stood guard while Mika, Luca and Gavril crept down the small hallway to the bedroom, ready for an ambush. Luca hand signalled 3, 2, 1 and opened the door. Nothing could have prepared them for what they walked into; it was a bloodbath, a horrendous massacre like a scene from a b-movie slasher.

Izzy was laying there, twisted on her side, naked and facing away from them, giving them an unobstructed view of her sliced and mutilated back, the deep ugly gouges still oozing. As they stepped further inside the room and closer to her, the full horror became more apparent, she was covered from head to toe in blood, the splatter had sprayed up the walls and onto the ceiling. Her beautiful face was swollen almost beyond recognition, battered black and blue.

Mika's heart stopped mid beat, his feet froze to the spot, he could not breathe, this could not be happening. The tears he'd fought so hard against defied him and cascaded down his face, the pain was immense. It was as if his heart had shattered, piercing him from the inside.

"Izzy......God, No!" he cried out as he ran to her. He almost tripped over the dead carcass of Adair Nano, lying in a pool of blood with his throat sliced wide open with that lifeless stare in his eyes. He didn't give the body a second glance before kicking it away and falling to his knees. He gently brushed her fringe out of the way, "Izzy, Christ my Angel I'm so sorry," he croaked out barely a whisper.

Luca and Gavril were left standing just inside the room, not knowing what to say or do, both deeply affected by the awful sight in front of them, and they could feel Mika's despair and devastation. Luca's own heart was breaking; sorrow filled his soul for this wonderful Angel, the torture she must have had to endure and with his face slick from his own tears, he watched Mika cry his heart out. The silence was broken by the sound of a wheezing, "Mika?"

Mika's reaction was more panic than relief, "Angel, baby I'm here, it's me," he kissed her hand, his eyes never leaving her, "Call 911 NOW!" he screamed out, knowing she'd never make it back home.

"Helps coming, stay with me Angel," he begged her to hold on.

"I did it, I killed him!"

Walking out of the room, Luca turned to Gavril, "Go tell the men to head back to Detroit before the cop's show up." He then returned to Alex in the kitchen, "Go bring Mika's car and park it out front." Alex needed an answer and before he had chance to ask Luca gave it, "She's alive but only just, now go!"

Luca pulled out his cell and called 911. Five minutes later Alex and Gavril were back, "Everyone has gone," and by the anger on Alex's face Luca gathered Gavril had told him the extent of Izzy's injuries. All three walked to the slaughter room, Luca whispered to Alex, "It's really bad," a small warning for his younger brother.

Luca coughed, getting Mika's attention, "Rescue is on the way, she still hanging in?"

Mika answered with a weak smile, "My girl is a fighter."

"Mika I'm sorry but we need to get our stories straight before the cops show asking questions!" Mika nodded in agreement. They all decided the story was basically the truth, that Adair Nano, the son of a dead Albanian mobster who had been killed by the late DPD Detective Nicholas Bays, in the drugs bust that claimed his own life had taken and tortured Isabelle Bays, the late Detective's only child. She had become Adair, the sick psychopath's obsession and he had stalked her for months, eventually kidnapping her three days ago, all in the name of vengeance and retribution. It appeared as though she had fought him off and killed him before he could finish her.

The sound of sirens wailing in the distance grew louder, and within ten minutes the cabin was lit up like the fourth of July with red and blue flashing lights. The paramedic's couldn't hide the shock on their faces at the gruesome sight that greeted them, none asking questions, just solely focused on the critically injured woman fighting hard to stay alive.

All four men had been separated and spoken to by the police and all told the same story but all slightly different. Mika refused to leave Izzy's side no matter how hard the police tried. CSI arrived on the scene and when the medics had Izzy strapped to a gurney ready for transport to the hospital, the cops allowed Mika to go with her. The others agreed to remain behind for more questioning.

CHAPTER TWENTY

The hospital had a medical team waiting for them when they arrived and Izzy was instantly surround by people in scrubs shouting in medical jargon that Mika didn't understand.

He felt a gentle hand on his arm, "Excuse me Sir, would you please come with me, we need the ladies information?" The petite nurse sounded sympathetic but he just stared at her. "Sir please it's really important, the doctors will need it?"

Mika finally acknowledged her and nodded. She showed him through to the family lounge, "Can I get you some coffee?"

"No, no thank you I'm fine."

"OK then, can you tell me your name and her name, and her date of birth if you know it?"

"I am Mikhail Remizov and she is Isabelle Natasha Bays, she is twenty three and was born on the fourteenth of August, ninety three."

"Thank you and do you know of any medication she is on and if she has any allergies?"

Mika smiled to himself, he knew everything about her, her favourite colour, perfume and food, he knew more about her than she herself did.

"No allergies and the only medication she is taking is the pill."

The nurse thanked him again, "What relation are you to her?"

"I'm her fiancé and next of kin," he may have exaggerated, but it was the only way to ensure he was kept in the loop.

"Sir the doctor will be with you shortly to give you an update, are you sure I can't get you something, it's going to be a while?"

He accepted the offer, "Coffee, strong and black thanks," and she smiled as she left him alone.

The feeling of powerlessness was one he had never felt before; all he could do was watch the hands on the clock move so very slowly, even that had more control than he did. Mika's patience was wearing thin and he was about ready to explode when Alex walked through the door.

"Any news yet?" he asked gingerly.

"Nothing yet, you?"

"The cops have finished with me for now but are still talking to Luca and Gavril," he chuckled. "Actually the cop who took my statement gave me a ride here; he needed to speak to the doctors."

Before Mika had chance to ask more questions the doctor from the ER entered the room, "Mr Remizov?"

Mika stood, "Yes, and this is my brother Alex."

"I'm not going to lie to you or sugar coat it; she is in really bad shape. On top of her injuries she has a severe case of pneumonia, her lungs are a mess and we have had to ventilate her to help her breathe. She is going to need surgery to fix her jaw and her back wounds are infected and need to be surgically cleaned and stitched. The good thing is she is alive and we have sedated her so she is not in any pain. It's going to be a long road to recovery, both physically and mentally I'm afraid."

"Can I see her?"

"As soon as we get her settled someone will come and get you." The doctor shook Mika's hand, "By what the police said, you made it to her just in time."

"I just hope it was soon enough," he said, barely hiding the fear in his voice. A short while later Mika was taken to the ICU where he saw his beloved Izzy with tubes, wires, drips sticking out of her and machines bleeping and keeping her alive, it was one sight he would never forget and it would haunt him forever.

Laying his head on the bed by her hand he sobbed his heart out, losing his parents hadn't hurt this much, and he kept thinking to himself was history repeating itself, like father like son? Would they both end up losing their one true love? He had to stop himself thinking about her dying, not now, not ever, she will make it, she will break the cycle, she is stronger than anyone Mika had ever known.

The days merged together until he lost track of what day it was. The police had let Luca and Gavril go; the Battle Creek PD had joined forces with the Detroit PD. When the DPD heard about Isabelle and what she had been through, they had come to the conclusion that no charges would be filed against her and she had acted in complete self defence. The police had discovered more damning evidence against Adair Nano; he had been in and out of mental institutions all his life and was a very dangerous and disturbed man.

I came round to the sound of voices, and opening my eyes caused me to squint at the bright lights. It took a while for my vision to clear, and eventually I could make out two figures standing by the door, one was Mika and the other I guessed a doctor. I couldn't make out what they were saying and neither had noticed I'd woken up.

"Hello." My voice was all husky and under different circumstances it would actually sound sexy as hell, well maybe. The pair turned quickly to me.

"Angel you are awake!"

Angel, how I'd missed him call me that and it made me smile, until the pain in my jaw stopped me and made me cry out. That's when the doctor told me what had happened, Mika sat holding my hand reassuringly, and I could tell he knew what was coming.

The maxillofacial surgeon had screwed plates at the fracture sites on my jaw; he'd done a remarkable job and apparently no scarring. The plastic surgeon had worked on my forehead and back. The head wound, once it settled down would be barely visible, just a faint line, but my back was a whole different story and I'd need a lot more procedures. Thankfully the pneumonia and the infection on my back had cleared up due to the strong cocktail of IV antibiotics. Physically I was healing superbly Dr Cole had said, but he was still worried about my mental state of mind and recommended I see a psychiatrist once I got home. The way my face screwed up at the thought of it made the doc say firmly, "It's nothing to be ashamed or embarrassed about Izzy. PTSD is not a laughing matter; trust me as a retired veteran I know!" I promised him I would go and I really meant it.

Mika felt that the day she woke up was as if God had answered his prayers. Just before Dr Cole left he had told them he would inform the police she had come round and that they would want to talk to her. That gave Mika just enough time to tell Izzy what they'd told the cops, as he finished and was kissing her forehead Detective Downing and a female DPD officer walked in.

"Miss Bays I'm pleased to see you're awake, we're sorry about this whole torrid affair but we do need to speak with you alone?" he glared at Mika.

Mika leaned over to her, "Angel I'll be just outside."

She squeezed his hand, "I'll be OK." He stepped out into the corridor closing the door behind him.

An hour later the Detective walked out, "Jenkins give me a minute with Mr Remizov?" The female officer nodded and walked away. Mika followed him into an empty room and Downing closed the door. "Mr Remizov, don't be fooled, we know all about you and your connections. Luckily we have nothing linking you to this terrible crime. Isabelle has confessed to killing Nano and personally in my eyes its good riddance to that psychopath, but trust me if we did, you'd be in jail awaiting trial. My Captain always said Detective Bays was a good cop and Isabelle is one of our own to protect, but I can't work out why the fuck she has chosen to be with a two bit gangster like you? Listen and listen real good, protect her with your life – hurt her and I'll make sure you spend the rest of it in a 6' by 8' cell, do I make myself clear?" Mika had to look at this cop with respect, this pig had balls!

"You have my word Detective, nobody, not even me will ever hurt her again." Downing left, his parting gesture was a manly chin lift as the elevator doors closed.

CHAPTER TWENTY-ONE

Finally after another week I was cleared for discharge, with bags of medication and leaflets about after care and what signs to look out for, as well as two names of shrinks in Detroit recommended by Dr. Cole. I was so ready to blow this joint and get out of this hospital and town forever, I never wanting to step one foot back in it. Luca walked in full of the joys of spring.

"Hey pretty lady you ready to go home?"

"Pretty! Hardly," I snorted, "but home most definitely."

Luca stood over me, "Angel you will always be pretty, in fact I'd say bloody gorgeous. I'm just thankful we get to take you home," he added with his voice choked with emotion.

Mika and Luca had been my only visitors while I'd been in hospital. Jazz had called everyday but she was really pissed off with Mika for not letting her come, but I was grateful to him for that, I didn't want her to see me like this, she would have been far too upset. It had been a frightening enough ordeal as it was and not just for me, I was still black and blue but at least the swelling had now gone down; still I was not a pretty sight and simply could not bear the look that would have marred Jazz's face when she saw me. Mika refused to leave me and had stayed in my room sleeping on the cot provided by the hospital.

While Mika pushed the wheel chair, Luca was my pack horse and carried all my belongings to the car, I was placed gently into the back seat and couldn't hide the grimace on my face.

"Sorry babe, the pain killers will kick in soon," Mika said as he kissed my head once again. He fastened the seat belt before going round to the other side and sitting next to me. This was going to be the most uncomfortable ride home ever – thank God for morphine. I fell asleep just as we left Battle Creek with Mika's arm around me. I was awoken by him whispering into my ear, "Angel we're home."

"Really!" I was totally shocked I'd only closed my eyes for two minutes.

"Shall I carry you inside?"

"No thanks that will hurt to much, I'll walk slowly," and that was no exaggeration, tortoise speed!

The door flew open and Jazz bolted out like a race horse; I braced myself for the impact and the impending pain.

"JASMINE, NO!" Mika yelled as he felt me tense up and maybe he over reacted a bit.

I felt sorry for her, "Its ok Jazz, just go gently," I said and managed to give her a small smile. By now she was in tears.

"Izzy my God look at you, I'm so sorry this happened to you but I'm so fucking proud of you for killing that bastard!"

I had my head in the crease of her neck so she couldn't see me smiling, but Mika sounded mad as hell.

"Jazz for fuck sake!"

I whispered so only she could hear me, "Me too!"

Everyone tried to help me inside, what's the saying to many cooks?

"Guys you are all not helping, just leave me be, I'll get there." I did eventually make it to the den; Jazz had made a little nest for me on the couch with pillows and comforters. "Before I get on there I need to use the bathroom and I would love a soak in the tub."

Jazz offered before I could ask for help but Mika told her no, before turning to me with a worried expression marring his face. "I'm sorry Izzy but I will be carrying you upstairs!"

It was probably for the best considering how long it had

taken me just to get into the house. It hurt but nothing like I'd imagined, and I had expected him to take me to my room, but he didn't, we went to his.

"I moved you back where you belong." I didn't argue, at least for now anyway.

Mika sat waiting in the bedroom while I soaked in the tub; I had major issues now with my privacy and was adamant that it never would be violated again. The hot deep water kissed my scars and soothed me, even if it did still feel like that dead fucker's blood was on me; I had showered in the hospital and scrubbed myself raw. I saw the state of my hair in the mirror properly for the first time and as stupid as it may sound it was that what really got to me. I made a promise to myself that as soon as I was up to it, I would get the abomination that was the mop on my head fixed. Some of the bruises had changed to that mucky green, yellowish colour but most were still black, the scar on my back was ugly and still angry red, but was beginning to settle down a little. I walked into the bedroom dressed in my PJ's and could feel my energy draining away, Mika must have sensed it because he had turned the covers down on the bed for me, and climbing in, I rapidly lost the fight with my eye lids.

The weeks that followed were full on, I had many visitors and one in particular was Mandy, she was now basically living here but then maybe that had something to do with Luca being here too? Jazz surprised me by getting her hair stylist to come to the house and give me a make over. I went for something totally different, she cut my hair into an inverted bob and dyed it dark mahogany, it was really severe but I liked it. The guys had been stunned but Mika hated it, even though he said he didn't. I was pampered and treat like a queen, but the tension between Mika and I was not only palatable and hung heavy in the air, it was uncomfortable to say the least. I had questions and he knew it. One Saturday in late January I walked into the kitchen where everyone was seated around the breakfast bar, the atmosphere changed, it felt like a storm was approaching. I looked directly at Mika, "Tell me about my father!"

He slowly stood up and walked out of the kitchen in the direction of his office, the rest of us just sat there in silence, I was about ready to pitch a fit when he came back in carrying an old photo album.

Before sitting next to me, he refilled everyone's mugs then began to tell the story I was so desperate to hear. He started with how he had found out, even Luca hadn't heard this and listened as intensely as I did and for an hour we all listened to him speak, none of us interrupted him. Nikolai Bazin was my Fathers real name, he had been Savas' best friend since they were children. Everything had changed when Natasha, my aunt was murdered; she had been Savas' one true love. Now it made sense why he always looked at me with such love and pain in his eyes, and looking at the photo's of her only confirmed it, it was like looking at pictures of myself.

Watching me grow up must have reminded Savas of his loss, and he relived that tragedy every time he saw me. My Father was Bratva through and through, he had only joined the police for the sake of the brotherhood but once he did he had taken the roll very seriously and he loved it, helping hundreds of citizens over the decade he was an officer. He had been well liked and respected by his colleagues on the force and had died a hero; nobody could take that away from him. The brotherhood had been deeply saddened by his death, especially Savas who mourned his passing every year on the anniversary. That was why I had been accepted and protected by the Bratva all of my life.

"OK, but why didn't you tell me the truth, after all it was your Fathers promise to keep not yours, and he died with that still unbroken?" I asked.

"That's true but when I became Pakhan that oath became my duty to keep."

My anger began to burn, "So you purposely kept my true

identity from me, I have lived a lie my whole life – you say you love me but how can you? You don't know the real me, fucking hell I don't even know me any more." I was raging.

"If I could go back in time I would, but I can't." Mika was trying but I didn't want to hear it and I just shook my head. "I'm sorry Izzy."

"What for, sorry I found out?" I spat with venom before storming out of the room.

Things didn't improve as the weeks passed by, I was constantly angry like I had permanent PMS. My shrink Dr Hurst was a true life line, at first I hated the thought of replaying that nightmare but after I had it was the best decision I'd ever made. Dr Hurst had me talking about my attack, my fears and my feelings and it got easier every time. I shocked him when he asked about how I was sleeping, he was probably expecting the usual, *I don't sleep, I have nightmares, I need sleeping pills*, but instead I told him I slept like a baby and had never lost a wink of sleep over the fact I'd killed a person, well a fucking freak as I put it. I began to look forward to my twice weekly visits to him; I felt as if he kept me grounded and sane.

Just as things began to return to some sort of normality I received a huge blow, basically the final straw. My Gran passed away, and even though deep down I knew it was a blessing, it still hurt and it meant I was officially alone, and that feeling of loneliness was suffocating. Two weeks after her funeral I was sitting in Dr Hursts' office pouring my heart and soul out and that's when I made a huge life changing decision. I had kept in touch with Anka Bjorkman since she had left Berkeley and returned home to Sweden. We'd been emailing back and forth and we chatted on Facebook, and when I rang her and told her what had happened she'd told me to get on a plane and fly to Stockholm. She was now living there where she had landed her dream job as a geography teacher at a private school.

Her apartment was in the City centre and her guest room

was mine for as long as I wanted. I was so excited when accepting her generous offer. Dr Hurst agreed with me but he did have one stipulation, I had to check in at least once a week by phone. Now all that was left was to let Jazz and Mika know.

Every night I slept in Mika's bed I was covered up, I had never let him see me naked, I couldn't even contemplate that and especially being intimate with him. Adair fucking Nano had done a hell of a job on me, I hoped that one day I'd be able to put that behind me, but for now it was a huge issue and I had to get there at my own speed. Thankfully Mika had never pushed me and I would always be eternally grateful to him for that. It just seems like we fell into a routine, where I would be asleep when he came to bed and if not I pretended to be.

I was sat waiting for Jazz to come home; Mika was out late on business again, I had made the atmosphere so uncomfortable here he hardly came home early any more and I couldn't blame him. When she walked in and saw me she knew something was going on, we'd all been on one hell of an emotional roller-coaster not just me.

"I knew you were planning on something, are you sure about this Izzy?"

"Yes I have to do this, it's the only way I can sort my head out and leaving not just Detroit but the States is the best thing for me right now."

Jazz looked as broken as I felt, "How long for?"

"I don't know, a month maybe two?"

We held hands while sitting on the floor, "I could come with you?" she wept.

Shaking my head, "No Jazz, I have to do this alone. But I promise to call and Skype you all the time." We cuddled and cried a river.

"When are you leaving?"

"My flight is the day after tomorrow."

"So soon," she bawled.

While we were still clinging to one another Mika walked in and like Jazz, he'd suspected something, but unlike Jazz he was furious.

"So you are running away – AGAIN?"

That cut me deep, "No I'm not, I just need to sort my life out, make sense of everything, please Mika understand?"

"You belong here, not fucking Sweden. Here!" he spoke with such bitterness.

"I used to think so but now I don't know, the only way to know is to leave and see if I find my way back, you have to let me go?" I pleaded with him.

"I DON'T HAVE TO DO ANYTHING OF THE KIND!"

His hatred hit me full on, I had expected anger and maybe rage but his next act stunned me. He picked up his keys and stormed out; slamming the front door so hard it rattled the windows. I felt like he'd punched me in the stomach, I called his cell but just got voicemail.

"I'm sorry I'm hurting you, that is not my intention at all, just give me a little time please. I love you."

Jazz tried to console me, "Just give him chance to calm down, he'll come around."

He didn't, he never came home before I left, and I never got chance to say goodbye, I just hope he didn't hate me because no matter what happens I would always love him.

CHAPTER TWENTY-TWO

Jazz drove me to the airport, "Why did you sell Bertie?" she asked.

"For the money, I won't be getting a pay check for a while."

She scowled at me, "That's bull shit and you know it. You're not coming back are you?"

I embraced her so tight, "Jazz it's just a car, yeah I loved him but I can always get another, and of course I'll be coming back, you're here, I'm gonna miss you."

"Izzy just promise me you'll be safe and come home soon."

"I promise I will and Jazz please tell Mika I'm sorry and that I love him, try to explain it to him why I have to do this. I can't bear the thought of him hating me."

"I'll try, but I do know he'll never be able to hate you."

We cried as we parted, "I love you so much," I told her, then walked away and hoped to God that would be the end of shedding fucking tears for a while.

It was the longest journey I'd ever made, nearly forty eight hours but I had arrived. Switching my cell on, I had numerous texts from Jazz and Mandy but nothing from Mika. I text them back to let them know I was here safe and sound before walking into arrivals to meet Anka. She was as gorgeous as ever, and the drive to her place was simply breath taking.

The City of Stockholm looked amazing, I couldn't wait to explore it, well once I had gotten over the cursed jet lag. Anka's apartment was fantastic, the views alone would simply make it, but the space and how she'd decorated it was fabulous.

"I'm so pleased you came," she was as happy as I was.

"Oh God me too, and you look as gorgeous as ever."

She giggled, "It's the fresh clean air of Sweden, it does wonders for your skin." She preened herself jokingly, making me laugh. "Izzy, I have to ask, what is your hair about?"

Self consciously touching it I asked, "Why?"

"It's cut nice but the colour is harsh, it has to go, you are fair and you know blondes always have more fun?"

That's one of the things I always liked about Anka, she tells it straight and I had to agree with her.

"It seemed like a good idea at the time but yes it does."

"Ya," she hugged me, "We will have some fun these next few weeks or how ever long you can stay. So from today no more sadness, its time to live, and Izzy we are only twenty four once," she sang.

Over the next few days Anka walked my feet off, what a marvellous City Stockholm is, the people are so nice and the history was to die for. It was also one of the cleanest and eco friendliest places in the world; I knew I had made the right decision. I Skyped Jazz on my third night and we chatted for a while and actually had a good laugh.

"You seem better already," she smiled, and I was. I so wanted to ask about Mika but decided not to, it wasn't fair to put Jazz in the middle and if she had any news she would have said so. With every day that passed I could feel my old self returning, growing stronger. Adair fucking Nano may have knocked me down but I sure as hell wasn't staying down.

After a month and plenty of money getting spent I checked my account online, just in case I needed to transfer some funds over from my savings. Talk about shocked when I saw the balance, my wages were still being paid in! I immediately phoned HR to query it, only to be told Mr Remizov insisted I still get paid. Since I hadn't left I was on sick leave and the company paid its employee's sick-pay. I text Mika to thank him and I also let him know I was feeling more like my old self and that I loved him. He never replied and that hurt, but seriously, what did I expect?

Spring in Stockholm was magical and while Anka was at work I walked around the City and its parks. Strolling down the Vattugatan I came across a tattoo parlour called *Skin Canvas* and before I knew it I was standing inside looking at the art work on the walls.

"Halla," a voice said, and lifting my head up I came face to face with a giant Viking of a man, like an inked Nordic God.

"Halla," I replied.

"Ahh, an American beauty."

I laughed, "Oh how original and how could you tell?"

"The accent gave you away." His voice was soothing and he made me feel at ease straight away. "How can I help you today?" he asked in a deep gruff voice.

"I would like a full back piece please?"

He looked pretty shocked, "Have you had work done before?"

"No!"

"And you want a full back piece for your first tattoo?"

"Yes, and it will be my only one so you better make it fantastic," I smiled.

He got very serious, "Hey lady I can guarantee that, but it will take weeks to complete and it will be very painful!"

Honestly I think he was trying to deter me but you already know how stubborn I can be.

"I have the time and as for pain, I've suffered worse pain than you could ever imagine, so trust me, your little needles will be like a tickle."

That made him laugh hard. "What's your name?" he asked

intrigued.

"Izzy."

"Hi Izzy, I'm Erik and it's a real pleasure to meet you," he held out his hand and I shook it.

Erik showed me all kinds of drawings and art work and all were amazing, but they were just not me.

"What do you want?"

"Something feminine, beautiful and colourful?"

He stared at me deep in thought. "Have you heard of water colour tattoos?" he asked.

I shook my head.

"It's softer and fits with what you are after, leave it with me and I'll sketch something just for you. Pop back tomorrow and we'll go from there, OK?"

"Ok." I was so excited I was on cloud nine. "So tomorrow it is then."

At ten a.m. the following morning I returned.

"Wow Izzy you are an early bird," Erik chuckled.

"I was so excited I couldn't wait any longer."

Talk about feeling like a kid and acting like one too. Erik showed me what he'd drawn and I was speechless, I just stood there and stared at this amazing piece of artwork with my mouth agape catching flies. He'd drawn a beautiful garden scene where bright flowers were in full bloom and vines were climbing up an arbour and in the middle of the lawn was a sundial, it really did seem like you could feel the suns warmth and smell the roses it looked so real. It was a kaleidoscope of colours, a true master piece, especially for me and something beautiful to hide my ugliness forever.

"So what do you think, is it colourful and girlie enough?" he nudged me.

"Wow it's perfect you are amazing."

"I need to measure your back for the stencil?"

That froze me to the spot. I knew he had to but it still caused a reaction and he saw the fear glint in my eyes.

"Come, we'll do this in the private room out back."

I simply nodded and followed him, well I tried to but my feet failed to respond to my brain's instructions.

"You ok Izzy, not having second thoughts are you?" he asked. I can imagine he'd seen many a person bottle it when it got to the serious bit, but I was different. I had never let anyone see or touch my back other than the medical staff at the hospital.

"No I'm not; I have to warn you it's not pretty."

Erik smiled, I don't think he believed me, "Take your shirt off but you can leave your bra fastened for now."

It took all the willpower I possessed to undo the buttons and I turned to face the wall before I slipped it off. I closed my eyes and I heard him take a deep intake of breath before gasping.

"Jesus Izzy, what the hell happened to you?" Of course he was going to have questions, hell I would want to know had the boot been on the other foot.

I'd only known Erik for twenty four hours but already I felt safe with him, some men just give off that vibe. They may be hard as nails and some even deadly but my instinct was I could trust this giant of a man, I knew he would never hurt me and I opened up to him.

"I was stalked and kidnapped by a psycho who signed his work!"

Erik was beyond shocked, "I hope to God they caught the evil bastard?" I could sense his rage at such a vile act.

"No need, I killed the fucker."

Erik touched my shoulder turning me around, it was the first time a stranger had touched me and I didn't flinch.

"You little Izzy, are one hell of a brave woman," he smiled, "and I hope to God I never get on the wrong side of you. But seriously, scarred skin is a bitch to cover and these are still red."

I was devastated, "So you are not going to do it?"

"Not today, I'll give you some of my own ointment cream to apply twice daily, it works miracles. Come back in two weeks and we'll check, but to be honest it's looking like a month at least, OK?"

"OK, how long will it take to complete and how much will it cost?" I asked.

"Around four months, it all depends how much you can endure in one sitting, and the cost will be about 12300 Krona, that's about $1500."

My two month stay in Stockholm had just jumped to seven but the price was a whole lot cheaper than I'd expected.

"That's great then, I'll see you in two weeks time."

Erik actually hugged me, "See you later little Izzy."

When Anka arrived home I had her dinner ready then I explained about my extended stay, hoping she would be OK with it and in fact she was over the moon.

"I love having you here and I was kind of dreading you leaving soon."

She was my personal Godsend; she applied the cream to my back, not once showing any disgust at the hideous scars. She also made me change my hair back to my natural honey blond, I had grown the bob out quite a bit, and I hadn't straightened it in a while so it was naturally wavy, definitely me.

I Skyped Jazz, with the time difference it was pretty difficult finding time to, so we'd usually text or Facebook message one another. She screamed when she saw me.

"Look at you, you look fab. I'm so pleased you got rid of that dark hair." I laughed.

When I told her I was staying for at least another six months she pouted and sulked a little, but seeing me smiling and giggling and just how well I was doing seemed to make her happy. I had to ask, "How's Mika?" I still hadn't heard so much as a peep from him in eight weeks.

"Oh he's working all the time and I'm at the bar so we hardly see one another."

"Oh," I tried not to sound too disappointed, "send him my love." The next bit hurt even to think about it but I felt I had to say it.

"I can't expect him to wait for me, so if he finds someone else I'll be happy for him, I would understand." Jazz looked at me chewing my lip and didn't believe a word I'd said.

"Well he hasn't, but I have!" she smiled.

"Who, Do I know him?" and I honestly expected her to say Max from the bar.

"Yes you do, it's Illa!"

I was shocked but so happy for her, Illa was a really nice guy, and he has a fine ass to boot.

"Look at you all loved up," I teased. We chatted for a while longer before we said goodnight, I really did miss her.

After a month of religiously applying the magical ointment Erik had given me he was happy to begin the one off masterpiece. So on May 2nd I had the first of my five sessions that would span out over four months. Erik thought it may end up being another month on top of his estimate depending on how I would handle the pain. I had other ideas though, not that I'm naive or stupid, I knew it was going to hurt but this time it was my choice, so I was prepared to grin and bear every single needle prick. Erik and I had built a strong bond and I had even grown close to the other guys at *Skin Canvas*. We had all gone out a few times, Joss had even convinced Anka to get a tattoo and gave her a very sexy tramp stamp in a Celtic design, which she loved and couldn't wait to flash it off.

By the end of July I had finally turned a corner and my life was my own again, even my phone sessions with Dr Hurst had been reduced to once a month. My head was in a great place but my heart was another matter and it wouldn't heal. I missed Mika dreadfully and it only seemed to get worse day by day. I had to do what I did, it was the only way to prove to myself one way or the other if I could forgive him for all the lies and deceit, and to see if I could accept my new identity, and I'm pleased to say I could. I am Isabelle Natasha Bazin, I am my Fathers Daughter and was proud of everything he stood for, whether it was legal or not, even for keeping his real identity from my Mom and I. He had only done it to keep us safe so how could I hate him for that, so if I could forgive my Father, forgiving Mika should be easy.

On Jazz's birthday I called her, I'd sent a parcel full of trinkets and gifts from Sweden and she loved it.

"I have something to tell you?" she said sounding about fit to burst.

"What?"

"I'm getting engaged!"

I squealed, "Congratulations I'm so happy for you both."

"The party is on September 3rd, will you try and come?"

I knew I'd be there but that will keep for now. "I will try I promise, so when's the Wedding?"

I could hear her smile, "April 20th, a spring Wedding and you'd better be back for that because you are my maid of honour!" We both screamed in excitement.

I only needed four sittings for Erik to finish my back.

"You surprise me every time Izzy," he chuckled.

"I'm a hard ass!" I replied sounding cocky.

"I've seen big men manage ten minutes before calling it, so yes you are. Right girl listen, it will take at least a week to settle down, so use that cream and one more thing!" He stood up and hugged me without touching my back, "You are done!"

I looked in the mirror, "Oh my God Erik, wow, that's amazing, and it's more than I could ever have hoped for."

I could feel a lump forming in my throat, "You will never understand just how much you have healed and repaired me, thank you," and clinging to him I cried tears of joy. "If you are ever in Detroit look me up?"

He looked down at me, "So little one, home is calling, when are you leaving?"

"At the end of the month, so we'll have to have a leaving party."

He laughed, "Oh yeah one last blow out."

Telling Anka it was time to head home was quite hard but she was so happy for me.

"Why don't you come back with me, Jazz would love to see you and I could really use the moral support?"

Anka seemed to like that idea. "I need a vacation, why not."

I couldn't hide my excitement and relief. We booked our flights for the 31st of August, which would give us a day to acclimatize before the party at *Red Square* and we also made reservations at The Concord hotel. To be honest I didn't know how my home coming would be met back at the Remizov's estate so staying at a hotel was the best option for now. Once I was back stateside it would be easier to find a new place to live and thankfully I'd have Anka to help me, for now anyway.

The day before we flew out I had my hair done, the inverted bob was long gone, it was still fairly short but so much softer and wavy. I actually looked liked my passport photo. I had bought a backless black mini dress for the party; I was so determined to show off my new artwork with pride since my back was no longer the ugly disgusting scar. Erik had also given me another tattoo, a tiny cherub just under my hair line on the back of my neck that was just for me, it was my little secret and I loved it. Anka and I were all packed, "Holy cow Anka, just how long are you planning on staying?" I laughed at her, she had more luggage than me and I was leaving for good.

CHAPTER TWENTY-THREE

Mika had watched Izzy struggle every day; it was devastating to watch knowing there was nothing he could do but just be there for her when she needed him. He tried to be a rock for her to cling to but she began to close herself off from everyone. She had gotten worse when he finally told her the whole truth, and everything he tried just pushed her further away. He decided to give her the space she seemed to need but that had been a huge mistake; it had erected an impenetrable wall that he could not pull down.

She would lock herself in the bathroom, never allowing him in or letting him see her naked and on more than one occasion he'd nearly kicked the door in. If anyone touched her she would instantly stiffen, flinching at the slightest contact. 'Give her time, be patient and she will come around' her shrink had told him. But how could he, his Angel was becoming a stranger, they shared a bed and the gap between them may only be inches but it felt like miles. Then the hairdresser came and dyed Izzy's hair that awful dark brown, which really didn't suit her, and the style made her look bitter and harsh, what the fuck had she done? Mika couldn't even speak when he saw her, he tried to smile, but he hated her hair and he wanted to kill the damned stylist for what she had done to her.

What finally pushed her over the edge was when her Gran passed. He and Jazz had gone to Milwaukee with her, he had been so worried. She was so quiet and withdrawn and he knew something had to give, but never in a month of Sundays had he expected what it would be. That night still hurt him deeply, when he saw her and Jazz sitting on the floor crying, if she had pulled a gun and shot him he wouldn't have been half as shocked. "So you are running away – Again!" He'd yelled at her, watching her fighting her emotions as she begged him to understand and pleaded with him to let her go.

The rage inside him was immense, he wanted to smash up the house and keep her prisoner here, locked up forever. He grabbed hold of his car keys, gripping them so tight it hurt the palm of his hand, he turned and turbulently marched out, slamming the door and drove off into the night. All he wanted to do was grab her, shout at her till he was blue in the face and shake the real Izzy back into her. Somehow he ended up at Alex's hotel, The Majestic. The valet parked his car as he walked to the front desk, "Good evening Mr Remizov, how may I help you?"

"I need a room and tell my brother to meet me in the bar?" The receptionist handed him the penthouse key-card before she called Alex. Mika sat at the end of the bar, "A bottle of Talisker and two glasses," he instructed the bartender, he planned on drinking himself into oblivion.

Alex entered, still straightening his attire; he had been balls deep in a sweet little brunette when his office phone rang. His eyes set on the twenty year old bottle of scotch.

"What's happened Mika?" he asked, knowing it had to be bad.

"Izzy is fucking running away again; she says she has to find herself, whatever the hell that means."

"Where is she, do we know?" Alex asked concerned.

"Still at home planning some fucking mission to Sweden….. Fucking Sweden!" Mika was so pissed off he slung another shot down while trying his hardest not to lose it.

"Swedish, that's what her and Jazz have been talking!"

Alex sounded so chuffed that he'd discovered the language the pair had been using to conspire in. Mika glared at him.

"Sorry?" Alex realised just how inappropriate his timing

was. "So why the hell are you here and not at home?"

"I couldn't stay, I was about ready to kill someone or destroy the fucking house."

Alex saw the penthouse card on the bar next to the bottle of Talisker and his cell, "So you are staying here tonight!"

"I'm staying here till I calm the fuck down, God Alex I love her with all of my heart so what else can I seriously do?"

Alex knew that was a rhetorical question so simply shrugged his shoulders. After Mika's cell rung for the fourth time he switched it off.

By two thirty Alex had to literally carry Mika up to the suite and he dropped him on the bed to sleep it off. Then he called Jazz who filled in all the gaps and after he heard the tale he actually thought Izzy's plan was a good idea. He understood she had to get away from them all and he just hoped she would work it all out and find her way back home.

That's exactly what he told Mika the next day when he came round, with one hell of a hangover.

"Mika you need to talk to her, she's leaving in the morning, if you don't you'll regret it?" Alex pleaded with him but to no avail.

"No, but if she needs to find herself so be it, let her go on this journey of self discovery. I really hope she finds what she is looking for, but I can not give her my blessing and I do not trust myself not to say something I will regret later. I will not interfere or try to influence her so my decision to not talk or text her is final, it's her choice to leave not mine. If she wants to talk when she returns then fine I will listen, but until then I will not communicate with her." Alex knew that look and no one could change his decision once Mika had made his mind up.

Jazz returned home from the airport upset and distressed to find Mika, "Oh so now you decide to come home, now she has gone?"

All Mika could do was wrap her up in his loving arms, "Princess I'm hurting too, and I'm trying my hardest to understand why she has to do this. I just hope she will one day find herself and come home."

Jazz sobbed in agreement, "She said to tell you she loves you." He squeezed her tight, "I love her too."

Mika received at least one text a week, usually short and sweet, telling him she missed and loved him. He must have stopped himself picking up his cell and calling her a million times, just to hear the sound of her voice. But he hoped that time away from him would make her miss him so much she would return home. Two months had passed when Jazz told him that Izzy had decided to stay for another six and he took the news pretty badly. In fact he had been livid; he'd waited like a schlep, like a fucking pussy. Well no more, fuck her; he felt like she had been pissing up his back, and he nearly phoned to tell her to stay in Sweden. Instead he threw himself into work; the East Coast project was well under way and would be soon close to completion, the hotels and resorts were fantastic.

As for the brotherhood, every person who had been involved with Adair Nano, no matter how small, had been hunted down and eliminated from the face of the earth. Between Delushi and the Brotherhood they had rid the city of any possible threat, leaving it to just the two syndicates. They now had a better acceptance of one another and Mika would even go as far as saying they respected each other.

Jazz and Illa walked into his office, Mika had been given the heads up from Katia but he was still pleasantly surprised.

"Boss I need to ask you something?" Illa looked nervous while Jazz giggled like a teenager. Mika was now intrigued, he didn't say a word he just gave him his deadly stare. "Boss, Erm well, err I'd like you to erm, you know well marry me!"

It was killing Mika not to burst out laughing; he had to cover his mouth with his hand.

"Boss NO! No I mean I love Jazz and I want to marry *her*. Holy shit sorry babe I'm totally fucking this up," he looked at her mortified.

Mika certainly wasn't blind he knew and saw everything, but decided to have a little fun.

"WHAT?" he bellowed.

"Mika, I love him, he nearly died for me, what more could YOU want?" Jazz yelled back at him.

Mika's face cracked and he laughed, "I'm teasing, I'm delighted for you both. You have my whole support and blessing. Congratulations."

Illa was finally able to breathe while Jazz launched herself at her big brother, "Thank you, I love you."

"So when's the big day?" Mika asked.

"We're having an engagement party on September 3rd and the wedding will be in the spring," she was so happy and that made Mika happy too, he needed some happiness back in his life. Jazz had stopped telling him about Izzy since he got mad but he did inquire if she was coming home for the party.

"I don't think so but she will definitely be here for the wedding." She didn't know if he was annoyed or relieved, but she was wise enough not to push it.

I could feel my nerves beginning to surface as the plane started its descent. Anka held my hand and smiled she didn't need to speak; I was just so pleased she was with me, I really needed her moral support. I left this City nearly eight months ago, sad, lost and angry but today I was returning happy, a little apprehensive but at peace with my issues. The sun was shining bright on Detroit, kind of like a warm welcome home and hopefully a good omen of things to come. As the wheels touched down I sighed, "Home."

We hailed a cab to the hotel and by the time we checked in it was close to five in the afternoon and safe to say it would be a very early night after nearly forty-eight hours travelling. The party was tomorrow night at seven so we had just over twenty-four hours to get ourselves refreshed and recharged. The next day we had a relaxing time in the hotels' solarium and had booked the works, from massages to mani and pedi's and then the beautician on staff worked her magic on us so all we needed to do was get dressed.

Once back in our suite I started feeling sick with nerves. "What if Mika is with someone else and what if he hates me and doesn't want me there?" I panicked. I knew Jazz and Alex would be pleased; they were the only ones who kept in touch with me, as for Luca I just didn't know.

"Stop it Izzy," Anka snapped, catching my attention, "You're thinking this out way too much. Everyone will be delighted to see you, and thrilled you look so healthy and happy like your old self. I can see what a change has happened to you in eight months and I have seen you every day. If Mika has found someone else, then, well girl you will just have to put a brave face on and be happy for him."

She was right and all I wanted was for him to be happy. As for me, well my new life begins right here, right now.

We had a real girlie time getting ready; Anka used her curling iron to add ringlets to my hair making it look natural and fabulous. My skin had a golden, sun kissed tan from the Swedish summer sun so my make-up was soft and subtle to bring out the blue of my eyes.

"Your face looks so angelic but your body in that dress looks sinfully sexy," Anka laughed. I walked to the mirror and turned to look at my back, "Wow your tattoo looks fucking amazing!"

It really did and I couldn't thank Erik enough. Anka was dressed in a cream trouser suit with no shirt just a jacket, she was so glamorous and at 6' totally dwarfed me, even in my 5 inch heels. It was nearly seven when I called Jazz.

"Hey girl, you all set for tonight?" I sang.

"Yes I think so, but I'm shitting it, I need you here."

"You'll be fine, just make sure you take lots of photos. What time do you need to be there, I'm not keeping you am I?"

"No we are already here, well Mika and Luca aren't yet but they will be soon."

"Have a wonderful night, I'll be thinking about you, I love you so much."

"Stop it, you're gonna get me crying, I miss and love you too." We said our goodbyes and I hung up. Looking at Anka I smiled, "She still thinks we are in Sweden."

"We have at least an hour, how about a drink at the hotel bar?" Anka asked, "A little Dutch courage will go along way."

"Great idea," I said, linking her arm we walked out of the room. At eight-thirty we were in a cab heading for *Red Square*, this was it, we pulled up outside and Anka got out first. Zack and Grant were on the door as usual and when they saw Anka their eyes nearly fell out.

"Close your mouths guys," I joked before they even saw me.

"Hey Izzy, wow how you doing girl, you look lovely as usual?" I just chuckled and hugged them.

"Wow Izzy that's some seriously cool ink!" Grant said rather impressed, as Zack turned me round to look, "Shit girl that's sick!" he added.

"Whose work is it?"

"A Nordic God called Erik from Stockholm." That just confused him; geography was not his strongest suit. "That's in Sweden!"

"Oh so that's where you've been, and this stunning lady is?" his eyes fixed on Anka.

"My very good and life saving Swedish friend Anka," and she

smiled and shook their out stretched hands, both huge men looking like infatuated school kids.

Grant opened the door, "Ladies have a great night," we thanked him and entered.

Instead of a band playing, Jazz had opted for a DJ and with it only being early the music was just a pleasant background sound while people laughed and chatted away. The place was packed; it had been decorated in gold and red tinsel with glitzy balloons, and a banner hanging across the bar read *Congratulations Jazz and Illa*. On the far side of the room was a table full of beautifully wrapped gifts, and people had plates mounted with food while congregating in small groups having a good time.

Anka's hand touched my shoulder and that's when I noticed people staring at us as their conversations stalled, talk about feeling like a goldfish in a bowl. It suddenly hit me and I started to panic a little. My head began to swim and my heart thumped hard in my chest. Jazz and her family were in their usual place by her office catching up on the latest gossip, while Mika and Luca were sat at a table surrounded by women, desperate for their attention. That's when Jazz noticed the lull in the atmosphere, she scanned the bar looking in the direction of where everyone was staring. Her eyes landed on the very tall and sexy Anka.

"Fuck me!" Jazz screamed, getting everyone's attention; Mika and Luca were instantly on their feet.

"What?" both asking.

Alex had seen the tall blond first, "Holy mother of God would you look at her? I want her to have my babies!"

Mika and Luca both laughed at him. Then Jazz's eyes locked onto her, "She's here, she's back!" was all Jazz screamed before disappearing into a sea of bodies.

CHAPTER TWENTY-FOUR

It felt like an eternity standing there being the focus of every pair of eyes in the place. Then the crowd parted like the Red Sea and I saw her.

"Izzy! My God," she cried, tears running down her beautiful face.

"Jazz... I've missed you so much."

I didn't want to let her go and all three of us clung together like old times. Then I heard a cough and turned to see Alex and Luca.

"Hey there!" I said sheepishly.

"Get your sweet ass over here now?" Luca held his arms open and I fell into them. He tilted my chin up so my eyes met his, "You look so much better, did you get everything sorted babe?"

I smiled at him, "Yeah I'm done, and I'm back for good."

As he kissed my head, Alex piped up, "Hey it's my turn," he said, pushing Luca out of the way.

"Fuck Izzy, your back!"

Jazz suddenly gasped, "That's fucking awesome, shit... it's beautiful." I felt her fingers run down the tattoo on my back and it didn't bother me now, it was a work of art not an ugly scar.

"That's why I stayed longer than planned to let Erik finish it, do you forgive me?"

"There is nothing to forgive, you're home and all better, that's all that matters."

The one person I hadn't seen yet was the one I desperately

needed to, to make amends with.

"Where is he?" I asked, almost choking on my own question.

"In his usual spot," and Jazz tilted her head towards the corner near her office. It was time, I couldn't put it off any longer and I had to make the first move, it was me who had left after all. The way we'd left it with him storming out and me not hearing a word from him in nearly eight months, I honestly didn't know what reception I was going to get from him, he might just ignore me? Would he just treat me like an old acquaintance, a swift hello before he moved on? I was so daunted by my own self doubting; still I reluctantly put one foot in front of the other and walked slowly over to him.

Mika just stood back and watched the excited commotion from afar; his fallen broken Angel had finally found her way back home. All that rage and animosity he had been carrying around like two lead weights for months suddenly evaporated the moment he first caught sight of her. Gone was the frown that had marred her face, and gone was that awful brown hair that she'd left with. The gorgeous bubbly blond who he had fallen head over heels in love with had returned. It took all the willpower he had not to push everyone aside and run to her, instead he waited patiently and let her find him.

He had been so entranced by Izzy's impromptu arrival he hadn't noticed the woman who'd suddenly appeared at his side, and was now rubbing herself against him, the sickly sweet smell of cheap perfume filled his nostrils.

"Hey lady, be a doll and fuck off?" he growled at her, to which she tutted and slinked off looking for her next target. Condensation dripped on to his fingers from the glass he was holding as he swigged the last dregs of his scotch down and he called to Max.

"Hey Max fill her up?"

Ignoring all the other people who were waiting at the bar for their turn, Max took his glass, refreshed it and handed it back.

"Thanks," Mika said, taking the much needed drink and walked back to the now empty table. The lights now dimmed for the disco had made the area around him pretty dark and unintentionally hide him, still he could see her and he watched her cautiously approach him.

I left everyone chatting with Anka, and Alex was practically drooling over her. The area near Jazz's office was dark and it took a moment for my eyes to adjust, then I saw him standing there watching me with his hands in his pants pockets. The anxiety that was building inside me was making my stomach somersault. The disco lights flashed and illuminated him, and seeing that perfect chiselled face stopped me in my tracks about a table's length away. I tried to gage his reaction as I stared into his eyes, physically shaking now as a single tear escaped and tumbled down my cheek, my heart felt like it had stopped beating. It seemed like an age before he finally blinked, took his hands out of his pockets and opened them up to me. The stress and worry lifted from my body as I ran into his wonderful embrace, feeling his strong arms cocooning me, he lifted me easily off my feet as if I was as light as a feather and crushed me to him. I could feel his desperation just as much as he probably could mine. My face was pressed against the crook of his neck, inhaling his intoxicating scent I'd missed so much, I didn't ever want him to let me go.

Eventually I slid down his front till my feet hit the floor and then he softly cupped my face and lifted it up to meet his. I could see the emotion swimming in his eyes and then he kissed me in a way I'd never been kissed before. I saw stars that caused my body to wake up from its year long hibernation, for a minute we both forgot we were in a public place. He had always kept that side of himself very private and never showed any affection to me in public, and I loved this new side of him.

Eventually our lips parted and I instantly missed the contact, shyly I glanced up at him. Looking into those eyes and at the face I had been in love with forever had proven one thing for sure; I was unequivocally in love with Mika and never wanted to be apart from him ever again. We still hadn't spoken a word and I decided to speak to him in Russian since the secret was out.

"Hi."

He raised an eyebrow comically, "Hi Angel, you finally found your wings and flew home?"

"No I flew back to you," I smiled. "I'm so sorry I hurt you, that was never my intention, but I hope you can understand why I had to go and I hope you can forgive me?"

His thumb gently stroked my cheek, "Angel look at you, you are full of life again, healthy, and even more beautiful than I remember, and you came back to me, how can I not forgive you?"

I threw my arms around him, "Oh Mika I love you so much and I'll never leave you again."

"Oh babe that is so true, and I love you more than life itself," and he kissed me again.

"We have company," he whispered in my ear, as he turned me around in his arms. Not letting me go he was about to wrap his arms around me when he realised my dress was backless and moved me forward.

"Fuck me!" he exclaimed as he saw my ink, "I need a better look at that." He grabbed my hand and dragged me into Jazz's office where the light was blinding. It wasn't just Mika and I, we were followed by Luca, Alex and Jazz.

"Izzy that's, well... wow... fucking amazing!" Mika gasped as his fingers traced down my spine, causing my skin to goose pimple and my panties to dampen instantly. His simple touch made me come alive and thank God I was facing away from them, I quietly composed myself while they examined my art work.

"When did you get back?" Jazz asked, snapping me back to reality.

"Yesterday afternoon, we're booked in at The Concord."

"Not any more," Mika's breath was hot as it caressed my neck.

"Anka can stay too, in your old room or maybe in my bed," Alex chipped in, lifting his eyebrows as he was walking out of the door, "I'll go let her know."

Jazz and I burst out laughing, which left Luca and Mika looking confused.

"She'll eat him alive," Jazz told them, and I just howled.

"Come on, it's my party lets get back out there?" she grabbed my hand and we walked back into the bar where the party was well under way. As soon as my eyes began to adjust to the light the first thing I noticed was all the teeth. Whenever the lights flashed I focused more and everyone was smiling at me, I was truly touched by the warm homecoming I received, never in my wildest dreams had I expected this reaction. Anka looked at me and mouthed, "You ok?" and the massive cheesy smile was my answer.

After a little while it felt like I'd never been away, Jazz eventually pulling me away from Mika's grasp, not even seeming to care about the deep growl he gave her.

"Oh shut up Mika, she's not just yours!" which did make me snigger. As the women, well the ones closest to Jazz and Illa, were sat around two tables that had been pushed together, the men stood guarding it, chatting amongst them. Mika was standing directly behind me, constantly touching me as if he was still convincing himself I was really here. I excused myself, "Nature calls," answering all the suspicious looks, well I suppose I'll have to get used to those for a while. When I returned I caught sight of Gavril standing alone at the bar, looking like he was fighting his own demons and I was pulled towards him like a magnet. I had caused this man so much anguish and grief; I knew Mika would have made his life pure hell through absolutely no fault of his own. I touched his arm gently to get his attention; his eyes were showing me so many conflicting emotions.

"Gavril... I'm so sorry for what I have caused," I struggled with a lump forming in my throat, "I should never have done what I did to you!"

He stared above my head not wanting to give me eye contact while he fought to gain control, "No you shouldn't have!" Then he had to pause a second, "That day will haunt me forever, not the day you tricked me but the day we found you and seeing what that fucker had done to you. Seeing you slashed and covered in all that blood..." he had to stop again. "I honestly thought he'd killed you, you were my responsibility, my charge to protect and I failed. Part of me died that day when I walked into that room; I have never forgiven myself for being so easily manipulated. But look at you now," he tried a smile, "I thank the Lord everyday for letting you live and making you such a survivor."

I couldn't stop myself flinging my arms around him, I never knew he was there to witness the worst time of my life, and he would always have a place in my heart.

"Thank you for rescuing me, and please forgive yourself, as well as me?" My own voice was once again strained with emotion, as he embraced me back.

"I'll always forgive you, but as for myself that may take a little longer," and he kissed my head softly. I half expected Mika to come barrelling over, but I had to give him credit, he just watched from a distance knowing what was going on. By the look on Mika's face he hadn't punished Gavril at all because Gavril had punished himself harder than anyone ever could have and Mika had respected for him that.

"Come over here and sit with me," I said pulling Gavril's arm, I suppose if he didn't want to I would never have been able to move him, but he grabbed his bottle from the bar and let me drag him to the table. Seeing the manly chin lift between Mika and Gavril as I reached over and picked up my drink, "I'm just chatting to Gavril," I informed Jazz before she had a chance to ask, "Ok babes," she smiled and the inquiring faces just dropped and carried on their conversations. I strolled back to Gavril, "Back so soon?"

"I'm like a bad penny," I joked, and we small talked for a while before he told me a story that floored me.

"I followed in my Papa's footsteps like many of the brothers in the brotherhood; he was one of the best minders the brotherhood ever had. Twenty four years ago he was assigned to guard and protect your Momma while she was still pregnant with you. He stayed close to both of you, watching and keeping you both safe from afar. When I was seventeen your Momma passed away and it affected my Papa very deeply, even though she knew nothing about him he knew everything about her and you. I remember you at the funeral looking so lost and Mika shielding you from the world even then. It was the only time I'd ever seen my papa shed a tear. Then he watched over you and your Grandmother, once you and Jazz left for college and with you being hundreds of miles away Savas assigned my papa to guard him and Petra, while Savas had the Pakhan of California keep tabs on you two. My Papa died in the same helicopter crash that killed Savas and Petra, so you can see Izzy, protecting you is in my blood, my DNA."

I was dumbstruck, "Oh my God Gavril, I don't know what to say? Thank you seems pathetic considering what you and your family have done for mine."

"We don't do it for the thanks; we do it to keep you safe and alive."

"Will you still be my minder?" I asked, I really wanted him to be.

"I really do not know but I hope so, protecting the Pakhan's future wife will be an honour."

Illa came and joined us, "Welcome home Izzy," he said as he kissed my cheek.

"Congratulations Illa, you are one lucky man!"

"I know, I still can't believe she said yes," he said looking over at Jazz. I left Gavril and Illa talking and made my way back to Mika's open arms.

"Do you think we can escape unnoticed," he whispered.

"Not a chance, maybe in about an hour or so?" I squeezed his hand.

"I can't wait that long, I want you all to myself."

I agreed, understanding totally, "I need to stop by the hotel and pick my things up?"

"Leave them; I'll get someone to collect them tomorrow." There was no way he was making a detour tonight.

"But all my clothes and personal things are there?"

"Izzy you have all of that at home." I knew it was pointless arguing, anyway I had the most important thing in my purse, my contraception pill just in case.

I could see Anka and Jazz chatting away then I caught a glimpse of Alex's disgruntled face. I leant over and whispered to Mika, "I'm going to go talk to Anka and Jazz."

"Don't be long, we are leaving soon," he told me in his sexy boss man tone and I got all giddy just at the thought.

"OK," I winked. Then I understood why Alex was looking so annoyed, Jazz and Anka were chatting away in Swedish and I added more fuel to the fire by joining in.

"So I hear we are now staying at the Remizov's mansion?" Anka chuckled.

"Yeah, you OK with that?" I had to ask.

"Too right I'm OK, me and my bitches all together again!" and that made us all giggle.

"Now Anka go gently on my brother?"

"Jazz you know I do not do gentle," she retorted looking towards Alex and giving him a sexy smile.

"Anka you're gonna make him blow his load in his pants!"

That made me choke on my drink.

"Fuck Jazz that's your brother!" I laughed so hard I nearly wet myself.

"What! I don't know why you're so shocked, look at him he's like a rampant dog, and don't even let me get started on my eldest brother; he's been dying to mount you all night."

Anka spat her beer all over herself and we all laughed together.

"Shit girls, I've missed you both so much," Jazz quipped.

"Ladies," Mika interrupted us, "Izzy, Vik is outside waiting for us."

That was my cue, "Well girlies I'll see you both tomorrow... Wait, how is Anka getting home?" I asked.

"She's coming with me," Alex informed us, and Anka's eyebrows lifted high at the double entendre that had innocently slipped out of Alex's mouth.

I chuckled, hugging her, "You are terrible," I whispered so only she could hear me, and she gave me a cheeky wink, "Have a wonderful night honey."

Outside Vik waited by a brand new Range Rover, "Well hello stranger, it's good to see you home and looking lovely as ever," he smiled, as he gave me a loving fatherly embrace.

"Hi Vik, you OK, how's Charlie and the kids?"

"Really good, she's ready to pop any day now, but hey we nailed it this time, a girl, third times a charm."

I gave him my biggest smile, "You must let me know when she arrives."

"Will do Izzy, is it home Boss?" he added suddenly all professional.

"Please Vik, and then call it a night."

"Sure thing Boss."

The journey took fifteen minutes and I had been a little apprehensive about returning before, but now it was a wonderful feeling driving up to the house, my home. Mika never letting go of my hand.

"What does it feel like coming home Angel?" he asked as he kissed the back of my hand.

"Like a dream, I wanted to come back months ago but I had to let Erik finish my tat, but it was well worth it." I was so proud of my masterpiece.

"He did a fantastic job, it's sexy as hell."

"Not only did he help me physically but mentally as well."

I felt Mika stiffen a little, "No, no, not sexually, no, with my confidence. You are still the only man who has ever touched me that way." That seemed to relax him a little. "Not even Adair Nano, he had tried but I threw up all over him, by the way that had been the best timed gift from God... ever."

Pulling up in front of the house we jumped out, "Night Vik say Hi to Charlie for me?" I said quickly as Mika dragged me up to the front door.

"Will do, goodnight," he yelled before he drove away.

Now it was just the two of us and we barely made it through the door before we started ripping each others clothes off desperate for naked contact. My legs buckled as he grabbed me by my hips and pushed me backwards until the wall stopped him. He effortlessly picked me up, forcing my legs apart, which made my dress ride up high. My whole body quivered in anticipation, this was not going to be gentle, tender love making but untamed, raw, hot primal sex. The craving we had for each other was consuming and I had never been this highly turned on in my life. His lips crashed down hard onto mine while his agile hand made short work of my drenched panties, and using his dexterous fingers he claimed my wet opening. Closing my eyes in euphoria I let my head fall back against the wall, as my nails dug into his shoulders trying to brace myself as he skilfully drove hard into me, thrusting his cock until he couldn't get any deeper. His pace increased but I matched him breath for breath, as his cock fucked my pussy, his tongue fucked my mouth, our bodies became one, in complete sync with each other and then I felt the first ebbs of my orgasm begin. My head was spinning from the blood rush and I could see a rainbow of colours. His shaft grew harder as he felt my muscles contracting and tighten around him bring him near to his own climax.

Screaming his name I came hard, which made him release his seed deep into me. I was still pressed up against the wall, he was the only one who would ever have this kind of power and control over me and I'd given it to him completely. As we slumped exhausted on to the floor we were still physically attached, and he kissed me.

"God I love you!"

"I love you more," I whispered.

He carried me upstairs not even caring that all our torn clothes were left strewn around in the foyer for all to see, he just needed to get us to our room so he could finish what he had started downstairs. Downstairs may not have been pretty but it was fast and straight to the point but the rest of the night was slow, erotic, and utterly sensual, one hell of a night to remember and one that I will relive for many years to come.

CHAPTER TWENTY-FIVE

Mika woke up with the biggest smile plastered across his face as he remembered last nights adults only adventure. He quickly turned his head to make sure it hadn't all been a dream. She was there, sleeping peacefully on her stomach facing away from him; the soft cotton sheets had ridden down and nestled in the small of her back hiding her sweet delectable butt. The sunlight filled the room and shone on her ink; it was even more exquisite in the daylight, a work of art to be exact, it reminded him of a quaint English country garden, it was so clear and crisp like a photo, he could virtually smell the fresh, scented air. Her hair was spread across the pillow and that's when he caught sight of a second tattoo on her neck that he hadn't seen before. He gently moved her golden locks aside to get a better look, it was a small but perfect angel complete with wings and a halo, he couldn't help himself and he kissed the angel on his Angel.

"Morning," the sleep laced, sexiest voice greeted him and then she turned over and gave him a mouth watering show, which caused the best and hardest morning glory he'd had in a long time.

"Morning Angel" he smiled.

After a physical morning workout and one hell of a stimulating shower, we were finally dressed and craving something other than each other, just then my stomach growled on cue as evidence.

"Hungry babe?" Mika asked as he heard the rumble. The sounds of laughter filtered up the staircase, "It sounds like we are the last ones up," I said.

"It is after noon, I'm surprised they haven't sent a search party out," he chuckled. I felt my cheeks flush, which only made him chuckle harder.

"Izzy you're so cute when you're embarrassed."

"Hey would you look at what the cat dragged in!" Jazz announced our arrival in her usual way. "Did you sleep well?" she asked with a devious glint. "Because I did *eventually* I think we had coyotes in the garden last night what with all that howling and screaming, it went on for hours."

Again on cue my cheeks lit up brighter than the ripest tomato and everyone laughed at my discomfort.

Mika pulled me to him. "My little sex kitten," he said proudly.

I composed myself and sat down, two can play this game!

"I need coffee now! So service me again boy!" I tapped the table with my finger nail and caused the kitchen to erupt once more.

"Yes Boss," Mika bowed.

"Ooh Boss, I like the sound of that, you can bring me toast as well."

Luca made the sound of a whip cracking, "All hail the new Boss," he chanted.

At breakfast the following day, Anka told me that Alex had planned on taking her out all day, to do some sightseeing and all the touristy things like going to see the Motown museum and Belle Isle and then ending the day with dinner at the new hip restaurant, The Element, which apparently had an eight week waiting list for a table, but somehow Alex had managed to get a reservation on short notice. God I did love the way dropping the name Remizov got peoples attention. I had never seen Alex act this way over a woman before, he was the typical love em and leave em on the same night type of guy and dating was simply unheard of. Anka was basically the female equivalent of him;

she would always leave men begging for more. She was most men's poster girl fantasy, the gorgeous tall blond Swedish goddess and because of that every other woman's ultimate nemesis. I honestly didn't know how this, whatever this was, was going play out, but it would certainly be entertaining to watch and for once I was just a spectator.

Jazz joined us for a quick breakfast, "There's a big NFL game on this afternoon so it's all hands on deck," she huffed trying to make out it was such a chore to have to go into the bar, but she wasn't fooling any of us. She grabbed her car keys.

"What no more shadow?" I asked.

"Oh I always have my shadow, but not like before," she smiled. "He is coming to the bar later, and I'll be staying at his place tonight. For some reason he's uncomfortable sleeping here, although I don't blame him really. Nothing like hearing your boss banging his old lady all night," she teased me.

"Oh shut up you," I giggled as she blew us both a kiss.

"Later bitches," she shouted as the door closed behind her.

Alex meandered into the kitchen looking rather suave and sexy in blue jeans and a casual shirt.

"Good morning ladies, you ready to go Anka?" and she winked at me.

"Have a good day you two," I called out as they left and then I was on my own. Mika had gone to the gym, I don't know where he got all his energy from and I don't suppose I ever will. I was still exhausted from the last two night's raucous activities, which my muscles could attest to. Luca still hadn't returned home from where ever, or who ever he was with, but I crossed my fingers and hoped it was Mandy.

Mika walked in around lunchtime, his dark hair still damp from the shower and wearing clean sweat pants that hung on his hips and a t-shirt with the gyms logo *Body Torque* that was tight around his biceps, God that man turned me on. It was a gorgeous day with the sun delightfully warm and the garden in full bloom.

"Do you fancy iced tea in the garden?" I asked him with a kiss.

"That sounds like heaven."

Finding a pitcher I decided to make a Long Island iced tea, the ideal tipple on a day like today. Mika carried the tray out to the patio table and as I handed him a glass I asked, "Mika, what happens now?" I was unconsciously chewing on my thumbnail.

"What do you mean?" he asked.

"Well do I still have a job?"

He sipped his drink, "If you still want it," he said, not sounding too happy.

"If it's going to be weird I can look for another job somewhere else?"

By his reaction I guessed I'd said the wrong thing.

"What, Hell NO," he barked.

"Why not?" I had a feeling but I had to ask.

"I'm sorry but Izzy you know why? You know everything now and the wife of the Pakhan will always have a target on her back. If you want to work fine, but it will be with me, and consequently when I'm not with you, you will have a minder assigned to you. Especially after what has already happened, and that is non negotiable, do I make myself clear?"

He wasn't asking, hell he wasn't even telling me, this was a direct order. The old me would have refused emphatically, I'd have argued till the death, but now I knew he was right. I did know every dark secret and had witnessed the danger first hand; I would bear the scars forever.

"Yes Mika, crystal clear. But I do have two questions?"

He looked at me with a raised eyebrow. "How am I not surprised." His lip twitched, I could tell he was fighting not to smile.

"If I have to have a minder I would like it to be Gavril?"

Mika frowned at me, his eyes looking suspicious, "Why?"

"He told me all about his father and the history between our families, and to be honest I was deeply touched and I really do feel safe with him."

Mika nodded slowly, "Ok I'll let Gavril know tomorrow. You had a second question?"

"Oh yeah, well err... the whole wife bit is a little fuzzy... when did you propose?"

I couldn't recall being asked at all. Gavril had said something at Jazz's engagement party about the future wife of the Pakhan and I was beginning to think Mika had asked me? I had been on a strong cocktail of drugs but surely I would have remembered something like that, especially if I'd said yes?

"Wait here, do not move," he said, as he vanished into the house and leaving me totally dumbstruck. I was so deep inside my mind palace searching for any clue, and coming up with zilch that I never heard him return.

Mika coughed getting my attention, "This isn't the way I planned this."

He took hold of my hand and inhaled a deep calming breath to steady his voice while I just looked at him totally befuddled.

"I wanted to do all that romantic shit women seem to really like," he kind of uttered while playing nervously with something in his hand. Then he dropped onto one knee in front of me, "Isabelle... I have loved you all my life, you were like another sister to watch over and protect, you have always been a huge part of this family even before we all knew why. That all changed for me the day you walked into the den and I saw you for the first time since you returned from California. That moment will be ingrained into my memory forever, you turned my life upside down and I fell in love with you and my love has grown stronger everyday since. When we found you that day in Battle Creek, it was the worst moment of my life, walking into that room and seeing you, seeing all that blood, I thought I'd lost you. I understood then what my father must have felt, seeing the love of his life murdered, but then you spoke my name, you were so brave and you are such a fighter. I ached for you, watching you struggling day by day, fighting the demons I could not slay, all I could do was be there for you when you needed me. My heart stopped beating the day you left, it was a very dark time for both of us. I know I had to let you go, I just prayed you would one day find your way back to me and you did. Before I even saw you at the bar my heart had begun to beat fast inside my chest again, it was like it sensed you were near. I swear to God I'll never let you go again, nobody will ever hurt you again, I will kill them like I have done before. So Isabelle Natasha Bazin..." he kissed the back of my hand, "Will you marry me?"

I couldn't speak, I couldn't see, I was blinking fast, trying to clear away those damn tears once again, I chewed my lip and nodded. Mika placed the ring on my finger and kissed me with so much passion it made my toes curl in wanting.

"I love you Angel, always have, always will."

I must have dreamed about this a million times and now it was really happening.

"Mika you are my world and you always have been," and this time we kissed like a romantic fairytale.

Touching the beautiful antique diamond ring was like touching a star, it was exquisite and I watched the colours sparkle from it as the sun's rays caught it, it was hypnotic. I had never seen a ring quite like it before, it was unique, just like me.

"That ring was my great Grandmothers, it came with her all the way from Russia, and it's been in this family for generations. My Nan gave it to my Father when he was going to propose to Natasha, but sadly she never got the chance to wear it. He has kept it in the safe in his office, still in the same box Nan had given it to him in. He never gave it to my Mom; I honestly don't think she knew about it. Dad showed me it the day he told me everything, he told me to take it and use it when I found the *one*; it's meant to be for your one true love and he had lost his. I knew he loved my Mom but I also know Natasha was the true love of his life. So Izzy this ring is our destiny, it was truly meant for you."

I stared at this mystical diamond ring that had been kept in the dark for decades and watched the sun's touch bring it back to life, fate sure is a powerful thing.

CHAPTER TWENTY-SIX

The next few weeks were completely manic and some days seemed to just blur into one another. Anka had returned to Sweden and I missed her something terrible, she had been my life preserver but she did promise to come back for both weddings and we'd skype as often as we could. Alex was like a bear with a sore head trying to put on an 'I don't care' face that didn't fool anyone. He told Anka what they had was just a holiday romance, which seemed to really hurt her, but Anka being Anka bit back and told him she hadn't expected anything less and she'd only wanted him for sex while she was away from home because here she didn't have to be the prim and proper school teacher and he hadn't been the only one on her visit, so he could simply just get over himself. I knew Alex had been her only one while she'd been here but I wasn't going to tell him that, well not while he was being a jerk about it. I did however want to crack both their heads together; the pair were as stubborn as each other.

One night we actually managed to have a family dinner, which was a rare feat these days.

"So when's the big day?" Luca asked, as all eyes focused in on Mika, even mine.

"We haven't set a date yet."

"We could go to Vegas if you like, make a weekend of it," I chipped in thinking it was a great idea.

Jazz dropped her fork and it clattered on her plate while the others gasped in horror, you'd have thought I'd committed high treason.

"Izzy do you realise what a huge thing a Pakhan's wedding

is?" Luca grinned as I shook my head, "It's kind of like a royal wedding, all the Pakhan's from the other states and Russia will be in attendance, and it's a massive celebration."

So that's a no to the quiet little ceremony then. Shit!

"How big are we talking?"

"Well Iz, it will put mine to shame," Jazz chuckled as she saw my face and read my mind. Her guest list was already three hundred.

I felt sick, "No, no, I can't do that, Mika I really can't!" my voice so panic stricken I was nearly hyperventilating.

"Stop putting the fear of God in her," Mika snapped as he walked over to me and knelt by my chair. "Angel, do you trust me?"

"You know I do."

"Yes there will be lots of people in attendance, but baby it's only one day and it will be full of love and happiness. I can't wait to tell the world you are my wife," he said as he reassuringly stroked my hand. "Sweet heart, you have faced true fear head on and survived against the odds, you are my ultimate fighter so guests bearing gifts should be a walk in the park."

I could feel my blood pressure begin to lower just by the soothing tone of his voice. "You are right, it's our wedding day and that's all that matters." he kissed the back of my hand and smiled.

"Hell girl, we can do Vegas for a double bachelorette party?" Jazz screeched, causing all the men to suddenly look unimpressed.

Luca whispered to Mika, "Hey, you and Illa could do the same on the same weekend?" He wasn't quiet enough and Jazz spat, "Hell No! Girls only weekend, you guys can do Reno or Atlantic City?" We both knew we'd lose, how could we win when the brotherhood was calling the shots.

As I walked into the kitchen on Monday morning I was

handed my favourite mug filled with hot steaming coffee.

"Thank you Sonja, you are a star." I sipped the hot black liquid gold and then sighed. Mika had left for work already and Gavril was sat in his usual spot watching the news on TV "Morning G," I called.

"Morning Z," he winked asking, "So what's on the cards today?"

"I really need to go to the gym; it's been weeks since I worked out." I hadn't been since Stockholm, Erik not only owned *Skin Canvas* he had a part ownership in a small gym. Definitely not the stereo typical health spa that had ever green plants and aromatherapy, it was more of a male dominated, testosterone filled iron man gym, with its gun metal grey paintwork and the equipment wouldn't look out of place on a sci-fi movie set.

Erik knew all about my life and was the only outsider who knew everything that Adair Nano had done to me. He worked with me at the gym, building up my strength and agility and had given me definition without the bulk. Of course Mika had noticed how toned my body was and although he did appreciate it, he was a typical man saying have you been going to zumba or whatever it's called? Yeah Id' lied; Erik had been training me three times a week for five months in Krav Maga, an Israeli self defence technique used by the military and Mossad. It was a mixture of aikido, judo and boxing along with fight training. It was gruelling and I had never worked so hard but Erik told me I was a natural fighter, that must be the Bazin DNA. I loved it and by the time I flew back home I could really kick some serious ass.

"Yeah, which one would you like to go to?" Gavril queried. I could read his mind, *God what girlie spa does she want to go to?*

"Your gym."

"What?"

I laughed, "You heard me, the place you work out at?"

He looked confused, "They don't do aerobics or shit like that there!"

"I don't want that." Then I told him all about Erik and he seemed very impressed.

"Krav Maga, that's some pretty serious shit Izzy."

I couldn't help my smile, "I know, do you know it?" I asked hopeful.

"Yes I do."

I was all excited by that, "Will you carry on my training since I don't have Erik?"

Gavril gave me a really proud grin, "It would be my pleasure and what ever keeps you safe?"

That led nicely into my next request, "Good I'm pleased you feel that way because I'd also like to learn how to shoot?"

He now looked unsure, "I'll have to run that one by Mika first, but for now let's hit the gym."

We pulled up in a part of town I'd never been to before, the surrounding buildings looked derelict and in need of repair. If I'd have been on my own I wouldn't have even stopped the car let alone gotten out. Gavril walked to the heavy looking metal door that had red paint flaking off in patches.

"Ready?"

"Shit, is this it, is this your gym?" I was astonished, which made him laugh.

"It's inviting isn't it?" He pulled open the door to reveal a large sign, which read *welcome to Body Torque.*

From the outside you would never have believed what was on the inside, "Why is it so hidden away?"

Gavril looked disappointed, "Because we don't want outsiders." I could have kicked myself, I knew that!

The gym was very much like Erik's but ten times the size, it had the same grey colour scheme, similar state of the art equipment and the aroma of male pheromones and sweat heavy in the air. I counted ten men working out and recognised most of them, even if I didn't know them by name. In the middle of the room was a cage fighting ring with three men inside I didn't know at all. Two guys fighting looked younger than me and I gathered the older one was the trainer and as soon as he spotted us he exited the ring and hobbled over towards us.

"Gav, morning, and who may I ask is this?" he seemed a little put out probably because I was a female.

"Riku, this is Izzy."

The man's face changed to one of shock, "Mika's Izzy?" Gavril nodded.

"Hello Izzy welcome, I'm Riku the gym's manager, how can I help you today?"

"I need to train, it's been weeks since I worked out last, Gavril is going to help me."

He looked at Gavril for confirmation, "She's learning Krav Maga and I want to see how much she knows?"

The smile Riku gave me was so patronizing I wanted to slap it off his face, "Oh I'd like to see that," he sniggered.

"I'll gladly show you, where can I change?"

"We don't have a female changing room but you can use my office, that's where Katia leaves her things when she comes."

"Thanks," I said, trying to sound grateful but it came out more annoyed instead.

Quickly stripping I changed into my usual work out gear, black Lycra three quarter cut off's, a sports bra and a black Y-backed t-shirt that showed off my artwork. I tied my hair into a high pony tail that flashed off my little guardian angel and walked out bare foot to find Gavril already waiting for me by the cage. He'd changed into shorts and a tight white vest, he was covered in ink. I don't know why that surprised me, probably because I'd never seen him in anything but a suit.

"Izzy lets see what you've got?" He sounded really encouraging and that made me feel excited.

After thirty minutes every man in the place had stopped their work out's and were now circling the cage watching and cheering me on. Not to sound too big headed but I shocked the shit out of Gavril and Riku by my knowledge and ability. My sparring partner was a guy called Jack who had been in the cage when we'd arrived; he was cocky to start off with when Gavril called him into the ring to fight me.

"Gavril there is no way I'm hitting the Boss's lady."

"Ha... you better try to or else she'll kill you."

After I'd knocked his ass on the canvas a few times all his cockiness evaporated and he really tried to fight me, a few times he landed a good punch but I never hit the floor once.

"Shit Gavril, did you know she was this good?" Riku asked.

"Fuck no, I had no idea," he was literally fit to burst with pride.

"Where the fuck did she learn Krav Maga, she's so fast and agile?"

"Some guy in Sweden apparently."

Riku was watching on transfixed, "He must have been a pro," Gavril could only nod in agreement, "She has got some awesome moves."

The two of them stood in amazement. Riku sucked air in through his clenched teeth as she leaped up effortlessly spinning around and kicked Jack in the side of his head so quickly the poor young guy didn't know what hit him, till he was bouncing on the canvas once more.

Riku leaned in to Gavril, "She may be small but she's deadly."

Gavril heard his cell ring and went to answer, "Hey Boss."

"Where the hell is Izzy?" Mika yelled.

"She's with me, why?"

"Because I've called her five times and she hasn't picked up?"

Gavril could hear the panic in his voice.

"Boss she's OK, in fact she's more than OK."

That only made Mika madder, "Where the fuck are you?"

"At the gym, she's in the cage beating the shit out of poor Jack," Gavril snickered.

"WHAT, my gym?" He felt Mika's rage surging down the line.

"Seriously Boss you need to see her, she's fucking awesome."

"I'm on my way, and Gavril if she gets hurt *you will die!*" That was not an idle threat and it made Gavril's guts knot.

Mika must have driven like Mario Andretti to have made it to the gym in less than ten minutes. Izzy was so focused she never noticed him or Luca enter. Mika immediately saw the small cut above her right eye and felt his blood temperature rise. The men around the ring were all cheering as they watched Jack face plant the mat.

"Jesus Christ Mika did you know she could fight like that?" Luca asked in awe.

Gavril watched Jack take another pummelling and saw the instant the lights went out behind his eyes.

"Time!" he yelled handing Izzy a towel, "Riku take care of Jackie boy." He turned his attention to her, "Izzy! Holy shit girl," he hugged her spinning her around.

I was out of breath and panting heavily when Gavril spun me round, I so needed that. Talk about an adrenaline rush, I was so pumped.

"Izzy, Mika and Luca are here," he whispered, giving me a heads up. Looking round to find them I could not wipe the massive cheesy smile from my face.

"Hey guys."

Mika never gave me chance to leave the cage, he'd already entered and was now standing right in front of me cupping my face.

"You're bleeding!"

I managed to pull away from him, "It's a small nick, I'm fine, really," but he was going into full blown alpha mode.

"What the hell were you thinking Gavril?" he yelled so hard I swear he was going to burst a blood vessel.

"Mika, for God sake - it's my life, and this," I pointed around the cage, "was my choosing because I'm really good at it and I love it." That he could not deny.

"But Izzy you could get hurt really bad."

"That's true I could, but with what I already know and what Gavril will teach me, no one will ever do to me what that fucker Adair did ever again."

That seemed to strike a cord in him, "Angel you were amazing, where did you learn that?"

His voice had now switched to one of genuine pride.

"In Stockholm, Erik taught me."

"I really need to meet this man and thank him," he didn't seem jealous but was dead serious.

"You just might, because I'm inviting him and the guy's to the wedding."

That honestly made him laugh, "Let's get that cut looked at," he added.

As we stepped out of the ring I caught Mika giving Gavril a murderous glare.

"Hey you!" I stopped him dead in his tracks as I poked him hard in the chest. "You have two choices buddy, one: You can accept that Gavril is my teacher as well as my minder and you will not punish him whenever I get hurt. Or two: I go back to Sweden and let Erik continue to train me, pick one?" I snarled and by the defeated sigh that came from him I knew I'd won this fight and I winked slyly at Gavril.

Sitting in Riku's office while he cleaned and tapped the cut up, we chatted, my first impression of him had changed.

"Izzy you certainly put me in my place, you really impressed me, tell me about this Erik?"

Just thinking about Erik and the guy's made me smile, "Oh he's a 6'7, blond, mouth-watering Viking hunk who lives in Sweden, and he's a retired pro fighter and an artist."

I couldn't help but notice Mika who was now silently fighting his malevolence.

"It's a real shame he doesn't live here, I'd hire him on the spot," Riku said oblivious to Mika torment. "If you become a regular visitor to this establishment, that would be two women using the gym and I'll have to look at getting a female locker-room?"

"With a shower?" I pushed.

"I'll have to have a word with the Boss?"

We both looked at Mika and once again I heard that defeated sigh. Riku left us, satisfied with the first aid he'd just performed.

"Are you not changing?" Mika asked, probably hoping for a personal strip tease.

"No it's pointless; I'll shower and change at home, you could always join me?"

"Believe me babe I would if I could, but sadly I have a meeting at one, but I promise to share a bath with you tonight."

Outside, Mika watched Gavril and I drive away.

"What did he say to you?" Gavril asked anxiously.

"I'm getting a female locker-room and shower," I announced proudly.

Gavril nearly crashed the car he laughed so hard.

"Did Luca say anything to you?" I asked.

Eventually when he'd finally composed himself he told me all about the guy's who had been working out, and how I'd blown them away with my skills.

"Luca thought Mika was going to skin me alive, hell I expected that too."

This time I was the one laughing, "When are you gonna mention teaching me to shoot?"

Gavril looked aghast, "Shit Izzy, let the man recover from this first, one shock at a time, I promise I will."

CHAPTER TWENTY-SEVEN

Christmas was fast approaching again and tomorrow would mark the anniversary of my abduction. As I reflected on the past year I couldn't believe just how far I'd come and how much I had grown, both physically fitter and stronger than I'd ever been. Mentally I was mostly at peace with everything, but maybe I still had a few demons I needed to bury once and for all. I had started feeling like I was being pulled psychically and the reason why was I had to return to the place I'd been held and tortured in, my nightmares had started a few weeks ago and in the dream, the house was like Norman Bates' in Psycho, the big scary one up on the hill. I'd been told it was a small cabin in the woods but I needed to see it for myself and put that fear to rest. I wanted to go alone, it was my fear to face, no one else's but shit, could you imagine the apocalyptic argument that would create, and I didn't know exactly where the cabin was, I only knew it was near Battle Creek.

Hailstones pelting on the window woke me; Mika had already left for work so I took a quick shower and dressed in jeans and a warm jersey, with my furry Ugg boots that Mika really hated. I purposely chose warm and comfortable attire for a day of travel on a cold wet miserable day, and my mood matched the weather, dark and unpredictable. I heard the TV on in the kitchen.

"Morning Iz, what's on the cards today?" Gavril called out asking his usual question.

"Christmas shopping," I replied, only to get the normal male reaction, as he slumped back in his chair and sulked, "and I'm driving," that only pushed the knife further into his back.

We'd only been on the road thirty minutes before Gavril became suspicious.

"Where are we going?" he asked.

The guilt I felt from the deception made me feel queasy.

"Don't be mad?"

That was all it took to watch him visibly stiffen and get his full attention.

"I need you to tell me exactly where Adair's cabin is?"

"WHAT?" he yelled.

"Do you know it's a year today since I was taken there? Please, I need to see it; I have to exorcise the demons that have been plaguing me."

He looked angry but really sad at the same time.

"Stop the fucking car now."

"No, Gavril please, I've built this fucking place up so much in my mind that it terrifies me, I just have to see what it really is, a small insignificant log cabin and not Dracula's lair."

It was now Gavril's turn to fight his demons. "I understand Izzy, I do, but I have to call Mika, you must realise that?"

I did and I nodded, too choked up to speak but I never deviated from my mission and kept driving towards Battle Creek while Gavril called Mika.

"Gav what's she done now?" he said sounding amused, I must be gaining a reputation.

"Boss I've got you on speaker."

"Why?" Mika's voice once again changed to worry.

Gavril glanced over at me, "Well Izzy is driving to... erm... to Battle Creek."

"What, why, why do you want to go *there* Izzy?"

"Because I have to, it's the only way to stop the nightmares, I have to see the place," my voice croaked.

"Izzy pull the car over," Mika instructed and I started to get annoyed.

"Do you know what today is, do you realise it's a year since he took me, I have to do this"

"Angel why didn't you tell me, I'd have taken you, fuck Izzy I have nightmares about that place too."

I never thought about him being affected, and by the look in Gavril's eyes he had also been haunted by this place. Nobody had ever told me their side of that awful story.

"I'm sorry I thought you'd think I was just being a drama queen, I didn't mean to be selfish." I was so confused now, "Mika I still have to go."

"I know you do, Gav where are you now?"

"About three miles from the Gas N Go we stopped at."

"Right I know where that is, pull into the I-Hop and wait for me."

My heart grew, Mika was coming with me. "I love you Mika, thanks."

"Anything for you babe, you know that."

We found a secluded booth and ordered coffee; while we waited Gavril gave me his side of the story. From the moment he discovered Mandy driving Bertie, up until the time he walked into the room where they'd found me, and for the first time I felt sorry for someone other than myself. Seeing it from their point of view and for once it didn't register that it was me lying on the bed. I just ached for him, watching the pain in his eyes and holding his hand I squeezed it.

"I'm so sorry."

"Izzy I want to burn that fucking place to the ground."

He also told me the four of them had sat and talked about it, kind of like therapy and that made perfect sense, I had learnt it was better to talk about it than let it fester and consume you. He also told me everyone that had been involved in Adair's plan, no matter how small, no longer required oxygen as he put it, and that included Ruth. I had found out more in the last forty five minutes than I had in a whole year.

We sat in comfortable silence, contemplating our confessions. Gavril was the only person other than Erik and Dr Hurst I had told what had really happened to me and by the time I'd finished he was clearly fighting to keep his emotions in check. I completely trusted and respected this man and felt as safe with him as I did with Mika, I also knew my secret would remain just be that, a secret. As a black SUV appeared in the distance I just knew it was Mika and I received confirmation when it signalled to turn into the I-Hop.

"He's here," I nodded towards the approaching car, giving Gavril the heads up, "and he is not alone." I watched as three doors opened and Mika, Alex and Luca all stepped out, confusion marred my face.

"We all have, how did you phrase it, demons to slay." Gavril answered my unspoken question.

Let me set the scene for you, the I-Hop was pretty busy, full of people having lunch or just taking a simple break from driving, all quite happily chatting amongst themselves. Then the door opens causing the atmosphere inside the diner to change instantly, the air giving your skin goose bumps and the trepidation was quite palatable. Then three of the sexiest well ripped men in designer suits walk in making one hell of an entrance. The three are obviously related, all having the same mannerisms and those dark sultry *come fuck me* eyes, nearly every female and even some men in the diner were transfixed by them. The sexual static was tangible and you could see the fantasies playing out in their minds, simply by the expressions on their faces and speaking from experience we all love a bad boy and these men were certainly that, and more. That's what the arrival of the Remizov's caused every time they entered somewhere and I must say I did rather enjoy those moments.

From the moment Mika spotted me his eyes never veered from mine. "Izzy," he pulled me out of my chair and into his arms sounding so relieved.

I caught the look of envy on a few of the ladies faces as Mika wrapped his big powerful arms around me and that felt good. Soon all three were sat with us in the booth and Alex ordered coffee for them with a smile and a wink to the cute waitress.

"I have to ask but why are you guys all here?"

It was Mika who answered, "We all know what today is, did you honestly think we'd all forget that day. It was for me the worst day of my life, and I'm guessing that Gavril has told you that we have all sat down and discussed what happened on numerous occasions. Just like you needed to do with Dr Hurst, we needed to do the same but we did it the only way we could." He took a huge intake of breath, "There was a lot of bloodshed and lives lost over those few weeks, some I cared about but most I couldn't give a shit about and I would kill them again in a blink of an eye and still not lose a wink of sleep. You were the only one that mattered; I have seen and inflicted torture, caused inscrutable pain and committed cold blooded murder. It has never bothered me until that day, that fucking day I..." He couldn't carry on and I watched his lip quiver and eyes well up. It was my turn to be the strong one and comfort him, I held his hand, and kissed the back of it.

Luca took over, "We had never been on the receiving end before, until that day we walked in and found you. The room looked like a slaughter house and you were lying naked on that bed covered from head to toe in blood. We all thought you were dead; no one could have lost that amount of blood and survived. My heart broke at that moment. God only knows what it felt like for Mika?" Luca looked at his older brother then back to me,

"We hunted down and eliminated everyone who had any dealings with Nano, but the one we all wanted you beat us all to, and killed that sick fucker. To this day I still don't know where you found the strength, I am so proud of you Angel."

I felt all four pairs of eyes on me, watching me like I was under a microscope. This is what I needed to hear, to listen to everyone's own stories, and in some sick way it healed me.

I read the look that was on Gavril's face, he wanted me to tell them my side of this awful story and its true, the more you talk about it the easier it becomes. As I began to speak I felt the burden I'd been carrying around, lift. They knew most of what I'd endured but didn't know about the sexual abuse. Even though Adair had never managed to penetrate me with his disgusting rank penis I still classed what he did as rape.

Sometimes when I'm in a hot bath I can still see the teeth mark scars around my nipples, he'd bitten so hard that I felt sick just remembering the pain. He had stood over me and masturbated, ejaculating all over me calling me the vilest names as he came. His disgusting spunk had clumped and matted my hair, and as it dried the putrid stench made had me gag. Every time I used the toilet he would order me to spread my legs wide open, parting my lips so he could see. Nothing was private and he would stand there watching everything that came out of me, the shame and embarrassment I had felt was immense. The one time he had made me shower he made me do degrading things to myself, giving him his very own sick perverted private show and as I cried he pleasured himself at my expense.

When I finally finished I looked up for the first time, I had been focused on the salt shaker, not wanting to see their faces. I honestly don't think I could have told them if I'd been staring into any of their eyes. The expressions on their faces were disbelief and utter disgust and if possible, Gavril was even paler than the first time he'd heard it. Nobody spoke; I genuinely don't think they could find the right words to say. Luca abruptly stood up and excused himself from the table and headed towards the restrooms, and I felt the urge to apologize.

"I'm so sorry," came out as a whisper.

"Shit Izzy you have nothing to be sorry for," Alex sounded aghast.

"No, no, I'm not apologizing for what Adair did to me; he's the one who has to plead his case before God. I'm sorry you guys had to hear it, and causing you all such pain," my voice had been quiet and low but then I found it once more.

"Now I want to go to this fucking place and basically shut the damn door on the past forever."

Luca returned, his forehead and fringe still damp and the knuckles on his right hand were red and starting to swell, something had felt the wrath that had been burning inside of him. I stood up before he had chance to sit back down, it was my time to be strong and show compassion for the pain. I pulled this giant of a man down to my level and threw my arms around him.

"Luca, I won, I'm still here." I felt his lips kiss my temple, "Yeah Angel, you did."

As we all left the diner Mika asked, "Are you OK babe?"

"I will be," I said, trying my hardest to reassure him.

The mood in the car was quiet and sombre for the rest of the drive, I watched the scenery pass by while Mika and Gavril small talked. I think I zoned out for bit until I felt the car turn onto a dirt road, "Are we nearly there?" I asked.

"It's just over that rise," Mika pointed.

My chest tightened as we reached the crest of the hill and I got my first look at my *Bete Noire*. Gavril stopped the car a short distance away and Luca pulled up along side us. For a moment I just sat and stared out at the insignificant, small log cabin, the place that had scarred me both physically and mentally. It was now time to reclaim myself once and for all.

CHAPTER TWENTY-EIGHT

I stood in the middle of all the guys, who were uncon-sciously surrounding me like a protective force field, with each one covering a point on the compass, all waiting to see what I was going to do. A tattered bit of crime scene tape still on the gate fluttered in the cold breeze, if you didn't know what hap-pened here it was obvious it was something bad. I approached the door and again there was more evidence with an unbroken police seal stuck to it. Gavril tried the door and no surprise it was locked. He swiftly kicked at it and the flimsy lock held no resistance and flew open. As the rancid stale air hit us, "God that's bad," Alex gagged, raising a handkerchief and covering his nose and mouth.

I entered into a small den like room, to the left was a tiny kitchen and on the counter top as well as in the sink were dirty dishes that may have once contained food but all that remained was just a pile of mouldy rotten mush, but that alone couldn't be the only thing causing the God awful stench. Nothing so far was familiar, in fact with a little TLC and a good clean this would be a sweet little get away cabin.

To the side of the kitchen was a passage way and as I began to walked down it the smell got considerably worse.

"Izzy wait, let me go in first," Mika said, as he pushed passed me before I had chance to respond. Luca and Gavril followed leaving me standing outside with Alex who had his hand on my arm gently restraining me.

Mika walked back to me. "It's a mess in there," he said as he took my hand, "You don't have to do this."

"I do Mika," and pulling my hand away from him I walked into the room that had imprisoned me.

Stopping inside I instantly remembered this place and my tormented hell came flooding back. The bed had been stripped leaving just the stained mattress and the handcuffs that had tied me to the headboard were also gone, probably bagged and tagged with the sheets as evidence. Blood splatter had sprayed up the walls and onto the ceiling, which had now turned a shitty brown colour. Inching towards the bed I noticed the massive dark stain on the carpet where the sick fucker had bled out. Amassing as much saliva as I could I spat on the dried blood patch, "I hope you burn in the fires of hell for eternity!" My rage was reaching fever pitch and then I saw the door that lead to the place that haunted me the most.

Entering the doorway caused my nausea to increase and tears stung my eyes, then seeing that toilet and shower set the tears cascading down my cheeks, the room still made me feel dirty and ashamed. Mika sensed my mood change from utter anger to complete despair and he quickly scooped me up into his warm loving arms.

"Angel, you are still the bravest person I know."

I buried my head into his chest, not wanting to see this hell-hole anymore and sobbed like a child. He lifted my chin up and kissed the tip of my nose.

"This place needs to burn," I whimpered.

"I can arrange that baby."

"Then I'm done, get me out of here please."

I can't remember walking out but the next minute I was standing outside with the cold wind blowing through my hair. I just closed my eyes and let Mother Nature cleanse me by blowing all the ghosts away, healing me. The five of us stood and stared at this place that had given us all nightmares.

"I want to burn this evil place down to the ground, today," I said, feeling my rage resurfacing.

"Izzy I will..." I cut him off mid sentence.

"NO! Listen to me God damn it! I have to do this. Get me something that will set this place ablaze?" I snarled, I had mastered Mika's lethal tone and nobody dared argue.

Gavril disappeared round the back of his car and reappeared with a gas can.

"Let me prep the burn, I know where to pour the accelerant for maximum results." Not saying a word I just glared, "Izzy, you can light it I swear," he actually sounded afraid of me.

"OK," I nodded, as we watched him disappear back into the cabin.

"Do you know who owns this place?" I asked.

"The last owner died leaving no other living relatives, so the state will take ownership," Mika informed.

"So who owned it?" not letting it go, I honestly think he didn't want to tell me.

"Ruth's father," he finally said, as he watched me intensely.

"Oh I hated that dirty skank; I hope she's keeping that sick son of a bitch company in hell."

Gavril came back, "It's all ready for you to light it up," he said, as he handed me a bottle filled with gas with a rag poking out of the top.

"So this is a Molotov cocktail," I quipped nonchalantly and the guys seemed impressed as well as a little worried. I lit the rag and threw the bottle like an NFL quarterback and as it crashed through a window I screamed on the top of my lungs, ***"Have a drink on me you sick mother fuckers,"*** over the deafening whoosh so everyone could hear me as the fire took hold.

Gavril had a hold on me and pulled me back to safety as the feeling of absolute satisfaction empowered me and I watched this awful place being engulfed in flames.

"Let's get the hell out of here before the cops and fire department show up?" Luca wisely suggested.

We must have broken every speed limit because within ten minutes we were flying down the interstate heading home, my body was still buzzing.

"Izzy you ok babe?" Mika stared at me curiously, probably because I couldn't wipe the big cheesy smile off my face.

"Never better."

After 365 days, I had finally reclaimed my soul and the future looked bright and so much more promising.

Gavril followed Luca into the driveway and dropped Mika and I off, before heading home he got out and came around to me pulling me tightly to him.

"I'm so proud of you; I hope you have slayed all your demons now?"

I sighed into his solid chest, "Yes, and thank you for not just being my minder but my friend."

He kissed the top of my head, "I'll see you tomorrow?"

Mika called after him, "Gavril you have earned an extra day off."

"Thanks Boss, call if you need me," and we waved as he drove away.

As the four of us walked into the house we were met with the mouth-watering aroma of Sonya's beef goulash simmering away.

"Good you are all home, dinner will be ready in twenty minutes," she smiled at us.

That gave us just enough time for a quick shower and a change of clothes, the smell of smoke lingered around us and I really needed to wash the last remnants of Battle Creek down the drain.

Mika knew never to just walk into the bathroom when I was

in there, and now he knew the reason why.

"Hurry up water hog!" he yelled from the other side of the door.

I smiled at him as I opened it, "All yours," as I was met with a naked hunk.

"It's a real shame I'm so hungry or we'd never leave the bedroom."

My eyes devoured him, and he gave me a quick teasing kiss as he walked into the bathroom leaving the door wide open, "I'll be five minutes," he yelled as I heard the water turn on.

When he emerged I was dressed and chewing at the bit, "Come on I'm starving and if we don't hurry Luca will eat everything?" That wasn't a lie, Luca could eat like a horse, and he should be sixty stone and morbidly obese.

We all sat around the table and we were joined by Jazz and Illa. After a wonderful meal I was full and satisfied and as I leaned back into my chair I said out of the blue, "What about February 1st?"

"What for?" Alex asked.

"For me to become Mrs Remizov."

Mika beamed as he put down his fork, "That sounds like the best day ever."

That would have been my Mom's birthday.

"Are you sure, it's only seven weeks away?"

Knowing that would be cutting it close, "It's no problem at all Angel."

I had always dreamed I'd have a winter wedding with the snow making it all feel magical and mystical, it just seemed perfect to me.

The next day I Skyped Anka and seeing her beautiful face fill the screen was wonderful, I had missed her so much over the past few months.

"Hey sweet cheeks, how you been?" She sang.

"Fantastic, but missing you everyday, anyway I need to ask, what are you doing on February 1st?"

Shaking her head she said, "Nothing why?"

"Will you be one of my bridesmaids?"

She squealed her answer and so it was arranged, Anka would fly out and arrive on the Wednesday before the wedding. I had kept in touch with Erik and we would text all the time and spoke often, he was now like my *big*, big brother and I loved him so much. So when he said he and the guys were coming to the wedding I was more than overjoyed, he was going to see Anka and they would all fly out together. I was so excited when I told Mika but then he surprised the hell out of me by telling me to book and comp their stay in the Majestic where the wedding was being held, and everyone back in Sweden was thrilled by that news.

I remember the day Mika had asked if I had photos from my time in Stockholm and I showed him the hundreds I had saved on my laptop. He had been slightly stunned and that was putting it mildly. There were a few of the guys working at *Skin Canvas* and even some of Erik inking me that Joss had taken and I loved the total concentration on Erik's face. The others were all of us hanging out and lots from the club we all use to frequent, and if Erik wasn't cuddling me I was clinging on to him with of course those awful selfies. Erik and I were pouting and posing and you could tell even from the photos we had a really tight bond.

"That's Erik?" he asked, somewhat gob smacked.

"Yeah that's Erik," I said smiling, "My saviour."

He had helped me in the darkest time of my life, which wasn't just being taken to that cabin by Adair, but all of the fall out it created months after. I think Mika had a touch of the green eyed monster, and I squeezed his hand reassuringly.

"Hey, Erik helped me find my way back home and back to you," I said staring into his eyes, "And because of that I will always love him."

That was received with a warm smile.

"Izzy I can't wait to meet him and thank him personally for keeping you safe."

I couldn't wait for him to be able to.

CHAPTER TWENTY-NINE

Christmas came and went and all I could think about was the wedding, I shocked myself by just how much I was enjoying it. Our wedding was going to take place at the Majestic Hotel, the flagship hotel of the Redline Corp. The ceremony would be held in the spectacular conservatory room with its walls of windows, which let the light stream in and the views were out of this world, over looking the magnificent gardens and private lake. A few days prior to the big day, God granted me my wish and covered the city in a fresh blanket of deep snow, giving me the perfect setting form my winter wedding.

Mika had organised almost everything, including the guest list since mine consisted of ten people, seven from Sweden and three from Milwaukee, Rita my Gran's friend, her husband Les and their Granddaughter Ellie, who would be driving them here.

When I was told about the security arrangements I was a little astounded at first but once I thought about it I really shouldn't have been surprised at all. It was a massive undertaking with all the Pakhan's from other states and Russia bringing their own detail, and Mika's own men would be in full force.

The hotel would be closed to the public for a week and would be guarded better than Fort Knox; you'd honestly swear the President was going to be in attendance. Every contractor that had any part in the wedding arrangements was vetted to the moon and back, even all my guests. All of Mika's men wore the same style dark grey suit, earwigs and communicated by talking into their sleeves like the Secret Service or CIA agents, and even though you couldn't see, they were definitely packing more than one weapon.

I recognised most of the men from the gym and all smiled, some would even wink at me, which made my shadow growl back at them. Gavril was literally attached to my hip these last few days, he even came with Jazz and I to the bridal shop for my dress fittings. Actually, he was a real Godsend, giving us his honest opinions on all the gowns I had tried on and he'd played a major part in my final decision when I'd selected the perfect one, which we all agreed on was the most beautiful one of them all.

Jazz had jokingly said, "Gavril you are so coming with us when it's my turn to choose the perfect dress," to which he shook his head in complete despair.

The Wednesday I had been waiting for was here at last and as I sat in the passenger seat of one of the cars heading to the airport, I couldn't hold my excitement. My friends from Stockholm were scheduled to land at 3.45 p.m. and according to the website their plane was on time.

We parked up and Ivan, who'd been driving the other car came with us to the terminal to wait by the arrivals hall. If I had looked at my watch once I'd looked a thousand times, I would have sworn time had stopped. Then I heard Ivan gasp in awe.

"Shit! Gav, its Thor!"

Both men were taken a back at the sheer size of this guy who had just exited the sliding doors of the arrivals hall.

"Erik," I squealed as I ran to his open, welcoming, huge arms.

"Hey little one, I'm so pleased to see you."

We had a few seconds before the rest joined us and I was squashed in the middle of four Nordic blond Gods, practically blocking the way out. After all the greetings, kisses and hugs I finally found Anka, who had been catching up with Gavril and Ivan, both men seemed thrilled to see her again.

I quickly did the introductions, "Gavril, Ivan these four behemoths are, Erik, Joss, Mel and Si, the best tattoo artists in the world," and all four kissed me at the same time for that admittance, making the rest just laugh.

"These lovely ladies are Ima, who is with Mel, and Ava who is with Si."

Gavril and Ivan smiled and saluted them all, "Welcome to Detroit," Gavril said sincerely, while I just smiled like a deranged lunatic with happy tears in my eyes.

Gavril instructed the gang to follow him to the vehicles and as a true gentleman, he took Anka's luggage from her and carried it while the pair chatted. I was glued to Erik's side.

"I've missed you little one, Stockholm has been so quiet since you left."

"I miss you guy's every day," that was not a lie.

"Oh hey; I've got you a job offer!" I giggled.

"What... where?" he asked shocked.

"At the gym I go to, the manager was impressed by my Krav Maga techniques and asked who'd been teaching me, he was gutted when I told him you lived in Sweden, because he wanted to offer you a job on the spot."

Erik's deep laugh was wonderful to hear again, "It's always good to know you have options," he said, as he kissed the top of my head.

We pulled into the Majestic's parking lot and got everyone checked in and room cards issued. I had asked Anka to stay at the house with me but she declined saying, "I think it wiser if I stay here with this motley crew, you know the way Alex and I parted, it might cause a little tension at your home and I really don't want that?"

I could understand that, Alex had been in a foul mood ever since she'd left, he'd been like a bear with a sore head. You'd have thought it had been Anka who'd been the abrupt one and not him. Then when he found out she was coming to the wedding he'd become unbearable, asking me a ton of questions like, 'does she ever mention me?' 'Is she seeing anyone?' 'Is anything going on between her and Erik?' I answered all of them basically the same way, I don't know? I had never seen him so stressed out and I kept asking myself what will it be like when those two finally meet back up?

One thing was for sure, it was going to be entertaining to observe.

After the long flight, all the guy's were dead on their feet so they were heading in for an early night. We made plans to meet up tomorrow, have lunch here at the hotel before spending the day together and ending with them all meeting the Remizov clan for dinner back here at the Majestic. That would probably be the only time they would get to see Mika, Luca and Alex before the wedding, on Friday all the other guest's would start arriving and it would be madness ensuing. To be perfectly honest even I wouldn't see much of them till then either.

Anka had told the guy's all about the Motown museum and they all wanted to go and I never got tired of going there. Gavril and Ivan drove us where ever we wanted to go; Ivan had also been assigned to me until after the wedding to help Gavril out. Gavril actually allowed me to go unchaperoned inside the museum, he said, "You have four giants surrounding you, as well as Ivan and I outside so go, enjoy yourself and we'll be waiting here," as he ushered me inside.

Once inside Anka linked my arm, "I can't believe you're getting married in three days and you are as cool as a cucumber," she said, sounding impressed. Little did she know on the inside I was a nervous wreck.

"Well everything is sorted; all I have to worry about is not tripping up and face planting the floor, which had lately been a recurring nightmare."

"You'll be fine," she told me but my unconvincing laugh may have slightly ruined my cool exterior.

The day had been wonderful, relaxing and stress free. We walked around Belle Isle and even in the cold, it was picturesque, we had huge mugs of hot chocolate and marshmallows with cream to warm us all up, in a quaint little bistro as we watched the snow begin to fall.

"I hope it lays." I crossed my fingers.

We reminisced about my time in Stockholm, I truly did love all these guys, I wouldn't be where I am today if it wasn't for them, especially Anka and Erik, and because of that I had a big question to ask im once we were back at the hotel.

Stepping out of the car I asked, "Erik can I have a word, just you and me?"

He flung his arm around my shoulder, dwarfing me as he walked us into the bar. There was a blazing fire in the fire place and the heat was welcoming, making my face tingle.

Everyone else had headed up to the rooms for a nap before tonight, leaving just the two of us, a bartender and my shadow who I knew wasn't far away, I couldn't see him but I sensed he was around. We ordered a couple of beers and sat by the fire.

"I know we have only known each other a year but to me it feels like a lifetime. I was at the darkest point in my life when we first met and you helped me find the light again. You made me feel safe, protected and loved, and you built up my confidence and self esteem, giving me the strength to want to carry on, as well as an awesome tat! You were also the first person I felt truly at ease with and comfortable enough to open up and tell you what had really happened to me. Letting me pour out my heart and soul while you just listened and never once judged me, only wiped away my tears and by God there were plenty of those. You lovingly shielded me. Erik you are like the big brother I never had and I will always love you for that, you are and always will be a huge part of my life. So the reason why I asked for this little chat was that I have a request, I'd like to ask you... Will you give me away?"

The Lies That Secrets Desire

He was totally lost for words but his face spoke volumes and he nearly knocked over the table as he stood up pulling me to him, crushing me into his chest.

"Izzy I feel the same way about you, you are my family. Like you, I am the only one left but now I have a baby sister to look out for, to love and protect, always. I would be honoured and proud to walk you down the aisle but I'll never totally give you away." He gave me the most loving smile, "And if you ever need me, call and I'll come running."

That was all the confirmation I needed to hear, I loved this huge Viking so much. Out of the corner of my eye I saw my ever alert shadow standing watching so when Erik left me to rejoin the others Gavril escorted me home so I could get ready for tonight.

CHAPTER THIRTY

I was more apprehensive about tonight than I expected to be with sweaty palms and my stomach in knots, the whole nine yards and I just hoped and prayed that the two most important men in my life would get along. The bar inside the Majestic had been set up for dinner with a huge table dressed beautifully and although the hotel was now closed to the public, with the amount of activity happening you'd never believe it. Staff were all busy buzzing around, getting the hotel ready for all the VIP's who were due to arrive tomorrow, so it was less imposing to have a small get together and a meal in the warm welcoming bar rather than a large empty dining hall. All my Swedish friends were already there, eagerly waiting to meet the family. Anka and Erik had subtly told them about the elephant in the room, *The Mob* and thankfully they were all smart enough not to mention it.

Mika was usually the tallest person in any room so this must have been a first for him, he actually had to look up to see Erik's eyes.

"Welcome to my world," I whispered to him jokingly.

"Erik this is Mika, the love of my life, and Mika this is Erik my liberator and guardian."

Everyone in the room were all happily chatting away but slyly watching as the two biggest Alphas' in the room shook hands.

"Erik, there are no words I can say that will do justice for what you have done for Izzy and I. Thank you for keeping her safe, thank you for finding this lost woman who I am in love with, and breathing life back into her so she could return home and back to me."

Erik smiled and graciously nodded, "Mika we finally meet at last, thank you for the kind words but I cannot take all the praise, I was just the staff this little one needed to hold onto. I will always be that for her, she is such a warm and special person. You are one very lucky man; I hope you will never forget that?"

"I know and trust me I won't."

I was so overwhelmed my heart was fit to burst, these two men who loved me with all their hearts in complete admiration of one another, I couldn't have wished for any more.

Mika and Erik had hit it off and by the end of the night were both laughing, telling stories about my quirky little traits. Jazz then joined in and began telling them all tales from our mischievous youth, and our childish antics, some of which I'd forgotten about. Until she started talking about one story in particular, and I felt the colour instantly draining from my face.

"Oh my God! Jazz don't you dare?" I snarled but sadly I couldn't keep a straight face and that was like giving catnip to a cat, she couldn't stop herself.

So this is basically how I remember it. It had been the summer of Savas' and Petra's twenty fifth wedding anniversary and they had held and hosted a huge party at their home. Jazz and I had just turned thirteen and started to notice boys. Petra had allowed us to wear a little make-up, just some lip stick and blusher; we thought we were so grown up. It was the last summer before Luca left for college, and Mika was home on summer vacation. That was the year I started to see Mika differently and my childhood crush grew into absolute love and adoration. As Jazz and I stepped out into the garden we had found Mika and Luca straight away, talking to two girls about their own age and these two skanks were flirting outrageously with them. We walked towards the four of them and were given the cold shoulder; the big brothers did not want their baby sister and friend hanging around and messing with their mojo and made it perfectly clear to go away. I was mad as hell and maybe a little jealous as we both sulked and walked away. I was stood in the kitchen when I heard giggling coming from the hallway and poked my head out just in time to see Mika sneaking one of the girls upstairs to his room. I may have only been thirteen but I knew what they were going to be getting up to and made it my mission to stop it at any cost.

"So Izzy found my Mom and told her in a distressed voice that she had heard Mika slip in his bathroom and couldn't get to him because the door was locked from the inside."

By now my head was in my hands and I was cringing, that was until the table erupted in laughter and not by my mortification, but by Mika's reaction. Even I laughed when I saw his mouth gaping wide open and his eyes bulging out on invisible stalks.

"Holy Mother of God! You were the one who grassed me up?"

Flabbergasted he looked at me for confirmation and I nodded, blinded with tears of laughter.

"Fuck me Izzy, I still have nightmares about that day," he began to chuckle.

Jazz asked the question we were all dying to know.

"Why, what happened?"

Mika actually blushed.

"Shit this is gonna be good," Jazz winked at me all excited.

"Christ how do I say this in front of my future wife? Well shit, she caused it so here goes..." he suddenly erupted in laughter and it took him a good five minutes to compose himself.

"OK, OK, well the said girl, who will remain nameless, was on her knees. I'll let you all use your imaginations to fill in the blanks, but it was safe to say I had reached the point of no return just as my Mom comes flying right through my bedroom door.

The girl jumps up, choking and spits everything out all over my Mom's shoes, before locking herself in the bathroom, probably dying from embarrassment and leaving me standing there naked from the waist down with everything hanging out facing my very angry Mom. My Mom then proceeded to take her shoes off and throw the metal tipped heeled stilettos at me with perfect aim, they ricocheted off my head, and let me just say they hurt like hell. She went ballistic, totally banshee'd on me, cursing and yelling, I'd never heard her swear till that day, I always thought my Dad was the scary one but Mom put him to shame that day, she scared the shit out of me. Her parting words were, *'don't you dare let me see you again tonight and get my fucking shoes cleaned,'* as she slammed the door so hard it knocked the dart board off the back of it!" By now the whole table had erupted in fits of laughter, some were even crying.

"Do you know I made Alex's life a living hell for a year, I thought it had been him who'd ratted me out."

With tears in my eyes I turned to Alex who was nodding, "I'm so sorry Alex," before I burst out giggling once more.

"Never mind apologising to him, what about me, you scarred me for life?" Mika joked.

I leaned into him and whispered, "I have a lifetime to make it up to you," before kissing his cheek.

It was close to one in the morning by the time we all made it home, it had been a fantastic night and it couldn't have gone any better. I knew I had some grovelling to do, just like the saying goes 'what goes around comes around,' and it was time to pay my dues. The one thing I remembered that Mika should have done all those years ago was to lock the bedroom door.

Friday morning was surreal, the calm before the storm. Mika and I had a lovely quiet breakfast for once, we got to spend about an hour together before he left to meet and greet his guest's. I knew this would probably be the last I saw of him before the big event. The plan today was to get me moved into the penthouse suite at the Majestic, it would give me more time to spend with my friends and hopefully get a chance to see Mika as well. My only guest's still to arrive were Rita, Les and Ellie, who would be here some time tomorrow afternoon. Thank God for Jazz and Gavril, the two of them kept me sane, we had set up a makeshift headquarters in the suite for the bridal party who would all be getting ready there on Sunday. It was definitely big enough for the four of us and our entourage, which had grown since we had sequestered all the girls from the hotels salon to work their magic on us.

The flowers would be delivered to the hotel tomorrow and stored in the kitchens cold room, so the only thing left was my gown. Chantelle Weller the young designer, would be bringing it on Sunday and she would also be helping me get ready, that was everything sorted so in the words of *Retro 73…Bring it on!*

CHAPTER THIRTY-ONE

Mika was also staying at the Majestic but in another wing we literally couldn't get any further away from each other and still be in the same building if we tried. I heard through the grapevine that there was going to be an unofficial bachelor party held in one of the private banquet rooms, away from prying eyes and it was strictly brotherhood admittance only.

I sent him a text,

There better be no strippers!!!

He replied quickly.

No strippers, anyway you are the only woman who gets my blood pumping.

Nice answer, I had to give him that one.

I decided if he could have an unofficial do, so could I.

"Jazz, how about one last blow out?"

She jumped up clapping; so I guess that was a yes.

As we turned to Gavril, he was already on his cell, he'd actually grassed me up while I was standing in front of him and then he had the audacity to hand me the phone!

"Izzy, what are you up to now?" he had an amused tone in his voice

"Why- What do you mean, you make me sound like a naughty school girl?" I huffed.

"Well if the shoe fits," he chuckled back.

"Hey mister, we are just going to *Red Square,* I think the guys will love it and Jazz said there's a great band on tonight."

I heard him sigh, "OK, fine, but Gavril and Ivan will accompany you, and Isabelle, NO sexy dresses."

That made me smirk, "Will I get to see you before we go?" I asked hopefully.

"I'll meet you in the lobby bar for a drink around seven OK?"

I grabbed at it, "See you then."

At eight p.m. there were two SUV's parked and waiting for us out front, the valet handed both sets of keys to Gavril and Ivan. Before we made it to the cars, I tugged on Gavril's arm.

"Sorry you are gonna miss Mika's soiree and all those strippers!" subtlety was not one of my best qualities.

"I'd rather be going with you to *Red Square* than sit in a room full of all the top bosses trust me… and there are no strippers."

"Ooh, good catch," I teased.

"Come on give me some credit, how could I miss that blatantly obvious fishing expedition Iz?" he laughed.

Well the only way I was going to find out about tonight is if Mika was going to tell me, and was it really something I wanted to know?

The band playing at Red Square was real good and played all my favourite classic rock anthems, I was in seventh heaven singing along and dancing like a groupie. Gavril was doing his job and keeping an ever watchful eye on me and taking note of my alcohol intake. For once I was actually being good, only because of the ton of things I had to do tomorrow and you really do not want a hangover while you're getting waxed and plucked trust me. Throughout the night Gavril's cell had been beeping.

"You're popular tonight… a girlfriend?" I asked curiously.

"No, just a fretting husband to be."

That made me feel all warm and loved, even at his own do, he was still thinking about me.

If playing it cool was a recognised Olympic sport, Anka

would be a gold medallist. Alex had been trying his damnedest all Friday night but was failing miserably, she was polite and friendly, even if she was basically treating him like an acquaintance she'd met only once, she wasn't giving him an inch. Alex had thought what he had done was the right thing, he knew he'd hurt her by letting her think she meant nothing to him. In his own way he was protecting her, how could he possibly tell her the truth, look at what had happened to Izzy, he just couldn't put Anka at risk. Their family had secrets and it was different with Izzy, she had been part of it, even if she wasn't aware of it till recently. Anka had no idea and that's just how Alex wanted to keep it, well that was then, now it was a different story.

She was the only woman who made his heart race and his blood pump through his veins, she was in his dreams and played a major roll in his fantasies, she haunted him, she was his one true love. Alex knew Anka had lied to him about the other affairs she'd had while she'd been here, it was her own self defence system coming into play but if it *were* true he would have hunted them down and sliced them wide open, with a sadistic smile as he did it. He had to bring out the big guns if he stood any chance in winning Anka back, he needed help from his sister... God help him!

On Saturday morning he was sat in the kitchen waiting for her to get up, but when Illa came down dressed for the gym he'd asked, "Hey you heading out, is Jazz still in bed?"

"Hey morning, yeah and yeah she's still sleeping, see you later."

Perfect, he made her a fresh mug of coffee and took it up for her, knocking but not waiting for an answer he walked in.

"Jazz, wake up I've brought you coffee."

Jazz pulled the sheet down uncovering one eye, "Thanks, but why?"

Alex flopped down onto the bed totally deflated, "Sis I really screwed up, and I need your help!" Now he had her attention she sat up intrigued.

"Ooh do tell."

He told her everything, not leaving a stone unturned.

"Shit Alex, what do you want me to do?" she said sounding daunted.

"I just want you to talk to her, convince her that I did what I did with her best interests at heart, just get her to at least talk to me so I can at least try to get her to forgive me," he looked like an abused puppy.

"Alex, this deserves more than a lousy cup of coffee," he sensed her caving.

"Anything... anything at all, just name it."

"I can't think of anything, lets just say you owe me one... no two."

"Done," he snapped.

"Woo, hoo, I want this one in writing first, I do not trust you." Jazz had been burned by Alex on more than one occasion.

"Seriously Jazz?"

"You bet," as she found a pen and drafted a quick contract. "Sign here and initial here," she pointed to the crosses on the page before handing him the pen.

"Shit Jazz, you're like Sheldon off the Big Bang Theory." He signed and was now deep in debt to her, and may God have mercy on his soul.

Rita, Les and Ellie arrived just before four on Saturday afternoon and I was thrilled to see them both looking so well, they had done so much for Gran and I, and I couldn't thank them enough. I managed to spend a good hour with all of them, we had afternoon tea in the sun lounge and caught up. Ellie, their Granddaughter was a real funny lady with striking good looks, tall (well compared to me everyone was tall) ash blond hair, cut short in a pixie style that really suited her and those stunning almond shaped hazel eyes. She was a head turner for sure and Gavril had certainly noticed, in all the time I had known him he'd never once lost his cool until today, it was hilarious to watch.

On my last night of single-dom we decided to have a girlie fest in the penthouse. Jazz and Mandy were going to spend the night here with me so we invited all the girls, including Ellie, since Rita and Les had called it a night already. We had tons of junk food and enough bucks fizz to fill the swimming pool, so while we drank and ate we gossiped like teenagers, sitting around in PJ's and watching a Bradley Cooper marathon, it was simply perfection.

Jazz eventually got Anka alone, *Operation Redemption* was about to go live.

"Hey bitch," (the normal greeting between them) "Have you spoken to Alex yet?"

"We've said hi... Why?"

"Oh I'm just being nosy, you know me. I just thought you might, you know, hook up again?"

That caused Anka to burst out laughing, "What! Come on Jazz you know the saying, once bitten twice shy, so that would be a big fat no!"

Jazz had to change tactics and play dumb, "I thought you really liked him, had something special?"

That just seemed to piss her off, "I did until he treated me like a cheap two bit whore, I know he's your brother but Jazz he's a fucking asshat!"

Jazz knew this was going to be hard but it was more like mission impossible.

"I totally agree but before you give up on him for good and chew me a new one, will you hear me out?"

Anka gave her the dead eye, "Go on then."

"Great, so how much did Izzy tell you about our families?" and so it began.

Izzy had told her most of what had gone on with her but hadn't delved too much into the Remizov's or the brotherhood, but Anka being Anka had put the rest together quite accurately actually.

"So I'm guessing Mika is the big bad boss man?" she said.

"No, not at all, here in Michigan he is," as Jazz proceeded to tell her as much as she could and watched Anka's demeanour change right in front of her eyes.

"So you are telling me he did what he did to protect me?" she said, sounding astounded.

"Yes, in his mind he thought he was doing the right thing, Anka honestly I have never seen him like this before over anyone, he really does love you, he's been a gigantic pain in the ass for months now. All he wants is a chance to explain himself to you?"

Anka was touched, "Ok I'll talk to him, but I'm not promising anything."

Jazz clapped, "Fantastic, that's all he wants."

The hangover part one had just finished when I heard Jazz squeal and clap, so walking over to them I asked, "What are you two up to?"

"Oh nothing, just gossiping and ordering more supplies for the Bradley festival," Jazz said, as she flung her arm around me, "Now go put part two on, it's my favourite?"

You didn't have to ask me twice to put more Mr Cooper on. Just before two a.m. and four movies later, everyone left, apart from Mandy and Jazz. Mandy had a bedroom to herself, while Jazz bunked with me like old times; we chatted and giggled for ages.

"Hey Bride, time for some beauty sleep, cause you won't get

much tomorrow night!" she sniggered.

"True, I hope," chuckling back.

We were woken up abruptly by Mandy and room service wheeling in breakfast, "Rise and shine, it's a gorgeous day and I hope you have both recharged those batteries because it's gonna get Crazzy!" she sang.

Mandy was a morning person... we weren't. I glanced at Jazz and she looked like I felt.

"All that bucks fizz was a bad idea," I whimpered.

"Hey Izzy, there is a note and gift box for you?" Mandy handed it to me and I instantly recognised Mika's handwriting.

"What is it?" Jazz asked, now wide awake.

As soon as I read it I burst out laughing.

"Does my man know me or what?" The note said:

Just a small token to let you know I'm always thinking about you :) <3.'

Inside the box were eight Advil tablets, "Give me two of them," Jazz snatched them and swilled them down with her orange juice and I followed suit. After a quick wash and teeth brushed we all sat on the bed and ate breakfast.

"It's now nine so we have about an hour before the madness begins." Mandy was not wrong.

CHAPTER THIRTY-TWO

Mandy hadn't exaggerated at all, it was utter bedlam, organised chaos. The penthouse looked like a disaster zone, two hairstylists, two beauticians, a photographer capturing the moments I didn't want to forget and bless them, we had two hotel waitresses who were life savers, running around keeping us all refuelled, plus the four of us.

I managed to escape the pandemonium for thirty minutes and got to soak in the tub while the bridesmaids were being worked on and I tried to relax, a big emphasis on the word tried. Once I was dried off and dressed in my new ravishing lingerie and unflattering bathrobe, I entered the lounge to the sound of Lady Gaga booming out of the stereo, it certainly got the party vibe going.

Sitting back, I just watched the magic happen, all of their dresses were hung up on a mobile clothes rail, I had chosen for them a light gold metallic, boat neck design, classic floor length, highlighting the elegant and classy cowl back, it had a blend of old Hollywood vintage flair and the shining sequins were the perfect finishing touch. All three looked graceful and exquisite.

I had sequestered the master bedroom for myself to get ready in and just before the stylist and beautician were about to start on me, Chantelle arrived with my breath-taking gown. Only Jazz and Gavril had seen it, and she wheeled it in to the bedroom on the rail she had brought with her, keeping it hidden under its protective sleeve. Only when we were alone did she unzip it and like the first time I saw it, I was awe-inspired.

It was an Alencon and Venetian white lace, tulle ball-gown design, with a Queen Anne neckline and basque waistline. Chantelle had entwined flecks of the same colour gold as my bridesmaid's dresses into it, the satin buttons ran from the top down to the small of my back, leading into the chapel length train.

"It looks even more beautiful than I remember," I sighed, all dreamily.

She smiled impishly, "I've tweaked it and added crystals to make it sparkle like ice and snow, perfect for a winter wedding." She had made it look so delicate and even enchanting and I could not wait to wear it.

My hair was curled and pinned up in an elegant chignon with fresh winter flowers, twigs and mistletoe weaved into it with Swarovski crystals that looked like icicles. Stepping in front of the mirror I was overwhelmed and blown away by this wood-land fairy staring back, I looked so celestial, even ethereal; it was the first time in my life I felt beautiful, even my make-up was flawless. I could hear everyone outside getting impatient; I was dying to see them as much as they were to see me.

"Ready?" Chantelle asked. I nodded but before she opened the door she said, "Izzy good luck, I hope you have a wonder-fully long and happy marriage."

"Thank you, and the dress is more than I could have ever hoped for, you're gonna be a star."

Chantelle opened the doors, "Ladies here she is," and I walked into silence and mouths gaping wide open.

"Holy Mother... Izzy look at you!" Jazz gasped.

"Wow, there are no words to describe you, you are so beauti-ful."

Mandy sighed, "Just divine, gorgeous."

Anka just couldn't speak; she covered her quivering lips with her hand, fighting the tears back. The three of them were jaw droppingly beautiful.

"Oh, you three look like Goddesses, you wouldn't look out of place on Mount Olympus."

Even with them all wearing flats and me in heels they were still taller... there really is no justice in the world I chuckled to myself.

The suite's phone rang, "Madame, Erik said to say he is on his way up."

I thanked her just before Mandy again sang, "Well girlies, it's nearly show time," causing my insides to fill with butterflies.

Anka finally found her voice, "Isabelle, you are the most stunningly beautiful, angelic looking bride I have ever seen."

She pulled me to her for a wonderful cuddle then the other two joined in, "Group hug," Jazz giggled.

Erik knocked and walked in, "Halla!" he shouted before stopping dead in his tracks the moment he saw me

"HERREGUD!" that's 'Oh My God' if you hadn't guessed. When he got the use of his legs back he came over to me and kissed my cheek, "Beautiful, just beautiful."

The ceremony was due to begin at two, and like any good bride I was running late, but only by a quarter of an hour. We were all in the anteroom, adjacent to the conservatory room and I could hear the string quartet softly playing Vivaldi's 'four seasons,' as well as the low rumble of people chatting. On the table in front of us were all our bouquets as well as five glasses of perfectly chilled Champagne, a little Dutch courage goes a long way.

Last night before the girlie fest, Jazz and I were given a private guided tour of the now decorated huge conservatory room; it had been transformed and fabulously dressed for the wedding. When the manager unlocked and opened the door we were instantly hit with the wonderful aroma of the fresh flowers, I'd picked white and cream Roses, Golden gate Marigolds and Angelwing Jasmine finished off with mistletoe and holly. When the lights came on I was truly overcome, the flower arrangements were out of this world, all in ornate crystal vases, some on ceramic pillars with vines hanging down. Every seat had been covered in cream fabric tied with a gold ribbon, with a white cushion placed on the seat. To the left was set up for the band and to the right in front of the windows was a magnificent antique desk with another flower arrangement and where Mika and I would sign the register.

"It's amazing Iz," Jazz said, I still couldn't seem to form any words but I did wear a big grin like the Cheshire cat, I couldn't wait to see it full of our friends.

The manager entered the small room, "Are we ready?" he asked.

We all nodded and walked out, eager to make our entrances. The band began to play Beethoven's 'Ode to Joy' for the bridesmaids to enter and was much louder and made everyone inside fall silent. Jazz was the last one to walk out and she kissed me before she left. The big double doors then closed so that Erik and I could get ready, and Chantelle did her final touches before giving me the thumbs up. Then we heard Pachelbel's 'Canon in D' and the porters' opened the doors slowly before my cue came to walk in, and everybody stood up, I had to tell myself to breathe.

"Ready little one," Erik kissed my cheek.

"Yes," I beamed.

I had been right; the conservatory room full of people was amazing. As we walked inside I was met with unfamiliar smiling faces and even with my nerves playing havoc I still managed to return their gesture and smile back. Eventually in the sea of faces I recognised my small group of guests and I saved my biggest smile for them. Rita was dabbing tears away and even Joss looked choked up. Then I saw him, and everyone else seemed to fade away, the look on Mika's handsome face mirrored Erik's when he had first seen me, one of sheer adoration and reverence, but Mika's had something else that matched mine, pure undying love.

As Erik gave my hand to Mika, "I wish you both all the luck in the world," he said, then he whispered to me in Swedish, "Be forever happy little one, I love you," and he kissed my cheek before taking his seat.

"Angel, you are a vision of beauty, how did I become so lucky?"

I had to restrain myself from launching at him and kissing him like my life depended on it. A cough suddenly got our attention, bringing us back to the moment at hand.

"Shall we begin?" the official smiled.

The words, "You may kiss your beautiful bride," caused the whole room to erupt, making both of us laugh. My dream had come true and I was now officially and legally Mrs Mikhail Remizov.

Whilst the guest's were all being relocated to the Ball Room for champagne and cocktails, the rest of us were getting ready for the photographs. We had a few taken in the spectacular bay windows of the Conservatory room over looking the snow covered lawns and lake before we all made our way outside. Chantelle had designed faux fur wraps for my bridesmaids and I, which only added to the already fairytale feel. The guys all wore Armani charcoal grey suits with the same gold colour waist-coats and cravats that matched the girl's dresses, to go outside they all wore matching black knee length single breasted coats, which looked very smart and dapper against the charcoal suits.

Some poor soul had been out at the crack of dawn and shovelled a snow path to the orchard. The trees were heavy under the weight of the freshly fallen snow, which glistened in the weak winter sun. It was the perfect spot to capture our memories with a semi frozen lake as the back drop, it was simply magical. Even the two resident swans came up and made an appearance, which was captured on film forever.

Two waiters carried out trays of warm cider for us so we didn't catch hyperthermia. It took about an hour to complete all the photographs, and once back inside, Mika and I were escorted to a private room where we could freshen up and warm up before making our grand entrance. As soon as the door closed Mika pounced.

"Finally I have you to myself," which made me giggle like a teenage girl. "You look breathtakingly beautiful," he kissed me with so much passion my blood instantly warmed up.

"Behave, we haven't got time for that mister," I teased.

"I can make time."

Time seemed to stand still for a second until there was a knock on the door and Mika's reaction was priceless, he pouted and sulked like a child.

"Later my darling husband," I teased, kissing him quickly before the door opened.

The rest of the day flew by; the food was out of this world and the company sublime. I was truly gutted when it ended but at least I had the wedding night ahead of me and hopefully the memory would be one I could relive for many years to come.

Landing back in cold wet Detroit after three weeks in sunny, idyllic Hawaii was so anti climatic, talk about a downer and walking into the house it got worse.

Jazz was waiting in the kitchen, "Hey, finally the newly weds are home," she crushed me, "God I've missed you Izzy."

"What the hell am I, chopped liver?"

Mika huffed, put out.

Jazz chuckled, "Soz, I've missed you too bro."

As she hugged him I knew instantly something was wrong.

"What's up?"

Then she broke the news I knew was coming, but selfishly I'd hoped wouldn't. She and Illa had bought a house, even though it wasn't that far away it was still too far for me. I tried to put a happy face on but was failing miserably and I felt guilty as hell because she was so excited.

"When?" I asked.

"About two weeks, once the work has been completed," she giggled.

"Well then girl, we will just have to party it up for the next two weeks," even though I was losing her from the house I truly was happy for her.

"Yeah, like when we were kids," she giggled before leaving for work.

Well that was a nice welcome home…Not! That night at dinner it was just Mika and I, and after talking to him about me returning to work, I finally accepted the fact it was never going to be like it was, since now I was married to the *Boss.* I decided not to go back and, surprise, surprise Mika was quite happy about that, which really seemed to piss me off.

I spent most of my days with Gavril, he had become much more than just my minder, he was a dear friend and one who I could confide in and air my frustrations out on. I loved going to the gym, he was an excellent instructor and I was learning so much from him. Riku would always come and watch us when we were there, he was always encouraging me. My first impression of him had been totally wrong; I really liked him and his dry sense of humour. Not only did this dilapidated looking building house a state of the art gym, down in the basement was a huge sound proofed shooting range and armoury. It held a vault with a vast array of weaponry; the brotherhood had one hell of an arsenal. Mika eventually conceded and allowed Gavril to teach me to shoot. Before Gavril let me shoot anything, he had me learn all about gun maintenance and safety, he even had me sit a damned exam! Which thankfully I passed.

Just like fighting, firing a weapon came naturally to me and I got pretty good, pretty fast, which totally stunned Gavril, in fact in his words 'I blew his socks off!' I could feel myself changing everyday, no more the damsel in distress but a small, compact lethal package with near perfect aim and the hand speed of an MMA fighter. My favourite gun of choice was a Taurus 24/7 G but Gavril gave me a Ruger LCP, which fit snugly in my purse and I knew there and then that if there ever came a time I had to use it, I would not hesitate.

For now it was all hands on deck, getting ready for the second Remizov wedding. Instead of the original spring date, Jazz and Illa had opted for a summer wedding. Just like me, Jazz had always dreamed of her perfect day and hers was to take her vows in the beautiful gardens of her childhood home. When she told Mika he had been delighted and the icing on the cake was when she asked him to stand in for their Dad and give her away, he was fit to burst with pride.

CHAPTER THIRTY-THREE

Eight months later

After nearly a year of flying between Sweden and the States, Alex and Anka had had enough, so Alex finally proposed and she said Yes, both Jazz and I were ecstatic. The plan was for Anka to give notice and finish the school year in Stockholm then fly here in August and apply for a position here when she had settled in. The only down side was Alex had decided to move into the fabulous private apartment in the Majestic, but that was still a whole lot closer than she had been, so I forgave him. While Jazz and I were speaking to Anka on Skype one night, we hatched a fantastic idea, we would fly to Stockholm in July and help her pack and sell up, and I would get to see Erik of course. I thought getting Mika to agree to it was going to be impossible but I had to try, so when he said yes without any argument it caused my spidery sense to tingle, it had been tingling like mad these last few days. I could pinpoint the exact time it started; Luca had gone away on some secret business thing about six weeks ago. That wasn't strange apart from the lack of communication, Luca had even distanced himself from Mandy and hadn't called her once since he'd left, and she was so hurt and distraught. I was so angry with him, how could he do this to her, I thought he was in love with her? My heart ached for Mandy and after six weeks she was mad, and I mean mad. We wanted her to come to Sweden but she said no, it felt like she was pulling away from us. It was like déjà vu, watching what was going on between Luca and her; I had gone through similar things with Mika when he was trying to protect me in his own way, something was going down, but what?

Katia's voice came over the intercom, "Mika I have Delushi on line one, do you want me to put him through?"

It had been quite a while since the pair had last talked; Mika's once adversary and arch nemesis was now an ally of sorts and he owed Delushi a huge debt because through the information he had found out, had lead Mika to find Izzy.

"Yes Katia, put him through."

"Delushi, to what do I owe this pleasure?" now that was the big question.

"Mika how are you and that lovely new wife of yours?"

The anticipation hung heavy on the line, "We are both well thank you. I know you didn't call for a catch up so what can I do for you?"

"I need a meeting; I have a request to ask?"

Mika had a feeling the debt he owed was about to be cashed in. "When and where?"

"On your turf, say the *Vanguard* at nine?"

"We will see you then."

Mika was left wondering as he hung up. He called Luca and told him what Delushi had requested.

"Do you have any idea what he wants?"

"No, but it will be interesting to find out. Let Ivan know and tell him to pick us up at home around eight thirty?"

Mika had heard on the grapevine there was some sort of turf war brewing but he would let Delushi confirm that before saying anything.

Mika and Luca arrived home and walked into the kitchen to the sounds of Izzy's laughter, when she turned round, Mika nearly lost it.

"What the fuck?"

She was sporting yet another black eye. "Mika calm down, it was my own fault, I didn't expect the gun I was using to have such a recoil, it clocked me straight in the eye, trust me it won't happen again."

She was still laughing but Mika didn't find one iota of it funny.

"Angel, I have a meeting tonight after dinner, I'm sorry but Gavril will stay and keep you company."

She wasn't laughing any more, "Fine," she spat.

Dinner was a strained affair causing Mika to feel guilty. While he showered and changed, Izzy sat on the bed and watched, pouting, "Sorry for being childish but I just miss you."

"I know Angel, I miss you too, but I'll try and make it quick OK," and he kissed her just before Luca appeared at the door.

"Ivan is here," Mika nodded, "Love you," and he kissed her again softly before leaving.

The *Vanguard* was pretty quiet since it was still early. Mika stood in the office looking out of the one way window down into the club, while Luca and Ivan sat chatting about the latest of Ivan's conquests, Mika didn't miss those days at all.

"So Luca, what's going on with Mandy, you ever gonna claim her?" Ivan asked.

"Why?" Luca snapped, a slight twinge of annoyance coated his voice.

"Dude seriously, what the fuck is going on with you two, because if you don't do something soon someone else will, she is fucking hot?"

Luca was in love with her but was fighting his own demons, she deserved someone better than him, someone who could give her the life he couldn't. The white picket fence and house full of kids was just a step to far but still he couldn't let her go either.

"Stay the fuck away from her and you can tell any fucker who comes even close to her they will not see another sunrise?" he growled.

Ivan held his hands up in a surrender motion and laughed, Luca had unknowingly answered Ivan's question.

Delushi and Massimo were escorted to the office and once the pleasantries were done Delushi got straight down to business.

"Thank you for agreeing to this impromptu meeting, I don't know if you have heard but we are having major trouble with the fucking Calina Cartel. We have lost a few good men already, but that is not why I'm here. Javier Calina has put a hit out on my Zaira, my only child, I would die before I let anyone hurt her, but there is nowhere in my world I feel safe leaving her, I lost my Ariana five years ago and Zaira is all I have left. My request is that you please take her and protect her, keep my little girl safe until I destroy Calina once and for all."

Mika couldn't condone the man for wanting to keep his loved ones safe.

"I didn't even know you had a child?" Mika said, quite shocked. "You have kept her hidden well so far, why do you want my help now?"

Delushi gave him a haunted laugh, "A child? To me she will always be a child but my Zaira is twenty-five."

"Oh, then why don't you send her out of the country?"

"Javier is very clever, he found my secret weakness, my Achilles heel, her. But even he isn't stupid enough to mess with the Russians."

Mika accepted his answer, not many dared to mess with the brotherhood, only the ones who had a death wish.

"Mika, Luca, you do this for me and I will be forever in your debt?" Delushi was ageing right in front of their eyes.

"OK, I will take her, does she know the danger she is in?"

Delushi nodded, "Yes, she is aware and also knows I'm talking with you now."

"Where is she now?" Mika asked.

Delushi laughed again, "Room 2610 at the Majestic."

This caused Mika's eye brows to lift, he was impressed, "Call her let her know we are on our way, then say goodbye for now and no more communication till the threat has been eliminated!"

Delushi didn't argue, he knew Mika was right.

"Thank you Mika," he shook his hand.

"Delushi, I give you my word I will do my best to protect her, but if anything happens to her, be it on your own head!" Mika's tone was deadly.

"I understand and accept the risk," he said as he left.

"Get the car Ivan," Mika instructed, destination, The Majestic Hotel.

On the drive to the hotel, Mika gave orders.

"Luca, you stay with Zaira in the safe house, Ivan use the tech and find out everything on Javier Calina, leave no stone left unturned, got it?"

"Mika do you think this is wise getting involved with the Italians?" Luca asked concerned.

"No I don't, but Delushi helped us in the past and like him, I know what the need to protect the ones I love feels like, I just hope it doesn't blow up in my face." Luca and Ivan both agreed.

Alex was waiting for them at the front desk, "Ivan I need you to get the house ready in Highland Park, stock the cupboards and refrigerator," Luca told him, "Alex will drive us and we'll meet you there." Ivan nodded and quickly left.

Outside room 2610 Mika knocked.

"Zaira, it's Mika Remizov," he knew by now Delushi would have called her.

They listened to the lock being disabled just before the door opened cautiously slow, Mika couldn't speak for Luca or Alex but what greeted them was certainly not what he'd been expecting. Delushi was a balding, rotund man with typical Italian features, olive skin, dark hair and eyes. What Mika saw first was the most hypnotic pair of eyes he'd ever seen, not blue, not grey but a mix that created a silvery, ice blue colour, that looked like two glacial pools but he could also see the fear in them. He took in the rest of her, she was small, maybe even shorter than Izzy, slightly curvier with long jet black wavy hair and skin like alabaster, Zaira was definitely exquisite and Mika thought how in Gods name had Delushi created such a beauty.

"Zaira, I'm Mika and these are my brothers, Luca and Alex."

As her eyes flickered between them, she gave a shy smile "Hello," her voice was another shock, deep, husky and very sexy.

Mika explained what was going to happen and Zaira never questioned a thing, even when Mika asked her to hand over her cell. She wasn't stupid, she had already taken the battery and sim card out as she knew she had to stay off the grid and her father had called her from a burner phone through the hotels switch board.

"Luca will be staying with you till all this blows over, if you require anything just let him know," and Mika gently squeezed her shoulder. "I am sorry this is happening to you."

"Thank you, I know you did not have to help me," her husky voice was tinged with sadness.

Mika glanced at Luca; he was mesmerized by this woman, "Luca grab the bags," snapping him out of his trance.

"Sure... yeah."

After getting Luca and Zaira settled, Alex drove Mika home,

it was now passed one in the morning.

"Alex, pack Luca some clothes and essentials, and drop them off for him in the morning and the less people who know about this the better."

Alex nodded. Mika hoped Izzy would be sound asleep by now and wouldn't give him the third degree; he really didn't want to face that now.

Over the next few days Mika received all the Intel on Javier Calina, he was the ostracised nephew of Gerardo Ramirez, the Drug Baron from down south, Austin, Texas to be precise.

Javier had attempted to overthrow his uncle and failed catastrophically, leading to Gerardo having all Javier's followers executed. Because Javier himself was blood, he'd been given two choices, Death or exile and a contract had been placed on him if he ever returned down south, spanning all the way from Arizona to Virginia. Just by sheer dumb luck the fucker had landed here in Michigan and was attempting to do here what he failed to do at home, only this time the fool had declared war on the Italians. The Italians were a big family, kind of like the Russians in that aspect but nowhere near as brutal or sadistic as the Bratva. Delushi was struggling with the loss of man-power, but slowly his numbers were being replenished by other states sending reinforcements.

Six weeks into the protection detail and Izzy was already querying the absence of Luca, she been told he was away on business for the brotherhood. Then a package had arrived at Mika's office, inside was a decapitated snakes head and surveillance photos of Izzy, some with her and Gavril, some of her inside *Red Square* and a few of her sunbathing alone by their swimming pool at home. Mika's blood ran cold, this was Javier calling Mika a snake and that he knew they had Zaira, if Javier couldn't have her then Izzy would have to do. The minute Mika saw the photo's he knew they had been pulled into this war. Now that the brotherhood had joined in, it was just a matter of time until

Calina was found and eliminated.

CHAPTER THIRTY-FOUR

Jazz and I had come up with a plan of attack to get Mika to let us go to Sweden and we decided to hunt as a pack, after all there was strength in numbers. So tonight Jazz and Illa were coming to us for dinner and once our men had been fed and watered... Bam! We'd strike.

I was pumped up ready for a twelve round battle that lay ahead of us, but it was us who'd been knocked sideways when Mika happily said yes, without hardly any persuasion. I should have been like Jazz who was bouncing off the walls and smothering poor Illa in lip-stick but instead I was staring at Mika suspiciously. This man freaks out if I don't answer my cell quick enough and now he was letting me and Jazz go to another continent without any arguments what so ever! Something was very wrong, but before I had chance to quiz him Jazz interrupted me and was now swinging on Mika's neck. I didn't have the heart to quell her excitement, it was so funny watching her, she actually made me laugh – what a nut! But trust me, as soon as we are alone I would be.

The second Jazz and Illa pulled out of the driveway I was on him, "Mika, what the hell is going on?"

He turned and tried to give me that look, the one that puts the fear of God in others!

"Nice try buddy, now tell me?" I glared back, it was like a Mexican stand-off and I was not going to back down.

"OK, fine, there is something brewing, I'm not going into to much detail but what I will say is it's safer for you and Jazz to be out of the city, even better out the country for the time being."

Dread suddenly filled me, "Are we in danger?"

"Angel, there's always a danger around us, but a threat was issued and its one I'm not prepared to ignore."

I had a million questions, "Is this why Luca's been gone for weeks?" all I got was a nod.

"Enough now, I will book everything for the three of you tomorrow."

"Three, there is only Jazz and I?"

As soon as I said it out loud I knew it was stupid.

"Gavril will be joining you both and that's non negotiable," and it was me who nodded this time. Mika walked towards me and cradled me in his arms, "I hate the thought of you being so far away, but trust me Angel, when it's safe I'll have you on the first flight back."

Why did that sound longer than the three weeks we had planned?

"I always do trust you," I did but I also knew I was Mika's biggest weakness, his Kryptonite, so if being thousands of miles away put Mika's mind at rest I wasn't going to argue. Two days later all three of us were on route to Stockholm.

Luca was getting pissed off after eight weeks of babysitting Zaira. He missed his family, Christ he even missed Alex, but what shocked him the most was how much he pined for Mandy, even just the sound of the sweet melody tone of her voice when she answered her cell. He was feeling guilt ridden, even before this fucking mess with Calina he'd been withdrawing from her. Mandy was getting too close and Luca didn't want her involved in his world. He had pulled the old Remizov trick and pushed her away for her safety. She deserved the perfect life, the white picket fence and the 2.4 kids with a man who had a steady job who'd love her forever, that was something he could never give her. The only thing he could do was keep her safe and off the radar and that meant keeping far away from her. Luca was prepared to give up his future happiness to keep her alive and if that was without him, so be it.

Zaira had warmed up to him, at first she had been weary of not only this fucked up situation but of him as well. He was this tattooed Russian giant who until recently had been a mortal enemy of her family. Gradually over the weeks Zaira realised he was not a threat to her so her trust in him grew. They began to talk and shared personal things neither of them had ever told anybody. Luca learnt that she was in love with one of her father's loyal soldiers Savi, and she was absolutely terrified that Delushi would find out and do something to him. Luca reassured her that once the threat had been eliminated and she was safe, Delushi would not only be overjoyed to have his little girl back he wouldn't care about who she was in love with, all he would want is for her to be happy. Luca opened up about Mandy.

"Admit it Luca, you are in love with her?"

"Love, me no, I don't do the love thing," he laughed far to loud that he didn't even convince himself let alone Zaira, she just looked at him knowingly.

"OK, lets say this shit is over and we are back to our normal boring lives. Mandy has gotten tired of waiting and has found a new beau and you see them out, he's kissing her, those lips that used to be yours to kiss and he's lovingly touching her sweet face, tell me, how would that make you feel. Would you be pleased and happy for them, or would you want to skin the fucker alive for touching what is yours?" Luca couldn't answer; he knew it would be lie.

"Aha, skin him alive," she giggled, as Luca felt his cheeks heat up.

"Let's change the subject... Do you want to watch NCIS or Bones?"

Zaira screwed her nose up, "Greys Anatomy?"

"Fuck that shit, Dr sexy, I don't think so," he growled. They compromised and settled on Supernatural.

The Lydmar Hotel was smack bang in the city centre, it oozed luxury out of this world and I fell in love with it the second we walked inside. After a day to acclimatize and getting rid of the jet-lag we all invaded Anka and spent the whole weekend helping her pack up her apartment, the couriers were coming Monday morning to ship everything back home.

The following week, while Anka was working, I played the tour guide and showed Jazz and Gavril the treasures Stockholm had to offer, they were both in awe of this magnificent city. Then we arrived at *Skin Canvas,* I had made Anka promise not to tell the guys we were coming and wow did we surprise the hell out of them all. Erik nearly stabbed his client he'd been inking when his eyes landed on me.

"Fuck me, little one!" Yelling as he jumped up, the poor guy on the table nearly shit himself. Erik crushed me so tight I could hardly breathe.

"Oh I've missed you, you big hulk."

By the time he released me the rest of the guy's were waiting their turn, I felt like the baby sister returning home. We all made plans for dinner before we left them to get back to work.

By the end of the second week, my suspicions were pretty much confirmed, I'd missed my second period and was throwing up like clockwork every morning. Even my beloved coffee had forsaken me and now the smell of it turned my stomach. I had Anka secretly bring me some pregnancy tests and all five came back positive. I thought thankfully we'd be back home in a few days and I would make an appointment with my own doctor.

"Are you telling Jazz and Gavril?" Anka asked.

"No, not yet, I think I should tell Mika first, so don't say a word."

She crossed her heart and pretended to zip her mouth

closed, which made me smile.

Mika had spoken to Izzy everyday, he was missing her like crazy. Delushi was making headway in the hunt to track down Calina but not quick enough for Mika's liking. Then on the Tuesday, two days before Izzy and the rest were supposed to return from Sweden, all hell broke loose, which basically forced the brotherhood's hand and they declared war also on the Calina scum. Javier had signed his own death warrant by ordering a drive-by outside *The Redline Corp* office building with the soul purpose of targeting one person. The only woman who had a personal connection to the Remizov's and who wasn't in Stockholm...Mandy!

CHAPTER THIRTY-FIVE

Mandy and Joe left the office building just after five p.m. and stood outside chatting for a few minutes before going their separate ways. Mandy was heading to the pharmacy a few doors down the block to collect a prescription before returning to her car in the offices' parking structure, she never made it. Joe reported a black van with tinted windows speeding around the corner with its tyres screeching as it passed him; he turned and saw the muzzle of a gun poking out of the now open window as it closed in on Mandy.

He shouted, "Get Down!" to her seconds before the gunfire exploded then watched helplessly as she fell motionless to the ground. The van sped off as quickly as it had arrived and he was unable to get the licence plate. He ran to Mandy and saw she'd taken three bullets, one to the right shoulder, one in the stomach and the third was in the left hip, a diagonal line from right to left. He applied pressure to the stomach wound, trying to stem the bleeding and screamed for someone to call 911, the paramedics were on site quickly and so were the police. Joe gave a very vague statement, keeping the rest to himself until he called Mika.

Mika had just left the office and was nearly home when Katia called him, he had planned to spend some time with Luca tonight but instead he did a 360 and drove straight to the Henry Ford Hospital. He got Katia to send him all of Mandy's personal details so he could let the hospital and the police know. Upon his arrival he was taken to the private family room and while he sat waiting he thought hard about what had just occurred, was this just a sick ploy to get Luca out of hiding? Did this stupid fucker honestly think he'd come running with Zaira in tow? Mika planned his next move very carefully. He gave the police and hospital all of Mandy's information and he was told that her parents had now been informed and were on route. As for Mandy herself, she was holding her own and had been transferred to the O.R, they told Mika they would keep him updated, Mika thanked them and sighed to himself, the Remizov's had another strong woman who'd fight tooth and nail to survive.

He knew he had to tell Luca, if the boot had been on the other foot and Luca withheld it from him he'd kill him, brother or not. He rang Ivan and told him to pick up Illa and drop him off at Highland Park and bring Luca to the hospital, by Mika's tone, Ivan knew not to ask any questions. The instant Luca got in the car he rang.

"What's wrong, you hurt?"

Mika could hear the worry in Lucas' voice, "No, where are you now?"

"About two minutes out."

"OK, I'm waiting by the E.R entrance I'll see you soon," he still didn't say anything.

Mika was pacing the sidewalk waiting anxiously, and then he heard the heavy sound of running footfall and looked up to see Ivan and Luca sprinting towards him.

"Mika, for fucks' sake, what's going on?"

Mika looked at Luca before placing a supportive hand on his brother's shoulder, "Its Mandy, she's been shot."

"What?" Luca couldn't quite comprehend what he was being told.

"There was a drive-by outside the office, by what we can gather they targeted her." Watching his brother processing the information broke Mika.

"Fuck, no! Is she, is she alive, please God let her be alive?" his desperation hit Mika full force; he had stood where Luca was standing right now.

"She is, I ain't gonna lie Luca, it doesn't look good." Mika watched tears stream down his brothers' cheeks, he hadn't seen Luca cry since they were kids, he hadn't even cried the day they buried their parents. He pulled Luca to him.

"I'm so sorry, but I swear to you, that fucker will pay!"

Luca pulled back and looked into Mika's eyes, "You fucking tell Delushi that cunt is mine!" he spat, with pure venom and Mika didn't argue, "I will."

Inside the waiting room once more, all three men sat silently praying for sweet Mandy until a doctor came in.

"Mr Remizov?" Both Mika and Luca stood up.

"This is my brother and Mandy's partner."

"OK, they're still in surgery and will be for a few more hours yet but I thought you'd appreciate an update." Luca held his breath. "She was shot three times, her shoulder was a through and through, the leg GSW has shattered her hip and the Ortho team will be replacing that later. Her abdominal GSW is the one that has caused the most damage, they have managed to stop the bleeding and repaired her liver but the damage done to the pancreas was too severe to save so they had to remove it, that means from now on she will need to take daily insulin injections. The other major concern is her stomach, which was ruptured by the bullet and has leaked inside of her so the risk of infection is high. All I can say for sure now is, she is still here, you have one real fighter on your hands."

All three men absorbed the words the doctor had spoken.

"Thank you for letting us know," Luca said.

"I'll be back when I have more, as soon as we know you will," he added before he left.

An hour later the door opened again and a man and a woman were escorted in, the woman was an older version of Mandy, these had to be her parents. The three men walked over to them,

"Mr and Mrs Neal, I'm Mika Remizov and this is my brother Luca and good friend Ivan, I'm sorry we get to meet under these awful circumstances."

Mrs Neal looked at Luca, this was the man that made her baby girl giggle and blush whenever she talked about him, she focused solely on him.

"What happened, the police said she was shot, why?" She wept and it was Mika who answered.

"There was a drive-by shooting and Mandy was just in the wrong place at the wrong time." This did little to comfort them and only seemed to confuse them more, "I'm so sorry"

Mika added.

Mrs Neal looked at them all, "Please call me Val, and this is Brett, my husband, Amanda's father," she gave them a weak smile as she squeezed Mika's hand. "Please don't blame yourself Mika, it's not your fault, you didn't shoot her."

The words stung him, it was his fault she'd been shot, he may as well have been the one who pulled the God damn trigger.

Val turned her attention back to Luca, "I can finally put a face to the name, Amanda has spoken of you often, and I just wish we'd been introduced differently."

Her voice cracked as she spoke, which caused Luca to do something very unlike him, he pulled her to him and cradled her affectionately in his huge arms.

"Me too, Mandy is my world, my soul mate and my one true love."

It was the first time he'd admitted it out loud and it shocked him as much as he'd shocked Mika and Ivan.

The hours passed slowly and the only word so far had been she was still holding her own.

Mika leaned in to Luca, "I'm gonna go call everyone; I'll be just out front?"

There was one call he really didn't want to make but he knew he had to. He called Gavril first and he picked up straight away, Mika gave him a quick run down leaving Gavril aghast to put it mildly and Mika promised to keep him apprised on Mandy's condition.

"For fucks sake do not tell Jazz or Izzy, I'm calling her next. The situation here is far too unstable and you all have to stay there until it's safe here!"

"Good luck with that boss!"

Mika gave him an empty laugh, "I'm gonna need it."

After hanging up on Izzy, Mika felt completely wrecked and guilt ridden, she had cried, screamed at him and argued till she was hoarse, wanting to know what had happened so badly that she couldn't come home. Eventually she accepted the fact that if he didn't want her to come home there had to be a very good reason and she begrudgingly conceded.

The next person on Mika's call list was Delushi, "This has just become fucking personal, you may have lost men but that cunt has just crossed the line. So Delushi, from now I take the fucking lead and if you find out where the cocksucker is first, you call me?"

Delushi knew better than to argue and he agreed, "I heard, how is the girl and who is she to you?" he asked.

"She's Luca's girl and it doesn't look too good."

"Oh fuck!"

"Yes, you could say that, he wants Calina's head."

"You have my word and please send my best wishes to Luca?"

"I will."

As he hung up, Mika looked up at the sky and saw a shooting star and he made his wish, "Please save her."

Alex appeared at his side, "Mika, what do you need me to do?" he could see the stress and rage marring his brothers' face.

"Call in everyone; we are at war, I WANT THAT FUCKER JAVIER CALINA NOW!"

"I'm on it," Alex turned to walk away.

"Wait, take Ivan with you."

"I'll go bring the car round; I'll pick him up here." Mika nodded, returned back inside and told Ivan.

It was in the early hours of Wednesday morning when the surgeon came into the room, "Mr and Mrs Neal," all four stood up.

"Yes."

"I'm pleased to say that Amanda has made it through the surgery but the next 48 hours are still critical, I understand Dr Clark has already been keeping you updated on what was happening and the severity of her injuries, if you have any questions please ask?"

Mandy's father, who'd hardly uttered a word these past few hours as he seemed shell shocked and closed off, was the one who spoke.

"When can we see our baby?"

"As soon as they get her settled in the ICU someone will come and get you."

The heavy atmosphere seemed to lift slightly in the room.

"Thank you so much for saving our daughter," Brett added, as he shook the doctor's hand.

"Mr Neal we have made it passed this check point and although we still have a long road ahead of us she has proved to be one tough cookie. I really do hope the police find the people responsible."

Mika was hoping for a different outcome and he knew it would go his way. "Ok then, I'll pop back and see Amanda and I'll see you soon," he gave them all a smile and left.

"I'm so pleased you both raised such a fighter," Mika said, he smiled and actually got one in return, "Rob, Val, I know this is a dumb question but have you arranged for anywhere to stay?"

They both shook their heads, "It was the last thing on our minds," Val answered.

"Then please leave it with me, I'll arrange for a suite to be available for you both at the Majestic for as long as you need."

Val flung her arms around him, "Thank you so much, both of you."

"It's the least we can do."

Mika smiled again as a nurse walked in, "Mr and Mrs Neal would you like to see Amanda?" She spoke softly and the four of them followed her to the ICU.

Before entering, the nurse turned and prepared them for what they were about to see, yet still even with the words of encouragement, the sight of her still shocked them. There were so many wires, tubes and drips surrounding her, with monitors bleeping and flashing and Mandy was also connected to a ventilator that was breathing for her. The sad vision of her was more than Val and Brett could bear, they both broke down, and Luca was trying his hardest not to, but was slowly losing that battle.

Before Mika left, he went to Val and Brett, he patted Brett supportively on the shoulder and embraced Val.

"I'll come back tomorrow," and they both thanked him.

Mika knew Luca would be staying, "Luca walk me out," and he watched Luca fighting with the thought of leaving her but he still followed Mika out. Luca listened as Mika repeated what he had said to Delushi on the phone and what he had instructed Alex to do.

"Call me immediately if anything changes?"

Luca nodded and Mika clasped his brother's face in between his huge hands and stared directly into his sad eyes, "Brother, I am so sorry," then embraced him before exiting the building.

Mandy had spent nearly five weeks in hospital and now she was ready to be released. Luca had spent the entire time by her bedside and he finally confessed his true feelings to her. Mandy heard the words come from his lips she had be waiting for, "I love you." She listened as he admitted she was his one true love and the thought of losing her was more than he could stand. So the night before she was discharged he proposed and Mandy said yes. Pulling away and putting distance between the ones they loved to keep them safe had seemed at the time like the only solution, but all three brothers had been catastrophically wrong. The best solution to keeping them all safe was to have them close and to never let go.

It had taken weeks but finally they had Javier Calina. Every person who had been affiliated with this pathetic little cartel had quickly and quietly been disposed of and were now all pushing up daisies. All apart from the wannabe Kingpin himself, he was chained and securely locked up in the bowels of *Club Trevie's* basement in the medieval dungeon.

When he realised he was beaten he was terrified and actually begged for his worthless life. Delushi had thoroughly enjoyed informing him that Luca Remizov wanted a 'private chat' and he watched as the last bit of colour drained from the cowardly fuckers face. It was sheer bliss and pretty understandable really, Luca's reputation was legendary and had a far, far reach. Calina may have had an idea what was going to happen to him but Delushi could promise him that the real thing was going to be a whole lot worse than anything he could ever imagine. It had taken all Delushi's will-power not to kill the bastard himself, but he had his Zaira back home safe and unharmed. Not Luca, he had to watch Mandy fight for her life, so Delushi simply stood back and gladly watched on.

CHAPTER THIRTY-SIX

No one was talking about the situation back home so it was difficult to comprehend the severity of it. I knew it must be bad because Mika wouldn't have let me travel half way round the world without him for any other reason than to keep me, Jazz and Anka safe. Everyday when Mika called he said the same thing, "Soon Angel I promise," and I knew I was being unreasonable and down right selfish but I couldn't stop myself from kicking off and ranting at him, calling him all the names under the sun and for what? For loving me so much he wanted to protect me. As soon as I'd hang up I would cry my heart out, feeling awful and guilty. All I wanted was to go home to him, sleep in our bed and tell him he was going to be a daddy. I knew there was more to it than what Mika would say and I'd even tried to quiz Gavril but as usual I got zip out of him. Why are all the men in my life always so secretive and stubborn like that, it's so bloody frustrating sometimes?

Anka had moved into our hotel since she had sold her place and we should have been back stateside weeks ago.

"Izzy I can't believe you have a proper bump already, how far along do you think you are?"

"To be honest I had a feeling I was pregnant before we left, but if I'd have said anything Mika wouldn't have let me come...," now I wish I had, "but I think I'm about three months?"

"Shit girl we need to get you checked out." She was right, we still had no clue when we'd be going home.

"I know, I know, Jazz and Gavril are going to get tattoos done on Thursday; do you think you can get me an appointment with your doctor?"

"Leave it with me," she smiled, and so on that Thursday at 11 a.m. Anka and I walked into the medical centre.

The one silver lining about being grounded in Europe was nobody had ever heard of the Remizov's or the brotherhood, maybe if you drove north to Russia it might have been a different story but here in Stockholm they hadn't. So Gavril bless him, had relaxed some what and gave me a little more freedom, and that's how Anka and I managed to get in at the clinic on our own.

They ran all kinds of tests on me and confirmed my pregnancy and thankfully everything looked healthy and normal. The doctor made me drink a gallon of water so she could give me a sonogram to find out just how far along I actually was. Anka sat next to me and we all looked at the fuzzy monitor screen; I was completely lost and couldn't see a thing.

"Well Mrs Remizov, if you look here there is one baby," then she pointed to another part on the screen "and here is baby number two, congratulations you are having twins!" if I hadn't been laying down I'd have fallen down.

"TWINS!"

The doctor laughed, "Yes, twins, and by the size and measurements you are between 13 and 14 weeks."

Now I could see them on the monitor I couldn't take my eyes off my babies, "Is that why I'm pretty big already?" She smiled as she nodded.

"Oh wow Izzy, twins," Anka was grinning like a crazy person, and then I felt my face crumple and the tears fell.

"Sweetie what's wrong?"

"I just wish Mika was here."

"Oh Izzy, I know but we'll be home soon," and she gave me a desperately needed hug.

"When are you planning on flying home?" the doctor asked with a hint of concern.

"Very soon why?" she had me worried.

"You are in your second trimester now so you have about two months and then I would not recommend flying until after they are born."

It was me who was laughing now, "Trust me, I'll be home soon." If I had to fly home without Mika's permission I was adamant about that, still we made another appointment for next week just in case we were still here.

The next job on our list was getting me some new comfy clothes since I had nearly out grown all the ones I had brought. After a successful shopping spree we arrived back at the hotel only to be met by a frantically pacing Gavril, "Where the fuck have you both been," he sounded harsh speaking in Russian.

Anka and I had unintentionally forgotten to switch our cells back on when we left the medical centre, but still I snapped back at him for how he'd spoken to us.

"I've been to see a doctor!"

His anger was replaced by worry, "Why are you ill?"

"No!" He shook his head waiting for me to elaborate more, "I'm pregnant!"

So much for keeping it a secret until we got home but I suppose my ever growing bump would eventually give it away anyway.

"What, really!" his face broke into a wonderful smile and he pulled me to him, "Congratulations," he whispered in my ear.

"Don't you dare tell Mika or I will kill you."

"I swear I won't, when are you due?"

"January 3rd," I said, rubbing my cute bump.

"Wow,, that could be the future Pakhan in there" he chuckled.

"Well there is a 50/50 chance on both counts; I don't know the sex of them yet?"

That really confused him, "What?" I heard Anka snigger as we watched the total bewilderment on Gavril's face, "Oh yeah, it's twins."

Over the next few weeks all three wrapped me in cotton wool, Gavril being the worst one of them all a proper mother hen.

"I'm pregnant not sick, I'm not made of bone China," I yelled more than once, the little bit of freedom I spoke of before, Gavril had truly rescinded it, the only person who kept me sane was Erik. I was now four months and growing bigger by the day, there was no way I could hide it any more so I embraced it lovingly.

The night Mika called to say, "Angel, come home," was the best day ever, I screamed so loud down the line I nearly burst his ear drums.

"I gather you're happy to be coming home!" he laughed.

"You have no idea."

Straight after we hung up, I went in search of Gavril and when I found him he had already booked all our tickets.

"We fly out tomorrow, I thought you'd want the earliest ones available?" did he know me well or what. We went and informed the rest before I returned to pack, I felt like Dorothy, "There's no place like home," I sang.

The next day Erik and Joss met us for lunch before they drove us all to the airport. Leaving them was the only sad part, "Stay in touch little one and I'll come and see the tiny ones as soon as they are born," Erik said.

"Promise?"

"I promise," he held me tight, "Take care, I love you," he said and then kissed the tip of my nose. It was hard saying goodbye but this time it was Anka who needed all our support, we hadn't realised just how hard and scary it was for her, she was leaving not only her home or the city but the country she loved forever. Jazz consoled her and bless him Gavril cuddled her, while I talked about Alex and that put that wonderful smile on her gorgeous face once more.

Jazz said, "Just think, in a few hours all our men will be waiting for us, and personally I can't wait to see the look on Mika's face," she giggled as she rubbed my bump. My wardrobe choice for travelling had been deliberate; I picked a soft and comfy grey track suit and a tight white t-shirt that showed off my delightfully cute bump, which made it so obvious that even the village idiot could tell I was with child, or in my case children!

It was the longest trek home ever, we had to make two changes, the first a four hour stop in Heathrow and the second a two hour delay at JFK. I had never been so grateful for first-class with those comfy seats. I actually slept most of the way and only woke up for food. The seat belt signs lit up as we made our final approach into Detroit as the Captain announced that it was 12.20 p.m. and the weather on the ground was a warm and sunny 27 degrees, after being away nearly two months, we were almost home. As the wheels touched down my stomach fluttered, I had felt my babies move for the first time a few days ago but this time I put it down to excitement, so I stroked my bump and silently said, "Let's go meet your daddy."

Within twenty minutes we had retrieved our luggage and the old mother hen would only let me carry my own purse, but then who was I to argue. We left him guarding the bags while we found the rest room so we could quickly freshen up.

"Izzy you have to let me and Anka go out first, we have to see Mika's reaction?" Jazz basically begged with Anka nodding frantically behind her.

"For Christ sake, get rid of that jacket, it hides that cute bump," she said as she pulled it off. They stood and gave me the once over, "Fuck me, Mika's gonna have a heart attack," they laughed. Because I was so small and carrying twins I looked a lot bigger than if I'd been taller.

Gavril was leaning on the trolley with his cell in his hand, "They're getting impatient," he chuckled.

"That's nothing new is it," I responded.

Jazz told him the plan of action and he really liked the idea, so we watched Jazz and Anka walk out of the arrivals hall.

"How long do we wait?"

"Five minutes." I was so excited I could hardly hold myself together. Jazz was going to say the line for the bathroom was long, then my cell bleeped, "*Ready*" and that was our cue.

I saw him as soon as the doors slid open, that beautiful smile I had missed so much suddenly vanished and his mouth dropped wide open, it was beyond comical and better than I could have ever imagined. I laughed and posed sideways giving everybody the full view of my perfect bump. Mika's hand was now covering his mouth; I had finally rendered him speechless for the first time ever. By the time he walked over to me he was a total wreck, my huge lethal softie, and he kissed me like his life depended on it.

"Why didn't you tell me?" he finally found his voice.

"Because I wanted that reaction," I giggled.

"We're having a baby, I'm gonna be a daddy?"

"Yes you are, but not baby, try babies!"

"Twins! Really, oh my God, I love you." He picked me up and almost crushed me to him and I wrapped my legs around him as he planted kisses all over my face, I was in seventh heaven.

"Hey buddy, don't squash my nieces or nephews," Jazz laughed.

On the drive home, Mika sat in the back with me while Gavril drove, I showed him the sonogram pictures and confessed that I knew I was pregnant before we left, but since we were all back home safe and sound I was forgiven. He kept touching my bump in disbelief and he finally told me the truth about what had gone down here. I was pissed that I wasn't told about Mandy but I had to agree with him that I would have been on the first plane back. Then he told me about Luca's confession, I was over the moon for Mandy, she finally got her man, and the plan to convert the top floor at home into an apartment for them since Alex had now moved into the Majestic, that for me was the icing on the cake.

When the car pulled into the drive, Mika got out and collected my luggage and while I hugged Gavril goodbye the front door opened and out stepped Luca and Mandy.

"Thank you G, I'm gonna miss you not being with me 24/7." He kissed the top of my head before he let me go.

"Gavril my friend, you have earned a well deserved vacation," Mika patted him on the back, "I can't thank you enough for keeping my world safe." He truly meant it and his words touched me deeply as I listened.

"Fuck me, Izzy!" Luca's voice boomed out, causing me to jump in the air, he'd not only startled me he'd scared poor Mandy half to death, "Sorry babe," he gave a reassuring squeeze as he kissed her sweetly. I had totally forgotten they didn't know yet.

"Oh yeah," I laughed, "You're gonna be an Uncle."

He jumped off the steps and landed next to me and like usual he picked me up and spun me around.

"Luca, I have a habit of puking you know?" I was joking but it made him abruptly stop.

"A baby, wow," he sounded thrilled.

"Try babies," Mika corrected him.

"Twins, oh that's wonderful," Mandy cried, "I'm so happy for you guy's, congratulations."

By now her tears had broken free and I gently cuddled her, "I'm so sorry about what happened to you, I wish I'd been told."

"I know, but you're home now and pregnant!" she yelled and as we hugged again I caught a glimpse of Mika, he was puffed out all proud as punch. It had been a fantastic homecoming and hopefully the last one for a very long time.

EPILOGUE

Five months later

The past five months had flown gone so quickly, so much had happened there hadn't been a dull moment. Alex and Anka eloped to Vegas and got married just a week after we returned from Sweden, they simply couldn't wait any longer. From my point of view I didn't blame them, if I'd had my way it's exactly what I'd have done, but the rest of the clan were not so forgiving, especially Jazz. She'd felt robbed of a weekend in Vegas but Mandy saved the day by assuring her we'd all go for her hen weekend.

Speaking of Mandy, we all got to know her folks Val and Brett. They stayed with us quite often and had become part of our family. Her Mom and I helped plan her dream wedding, which was going to be in April, and unlike me she absolutely loved it. The house these days was always full of people again and I loved that.

For New Years Eve we all decided to have a small gathering at our home with only family and close friends. I was so big and simply couldn't face going out for the normal boisterous party at *Red Square*. At least at home I didn't have to get too dressed up since the only clothes that I was comfortable in were my PJ bottoms and Mika's big T-shirts. But just for tonight I decided to put on a dress, even though it looked more like a tent but hey I made an effort.

While soaking in the tub before hand I got my first contraction, I never thought too much of it since it was only one. Once dressed and my make-up done I stood looking at this beached whale looking back at me in the mirror and that's when the second one hit. Once it finally passed, I walked to my pre-packed hospital bag and placed it on the bed, knowing I would be needing it by the end of the night. I walked down the stairs to meet and greet everyone, and decided to wait till the third one hit before saying anything, I'd only had two in two hours so it was going to be a while yet, or so I thought.

I stopped and chatted to Val and Brett as I did the rounds, then I spotted Gavril and Illa and I waddled over to them. As I reached up to kiss Gavril my water broke, soaking his pant leg, it was as if I'd thrown a bucket over him. All three of us stared at the carpet in total shock at what had just happened, and then the third contraction came with full force.

I grabbed onto Gavril's hand and crushed it, "Fuck me!" I hissed. That's when I heard Illa yelling, "MIKA... MIKA!"

Everyone in the room stopped and turned to see what the commotion was; you could have heard a pin drop. Jazz was by my side seconds before Mika, Luca and Alex and when they saw me holding onto Gavril and panting they all froze.

"Mika go get her bag," Jazz said calmly but he just stood there, "Now!" she shouted and he ran, "You two go get the cars," it was comical when the pair ran into each other, it actually made me smile. "Men," Jazz huffed and made me laugh.

By the time Gavril and Jazz had me outside two cars came squealing to a stop just in front of us. Once I was safely inside with Mika by my side and Jazz and Gavril up front we set off with the rest following in the car behind. As we pulled up to the hospital there was a porter and a wheel chair waiting. Mika had called ahead and informed them we were on our way. On the outside he remained calm and composed and I suppose that was for my benefit, he kissed me, "God I love you Angel."

At 11.55 p.m. on December 31st, Deron Savas was born weighing in at 6lb 11oz and twelve minutes later at 12.07 a.m.

January 1st, Nikita Jessica arrived, weighing 6lb 9oz. Both were healthy and absolutely perfectly beautiful. It had been a very long time since I'd seen Mika cry, but this time they were happy tears, our babies had stolen his heart and captivated him, and he looked at them totally hypnotised. While I was getting cleaned up and stitched I told him, "Go tell everyone, they'll be dying to know."

He eventually looked at me smiling, "Oh yeah, but I don't want to leave." He was totally spell bound by his two little miracles.

"The quicker you go the quicker you can come back?"

"OK, OK, mommy, God you're so pushy," he laughed before kissing me as he begrudgingly left.

He was still in a dazed state when he reached the waiting area; Jazz saw him and stood up making everybody follow, "Well?" She was chewing at the bit as Mika let out the biggest smile ever.

"Izzy did fantastic, she was amazing, we have a boy and a girl."

Everyone piled on him for one big group hug. Slowly they all parted except, for Jazz who still clung onto him, she was one complete emotional wreck.

"Would you all like to meet the new additions to the family?" He was almost deafened by them all shouting, "YES!"

By 2 a.m. everyone had left, leaving just the four of us and Mika climbed in bed with me wrapping his arms around me and holding me close to him. We lay there, not saying a word, just looking at the two cribs that held our sleeping cherubs. The next generation of Remizov's were here, and so a whole new story begins.

The End